"LIKE AN ALCHEMIST,
[Nick Burd] finds the wonder in the ordinary."
—PETER CAMERON, author of
*Someday This Pain Will Be Useful to You*

"NICK BURD REAPS A BOUNTY
from *The Vast Fields of Ordinary.*"
—*VANITY FAIR*

"A BRILLIANT ACCOUNT
of alienation and angst in the heartland."
—*QUEST* MAGAZINE

"Somewhere between *My So-Called Life*
and *Twin Peaks* . . . bright and concise,
A BEAUTIFUL BLUR."
—*FLAUNT*

"BURD IS AN AUTHOR TO WATCH."
—*PUBLISHERS WEEKLY*

# DADE IS HEADING FOR A CHANGE.

I didn't want to stay at the house with things the way they were, but I had a feeling that the party wouldn't be much better. Pablo would be there with Judy, and none of the jocks would talk to me. I'd just move from room to room like a ghost, the way I did at every party. Sure, a few random people might say hey when they passed me by, but no one would stop to talk to me. I'd basically be scenery.

I got in the shower and scrubbed my entire body with mint shower gel, then rinsed myself and did it all over again. After the shower I stretched out on the bed and let myself cry for a few minutes in the soft flash of the purple Christmas lights that ran along the edges of the ceiling around my room. I told myself that it was okay that I was crying, that it was a necessary part of mourning, because that's what I was doing. I was mourning the end of everything that had defined my life up to this point: Pablo, my parents' marriage, this house and Cedarville and the very idea of home. My new home was in the life that was waiting somewhere on the other side of the summer. It was college and Fairmont and the great tower of adulthood that loomed before me. I stared at the lights and thought of these things until I wasn't crying anymore, until their mild flickering had coated me with a numbness that I was able to confuse with acceptance.

# OTHER BOOKS YOU MAY ENJOY

| | |
|---|---|
| *Catalyst* | Laurie Halse Anderson |
| *Dreamland* | Sarah Dessen |
| *Hold Still* | Nina LaCour |
| *If I Stay* | Gayle Forman |
| *Jerk, California* | Jonathan Friesen |
| *Looking for Alaska* | John Green |
| *Paper Towns* | John Green |
| *Speak* | Laurie Halse Anderson |
| *Twisted* | Laurie Halse Anderson |
| *Will Grayson, Will Grayson* | John Green and David Levithan |
| *Willow* | Julia Hoban |

# THE
# VAST FIELDS
# OF ORDINARY

## nick burd

**speak**
An Imprint of Penguin Group (USA) Inc.

SPEAK
Published by the Penguin Group
Penguin Group (USA) Inc., 345 Hudson Street, New York, New York 10014, U.S.A.
Penguin Group (Canada), 90 Eglinton Avenue East, Suite 700, Toronto, Ontario, Canada M4P 2Y3
(a division of Pearson Penguin Canada Inc.)
Penguin Books Ltd, 80 Strand, London WC2R 0RL, England
Penguin Ireland, 25 St Stephen's Green, Dublin 2, Ireland (a division of Penguin Books Ltd)
Penguin Group (Australia), 250 Camberwell Road, Camberwell, Victoria 3124, Australia
(a division of Pearson Australia Group Pty Ltd)
Penguin Books India Pvt Ltd, 11 Community Centre, Panchsheel Park, New Delhi - 110 017, India
Penguin Group (NZ), 67 Apollo Drive, Rosedale, North Shore 0632, New Zealand
(a division of Pearson New Zealand Ltd)
Penguin Books (South Africa) (Pty) Ltd, 24 Sturdee Avenue,
Rosebank, Johannesburg 2196, South Africa

Registered Offices: Penguin Books Ltd, 80 Strand, London WC2R 0RL, England

First published in the United States of America by Dial Books, a member of Penguin Group (USA) Inc., 2009
Published by Speak, an imprint of Penguin Group (USA) Inc., 2011

1 3 5 7 9 10 8 6 4 2

Copyright © Nick Burd, 2009
All rights reserved

THE LIBRARY OF CONGRESS HAS CATALOGED THE DIAL BOOKS EDITION AS FOLLOWS:
Burd, Nick.
The vast fields of ordinary / by Nick Burd.
p.   cm.
Summary: The summer after graduating from an Iowa high school, eighteen-year-old Dade Hamilton watches his
parents' marriage disintegrate, ends his long-term, secret relationship, comes out of the closet, and savors first love.
ISBN: 978-0-8037-3340-4 (hc)
[1. Coming out (Sexual orientation)—Fiction. 2. Homosexuality—Fiction. 3. Coming of age—Fiction.
4. Dating—(Social customs)—Fiction. 5. Family problems—Fiction. 6. Iowa—Fiction.]
I. Title
PZ7.B915985Vas 2009
[Fic]—dc22   2008046256

Speak ISBN 978-0-14-241820-8

Printed in the United States of America

*For my mom,*
*my dad,*
*and my sister*

∞∞∞

# Acknowledgments

Endless thanks to my agent Nicole Kenealy James and my editor Alisha Niehaus. Words cannot express how grateful I am for your guidance, support, and unwavering faith in this book.

I'd also like to thank Nicholas Job, Robbie Imes, Jane Beachy, Brian Rothman, Heather Kaufman, Jared Hohl, Zachary Woolfe, Jason Napoli Brooks, Caroline Rabinovitch, Dale Peck, Jim Freed, Jackson Taylor, Kathryn Musilek, Brian Fender, Ryan Day, Sheala Hansen, Caroline Cazes, Eric Luc, Cameron Honsa, Karolina Zarychta, the staff of PEN American Center, and my family.

# THE
# VAST FIELDS
## OF ORDINARY

*"To be nobody but yourself in a world which is doing its best day and night to make you like everybody else means to fight the hardest battle which any human being can fight and never stop fighting."*

—e. e. cummings

# Before

I spent a good part of my senior prom drawing *DH + PS* in a giant heart in the last stall of the Cedarville High boys' bathroom. It covered the entire wall and took two red markers and almost an hour to complete. Every now and then, groups of guys would come in and piss in a line at the urinals and talk about how they were gonna get lucky with their dates, but for the most part it was just me and the marker stink and the muted sounds of crappy hip-hop coming through the walls.

When I was done I went back to give it all one last look, to tell it good-bye and head home for the night. My black-tuxedoed and frilly-dressed classmates were standing around the dim gymnasium, their voices striving to rise above the thumping beat of the music. I was wearing a powder blue tuxedo that I'd found at a thrift store just three days before. The prom theme was "Out of This World," and there were silver cardboard stars hanging from the ceiling and a twelve-foot tall green blow-up alien behind the table where the punch and cookies were all spread out. Principal Dugan was dressed like an astronaut and making the rounds, saying hello to students who inevitably rolled their eyes or flicked him off as soon as he passed.

I stood at the entrance and thought, *Good night, everyone.*

But I didn't go. Instead I went over to the bleachers, where a few other dateless losers were sitting and watching. They were all scattered at a safe distance from one another as if their loneliness was contagious. I saw Fessica Montana sitting in the very top row. She was wearing a hot pink dress and glittery eye shadow, and her hair was overcurled. She saw me and gave me a little wave and a shrug as if to say, *Here we are.* I waved back and looked out at the crowd.

It was then that I saw Pablo for the first time all night. He was in the center of the dance floor with a few of the other guys from the football team. He was moving his shoulders just slightly, too cool to really dance, but far too popular to get away with just standing around. He and the other players were not-so-subtly passing a flask back and forth. A few feet away, Pablo's girlfriend Judy and the rest of the mall girls were shimmying into one another, screaming and laughing and in love with being watched.

It didn't take long for Pablo to notice me staring at him. The moment his eyes met mine I thought of the previous afternoon in his bedroom, the lights out and his mother moving around upstairs and our hands traveling frantically over each other's bodies like we were in a race against time. I waved at him. Pablo let his gaze linger for a moment longer and then turned to Bert McGraw. He grabbed the flask out of his hand and danced off toward Judy. I understood that this was his way of saying that I no longer existed to him.

I stood up to go. I looked at Fessica. She was staring at me, her sadness somehow pointed at me now. I wonder if she'd seen what had just happened, if she knew. She looked like she was about to come down and say something, but whatever it was, it wasn't going to fix anything, so I turned and left.

I drove home with my windows down and my yellow bow tie unraveled on the passenger seat. Outside the car, the night hummed, quietly alive. I moved unnoticed through town, first past the strip malls and the office buildings and then through the residential maze that made up the periphery of Cedarville. I felt like a galactic traveler who'd landed on some ghost version of Earth where all the people had disappeared. When I reached my subdivision it was dark, save for the globe-shaped lamps that stood at the foot of every driveway, and I noticed that ours had gone out. It was nothing more than a gray sphere on a black metal rod. In the absence of its light our front yard had become shades darker than the rest of the yards on our block, and later that night I dreamt our dead lamp grew arms and legs and lurched down the street like a robot.

# Chapter 1

My father, Ned, ran Cedarville's only luxury car dealership, and my mother, Peggy, was an art teacher at St. Jude's, the smaller of the two Catholic schools in town. When I was thirteen we moved from the country to Cedarview Estates, a new housing development in the eastern part of Cedarville. The houses were all painted safe colors. Taupe, beige, and dusty blue. At night their windows glowed with a soft golden light. My mother hated it there.

"It's like a village of futuristic lighting fixtures," she said. She was out on the front porch smoking a rare Marlboro Light. "Sometimes I feel like if I stare at them for long enough I'll start to see them moving real slow. Like glaciers."

My parents had initially moved out of Cedarville and into the country when they found out they were having me. My mother wanted to raise her kid in a farmhouse. She wanted an unnamed cat and a few chickens that she didn't know what to do with. She wanted the space and the sunsets, the weird bugs in the yard. I spent my days wandering off the porch into the cornfields that ran behind the house. I would stand in the middle of the field, close my eyes, and spin myself around to try to make myself as lost as possible. One evening at dinner my father told us that he'd heard good things about the new Cedarview Estates being built in town and that maybe we should think about moving.

"It'll be great to move back into town," he said. "We'll be closer to everything. Plus, a guy from work knows a couple of the guys behind the development. He said it's going to be gorgeous. Real state-of-the-art living style."

"I don't see anything gorgeous about cracker-box houses," my mother said.

"Well, we're not twenty-five anymore, Peggy," he said.

She slammed her silverware onto her plate and asked what that had to do with anything, and I took my food up to my room so they could fight in peace.

The house in Cedarview Estates was too big for us. We had three extra bedrooms and a huge basement that my mother had taken over with art projects. Headless mannequins painted blue. Black stick figures acting out Biblical scenes on shattered mirrors. There was a fireplace we used one Christmas Eve and a stainless steel refrigerator with a built-in flat-screen television. We had a pool out back and a man who came to clean it once a week. There were stereo speakers installed in the walls, and sometimes the house would sing.

I didn't mind the house and our new neighborhood. It took

some getting used to, but before long I saw it as I saw the cornfields that ran behind our old place in the country. It was a space to be explored and to disappear in. My parents, on the other hand, fought about the house all the time, about what it meant and what kinds of people it made them. My father thought it represented a new level of adulthood and affluence, like it was a giant arrow indicating that they were moving in the right direction. But my mother saw it as a surrender to normalcy, a rejection of the fantasy where she created sculptures in the barn and heard the voice of nature in the black silence of the rural Midwest evening.

One night my father and I were reading the paper in the living room when my mother's voice came through the intercom on the wall.

"I just want you to know that I'm in the master bathroom using the bidet. I can't believe this. Dade, if you can hear me, never, ever let yourself become this."

My father looked up from the sports page and gave a dismissive shake of his head before going back to reading.

My mother's fellow teachers referred to her as The Hippie. She had long sandy blond hair and always wore flowing peasant skirts and gauzy tops that revealed the teenage girl slimness in her arms and shoulders. Her eyes lit up when someone told a clever joke or when she noticed that one of the flowers she planted in the backyard was beginning to bloom. But there were many days when the light behind her eyes went out and it seemed like the world she saw left her hopeless and disappointed. We'd been in the house for a year when she made an announcement at the dinner table.

"I'm going to start seeing a psychiatrist," she said. "I just wanted everyone to know. It's no one's fault. I'm not blaming anyone. It's just something I need to do."

My father stopped chewing his veal cutlet for a few seconds and studied my mother's face, maybe waiting to see if this was some sort of joke. My mother looked over at me and gave me as warm a smile as she could muster.

She said, "How's the veal, honey? Is it good? Do you like it?"

The doctor prescribed her some pills, and over the next few months it seemed like she was refilling her prescription as often as the pool guy was stopping by. She'd spend hours on the sofa watching old movies on cable. Other times she'd lock herself in her meditation room with an expensive merlot and play Fleetwood Mac albums all day, "Everywhere" and "You Make Loving Fun" at hostage situation levels.

"Life is good at the capitalist compound," she said one day on the phone to her sister in Phoenix. She was standing at the kitchen sink and looking out the window at our yard. "The garden's in bloom, the sprinklers just kicked on, and the pool boy will be over any minute. Oh, and I just took a Klonopin. So yes, life is good. Life is very good."

She started lying by the pool during the summers like some zoned-out starlet. She went unconscious in the sun and then murmured things that didn't make any sense. At dinner she sometimes talked about adding on to the house, but suggestions like these always had an edge, like she was trying to spite her former self, the one that never wanted to move there in the first place. But soon her feelings about our new life faded, or at least moved beneath the surface of it all, and she and my father began to fight over stuff like why she bought Mountain Mist scented detergent instead of the Spring Breeze my father preferred and whether a lawn should be watered in the daylight or the dark.

∞

My parents were always going on about wanting me to have a good work ethic, so we spent the day after my fifteenth birthday driving around and getting applications from every fast-food joint, movie theater, and grocery store in town.

"It'll be good for you to make your own money," my father said. "And when you get your first paycheck, I'll take you down to the bank and we'll open you your own checking account."

I nodded and stared out the window at the passing strip malls and restaurants. I found the idea of work terrifying and depressing. I saw the way my father sometimes looked when he came home from the work at night. He'd shuffle into the kitchen with tired eyes and a loosened tie. He'd grab a beer from the refrigerator and lean against the counter as he downed it, as if each drop of beer went toward erasing his day and put something better in its place. Then there was me sitting at the kitchen table, eating potato chips and flipping through a music magazine, the idea of going to my room and downloading porn a vague notion in my mind as always.

"How was your day?" my father would ask me.

"Fine," I'd say. "How was yours?"

"Oh, fine. Some private school girl threw a fit when her dad wouldn't buy her the Mercedes she wanted and I thought I was going to have to call the cops, but other than that it was fine."

I tried not to look at him as he finished his beer. Sometimes I'd get up and go out to the pool and leave him alone. Other times I'd put on my headphones, turn up the volume, and hope that the music leaking out of them would be enough to send him to another room.

My dad was a loner. It was one of the few things we had in common. He golfed alone, went to movies alone. He had colleagues at the dealership, people that could probably be considered friends, but he rarely associated with any of them outside of work. He stayed at the edges of parties, blank-faced and silent with a sweaty glass of scotch, but ready with a smile and a line about the weather whenever someone approached him. He was handsome enough, an ex-jock who'd somehow held on to his solid physique and unremarkable charm. You could tell that somewhere inside him was the genuine desire for a connection, something to pull him out of his self-imposed isolation, but the fishing trips and tennis games he suggested to other husbands always went unfilled in the end.

I ended up getting a part-time job at the Food World supermarket by the mall. I started out as a grocery bagger and by senior year I was working as a stock boy with my friend Pablo and a few other guys that went to my high school. We spent most of our time smoking cigarettes in the milk cooler and talking about how we were underpaid or pretending to be interested in the twins—Jessica and Fessica Montana—that worked in the video rental department.

The twins were a year younger than us in school. They were both just five feet tall, with chipmunk cheeks and wide blue eyes. Jessica had a smile so constant that after the senior play my father asked me if the girl who played Ophelia had some sort of personality disorder. She kept her hair dyed a sunny blond and enjoyed a status at our high school as one of the minions of Pablo's hyperpopular girlfriend, Judy Lockhart.

Her fraternal sister, Fessica, wasn't quite as pretty. Her real name was Francesca, but sometime during her time in the Cedarville Public School System some smartass had started calling her Fessica as a joke and it stuck. She had a nose that reminded me of a deformed mushroom and a mouthful of blue braces ("They're not blue. They're sapphire."). She always wore her dull brown hair in a ponytail and slouched through the aisles of Food World or the halls of Cedarville High as if she'd just been resurrected that morning and in her death haze had forgotten to shower. She wore what Pablo called "typical nerd gear," stuff like really tight stonewashed jeans and T-shirts with airbrushed horses bucking dramatically across her chest. Pablo liked to stop by the video department where she worked and tell her how unusual her name was.

"What is it?" he'd ask. "French? Canadian? French-Canadian?"

"I've told you," Fessica would reply. "Fessica is not my real name."

"Well, Fessica is a very special name," he'd say, taking her hand and bringing it to his mouth, "and you are a very special girl."

Pablo's family had moved to Cedarville from Arizona at the end of our freshman year. By junior year he was student council secretary and the Cedarville Warriors' star quarterback. Girls tended to swoon over him. A few even lamely referred to him as the Sexican. He was six feet tall with skin the color of a dirty penny and hazel eyes that were the main focus of my jack-off fantasies. He was dark and broody, not at all like the other jocks that ran around tackling each other and screaming each other's bizarre nicknames down the hall. I saw him in the halls at school and occasionally we passed each other in the aisles at Food World, but we didn't become friends until driver's ed class when we were paired up for a presentation on centrifugal force. We worked on the project all night and then smoked a joint in his bedroom while listening to the Mexican hip-hop he was obsessed with. We were stoned and spacing out on his bed when he reached over and started fondling my crotch. I was sixteen at the time, and I knew I wasn't straight. I'd known that for a fact since I was ten and my babysitter Kendra Kaufman let me stay up late and watch *Night of 1,000 Werewolves*, one of Johnny Morgan's first films.

"I want to marry Johnny Morgan," I told her when the credits were rolling.

"Kid," Kendra said, "don't tell your parents I let you watch that movie, and *definitely* don't tell them what you just told me."

I always thought there was the distant possibility that I could maybe sleep with a girl, but I never found myself staring at them the way I stared at the guys running around the track at school or the shirtless models in my father's issues of *GQ*. I practiced saying I was gay to inanimate objects around the house. I told the soap dish in my bathroom, the ceiling fan above my bed, the blue drinking glass I favored above all the others simply because over the years its entire family had perished one by one during various interactions with hard surfaces around the kitchen and I'd convinced myself our solitude was linked.

"I'm gay," I told these things. "I'm a homo."

I would then wait for the orphaned drinking glass to shatter, the ceiling fan to drop, or for the soap dish to let out a bloodcurdling scream. But nothing ever happened. The world went on as ever.

"We don't tell anybody about this," Pablo said when we were finished. He was sitting on the edge of his bed, slipping a worn green T-shirt over his head. "Especially not Judy."

I never allowed myself to call him my boyfriend even in the silence of my own mind. Our sexual encounters always lasted less than five minutes and ended with him looking even more depressed and pissed off than usual. Afterward we'd lie there in silence and I'd wonder what would happen if I asked for something more even though I wasn't exactly sure what more was. Despite it all, there were days when I entertained the idea of him and me somehow getting away from Cedarville and being together in some weird vacuum where the cigarettes I bummed him and the doors I held open were enough to make him love me.

∞

I didn't have many friends at school. I spent most of my time in my room writing and listening to music. I wrote weird little stories and poems, pieces where boys floated out the windows of their houses and hovered over their neighborhood. If I hung out with anyone, it was with Pablo and his jock buddies, but it was an unspoken rule between us all that if Pablo wasn't around, then I shouldn't be either. I was the odd man out, the one that was only spoken to when someone needed to copy my algebra homework or borrow a dollar for the pop machine. When they did speak to me, they always called me Dave to piss me off. Sometimes they made fun of me for wearing polyester pants and T-shirts I'd found at thrift stores around town. They told me my hair was too long, that I tossed it like a girl. I was never allowed to say anything because then I was the crybaby, the one who couldn't take it, and that would only prove a terrible point. It all came to a head one day during lunch when Bert McGraw, one of the linemen for the Cedarville Warriors, was going on about how, Mr. Stone, the art teacher, had given him a D.

"That white-haired faggot," Bert said. "What a frickin' perv. I should go to Dugan's office and tell him that his homo ass tried to fondle me in the darkroom."

A series of caveman chuckles rippled up and down the lunch table, and Bert high-fived the player sitting to his right.

And then without thinking I said, "Mr. Stone is a decent guy. Go talk to him. He'll figure out a way to help you raise your grade."

Bert stopped chewing and dropped his shredded beef sandwich onto his plate.

"Who is this kid?" he asked the table like he'd never seen me before. His voice got louder as he spoke. "You think Mr. Stone is cool? You think that hippy piece of turd is cool? What, fag? Did you blow him after class or something?"

At this point, he was yelling. The lunchroom went from midday pandemonium to complete silence in five seconds flat. Everyone stared over at the table in the center of the Cedarville High lunchroom, stared at the table of blue-and-red-uniformed football players and the one outcast at the end in the brown plaid pants and the slim-cut cowboy shirt whose silver threading screamed queer louder than Bert's booming apeman voice ever could. People at our school stopped everything to witness a good fight, and Bert McGraw raising his voice during lunch was a good sign that shit was about to go down. A few of the other players were red-faced trying to contain their laughter. One let out a sort of choking grunt of a laugh. Pablo glared at Bert from his place beside me.

"Are you a faggot, Dave?" His voice echoed throughout the cafeteria. "It's what everyone wants to know. Let's clear it up once and for all. Are you a homo, homo?"

His cheeks puffed with half-chewed bites of food. His eyes were crazed. Jessica Montana and Judy Lockhart and all the rest of the mall girls were craning their necks from a couple tables down. There were scattered whispers, muted giggles. Fessica stood up from the nerd table in the far corner of the lunchroom and stared. I looked down at my plate, at the undercooked fries and gray cottage cheese.

"Dude," I said to Pablo out of the corner of my mouth. "Help me out."

Bert turned to Pablo. "What, Soto? Is this little faggot your bitch?"

One of the players at the far end of the table let out a sharp burst of laughter. The sound triggered something in Pablo, and suddenly he lunged across the table and grabbed Bert's face with his left hand and punched him in the temple with his right. The sound was sick and fleshy. The lunchroom erupted with yelling and cheering as Pablo made his way over the table, bringing Bert to the ground on the other side. Principal Dugan and two of the security guards raced into the lunchroom, and I covered my face as they approached, covered my face until the two of them were being dragged out of the lunchroom, and even then I was just peeking through my fingers.

Pablo and Bert both got suspended for fighting. People started talking more than usual. Someone wrote FAGIT! on my locker. The misspelling would've been funny if it weren't so tragic. I left it there for the last month of school because there was the sense that wiping it off would only force something worse to take its place.

I drove over to Pablo's house to see him on the second day

of his suspension. The front door was open when I got there. I could see him through the screen door sitting on the couch in his gym shorts. He was watching some trashy daytime talk show. I knocked and he pretended not to hear me. I waited a few seconds and tried just walking in, but the screen door was locked.

"Dude, let me in."

He didn't move, didn't even look over at me. I kneeled and pressed my face up to the screen. His house smelled like incense and weed. He'd probably been smoking all day and now he was trying to cover up the scent before his mom got home from the hospital where she put in fourteen-hour days as a nurse.

"I just wanted to see how you were doing," I said. "And to say thanks for standing up for me the other day. That was cool of you."

He didn't move. There was a woman screaming on the television. Every other word was bleeped out.

"Dude, come on. Let me in."

He looked over at me, kept his eyes on me for a second. He stood up and slowly moved toward the door in that lazy straight-boy swagger he sometimes had when he stood up, like he'd forgotten how to walk properly. He stared at me through the screen door for a moment before letting me in. We stood there looking at each other in the entryway.

"People've been saying that Dugan may not let you walk at graduation. Is that true?"

"I'll walk."

"Oh," I said. "I was worried."

"Don't."

"Don't what?" I asked.

"Worry about me. It's stupid. I don't need it."

"But I care about you," I said.

"Don't say that to me."

"But it's true."

"Well, don't say it." He looked out the screen door out at the single-story houses that made up his crappy neighborhood. Toys littered the unmowed lawns like bright dead animals. "I feel like this is like some *thing* for you or something."

"I don't get it," I said.

"You're too needy. I already have a girlfriend. I don't need another one."

"That's so not true," I said. I brought my chin down to my chest. I didn't want him to see my face. We didn't say anything for a bit and then I blurted, "I love you."

I peered up at him to see his reaction. He'd screwed his face up into a look of disgust. He moved forward and grabbed me, pushed me against the wall, and raised his fist back behind his head. He was ready to punch me. I thought back to the first time he'd touched me, of all the times he touched me, of the way he pushed my face away whenever I tried to kiss him and how that didn't stop me from trying over and over again.

"Take it back," he said.

"No."

He smacked me across the face. Hard.

"Take it back. Now."

"I take it back."

He slapped me again.

"Stop! I said I take it back!" He backed away and looked me up and down. For a moment I thought he was going to apologize, but instead he said, "Get your faggot ass out of my house."

Driving home I couldn't cry even though I wanted to. I sat at an empty intersection and just stared at some power lines, at the way they looked against the trees, the black cords almost getting swallowed in the deep green of the leaves. Our entire relationship appeared in my mind as a glut of painful moments. I finally fully realized that my fantasy of making him fall in love with me was foolish, maybe even insane. He was a knot I could pull at until my fingers were raw and bloody, a knot that I could never untie.

# Chapter 2

It was one week after graduation when I heard about Jenny Moore. I came in from mowing the lawn to find my mother leaning against the kitchen counter and watching the built-in television on the fridge. A freshly poured glass of Fresca sizzled on the counter next to her.

"Are you watching this?" she asked me. "This little girl disappeared while playing in her backyard." She walked over to the sink and lit her cigarette on the apricot-scented candle burning on the counter. "Last name's Moore. They say she's autistic. God, how horrible. Can you imagine what her parents are going through?"

I couldn't, but I didn't say so. I took a bottle of water from the refrigerator and sat at the kitchen table. My mother cracked the window open and let the smoke creep out into the humid afternoon. Outside the window, the sky stretched like uncharted territory over the skeletons of the mansions they were building off into the distance on what once had been farmland.

"God, I miss the summers on the farm," she said. She rubbed her eye and ashed her cigarette in the sink. "Why is this making me so sad?"

A newscaster was interviewing a neighbor of the missing girl. She was asking how anyone could do this. Hopefully they would find her safe and sound.

I couldn't think of anything to say, so I said, "That really sucks."

"Do you think they'll find her?" my mother asked.

I took a drink of my water and looked out the patio door toward the pool. She turned on the faucet, put her cigarette under the water. Neither of us answered her question.

∞

I had dinner that night with my father at the Cedarville Country Club. He was trying this thing where just he and I had dinner together one night a week. We'd put on our ties and we'd get into the Audi and he'd say, "Well, where should we go? The country club?" and I'd say sure and then the next thing you know we're eating sea bass in silence on the deck of the Cedarville Country Club, while below us drunk old men wearing ugly pants puffed on cigars and sped around in their golf carts.

"The sea bass is better than it was last week," my dad said. "That comment I made to the waiter last time must have really gone straight to the top."

"It's not really sea bass," I said. "I saw this thing on TV where they said that what restaurants call sea bass is actually some other fish. I think real sea bass is, like, almost extinct."

He shot me a look and went on chewing his food with tiny controlled bites. I took a sip from the vodka tonic he'd ordered me and prayed for time to speed up. He was so different now than he had been when I was a little kid. I had images of him with long hair sitting on the porch of our farmhouse while he laughed his way through "Puff the Magic Dragon" for me on his guitar. I remembered when there wasn't age in his voice.

"So," he said after the waitress took our dessert order. "Are you excited to start at Fairmont?"

"I guess," I said.

"I remember my days at Fairmont. There's nothing like it. You'll have the time of your life. And Michigan is beautiful in the fall. And in the winter too. Hell, it's always beautiful."

"Yup. Can't wait."

"You know, it's sort of your last summer at home. Actually, in a lot of ways it's your last real summer."

He'd uttered basically the same sentence every week for the last month. The rapport between us was sad enough behind closed doors. It pained me to put it on display in public.

"I don't feel like it's my last real summer," I said. "There'll be other summers. Next summer."

"Well, next summer hopefully you'll have an internship or a job of some sort," he said. He leaned back in his chair, picked up his scotch. It was a position he often took when he thought he was bestowing some sort of wisdom upon me. "Jack McDuffy's got that law firm in Chicago. You remember Jack. I'm sure I could get you a job filing or something. Chicago would be nice in the summer. You've got the lake."

"That'd be cool."

He looked out over the golf course. "I'll make some phone calls."

"Cool."

I didn't know what was worse, us talking or not talking. I took a big swig of my drink and followed his gaze onto the course. A golf cart had turned on its side. The old man riding in it climbed out and stared at it with his hands on his hips as if it were a dog that wouldn't sit.

"Have you decided on a major yet?" my father said, his eyes still fixed on the overturned cart.

"I want to write," I said. I'd answered this question dozens of times before, but he kept on asking like he was hoping my answer would change. "Probably English lit. At least for now."

My father nodded slowly. He looked out at the man on the course, who was now kicking his golf cart. My father shook his head in disgust, brought his attention back to the table. The sun was setting behind the grove of trees on the west side of the course, and the sky was a mess of blues and purples with gauzy clouds pulled across it.

"It might rain," my father said as if I'd stated something to the contrary.

The waitress placed two pieces of key lime pie on the table. She was our waitress every week, a chipper girl named Cindy who wore sparkly barrettes and electric blue eye shadow. She had a voice like a parakeet, and my father waved her away before she could put it on display.

"Listen, Dade," he said. I knew something big was coming by the way he leaned forward in his chair, by the way his eyes met mine. He usually never looked me in the eye. My first thought was that somebody had died. But when? And how? "You know I love your mother very much. Hell, you know I love you very much."

I couldn't remember the last time he said he loved me. I put my hand in my water glass and played with the remaining ice. I thought about taking each piece out and pitching them over the edge of the patio to distract myself, but I didn't. I told myself that I had to be there with him. He told me there was a woman named Vicki that he'd met at his poetry class.

"What poetry class? When did you start taking a poetry class?"

"A few months ago," he said. He leaned back in his chair and shrugged. "It was something to do. Your mother is always try-ing to get me to be more creative, so I signed up for a Thursday night poetry class at the community college. I didn't want to tell anyone. This is just for me. I saw how you seem to get so much out of locking yourself away and writing your feelings down. I thought I'd do the same. Doesn't that make you happy?"

I let out a little noise of disgust that was a bit more forceful than I'd intended, but any guilt associated with it on my part faded as fast as the sound itself. The thought of my father in his dark den writing bad love poems for a woman named Vicki while my mother did her Peace Pilates in her meditation room made me wish I'd asked Cindy for another drink.

"I care deeply for Vicki," he went on. "I really do. She's nice. And not too . . . *serious*. She's fun. You'll like her."

"What do you mean I'll like her?" I said. "Is she here?"

"No," he said. He turned his scotch glass in little circles and chuckled to himself. "No, she's not here. But you'll meet her someday. She's very nice."

I stared at the key lime pie. It was a bright artificial green. I thought I could feel other club members looking at us. I wondered if this sort of thing happened all the time, if every few weeks some father sat his kid down and told him that he was having an affair. He leaned across the table.

"Listen, kiddo," he said.

"Why are you calling me kiddo?"

He brought his chin down and gave me a disappointed look. "Dade. I'm not going anywhere. I'm not divorcing Peggy. Hell, she's known about Vicki for months now."

"I don't believe that."

I crossed my arms and looked back over the golf course. People were heading back to the clubhouse, probably to drink cocktails and slap each other on the back over some fantastic putt on the nineteenth hole or some other bunch of bullshit. I knew my parents' relationship hadn't been in the best shape for the past few years, but that didn't make this any easier. I thought of every divorce I'd ever known, the divorces of neighbors, distant family members, and celebrities. I wondered if it came to that, which one of them would leave the house and which one would stay, if the ghost of the one that left would always haunt the halls, leave toothpaste spit on the bathroom mirror, forget to completely close the refrigerator door.

"I just wanted to tell you," he said with a helpless shrug. "These nights out are meant to bring us closer. I want to feel close to you, Dade."

I thought about saying that this was a pretty messed up way to bring us closer together, but there was the sense that the comment would be wasted on him, so I didn't say anything. Cindy was standing at the table next to ours explaining what wasabi was to a pair of very old women, one of whom was holding her menu upside down. Somewhere someone laughed a laugh that morphed into a series of snorts, and inside the club the piano player was playing "Moon River," a staple in his set. I tried to focus my attention on these small things, but my eyes kept going to my father's hands. He was turning his glass in counterclockwise circles on the tablecloth, and something about this made me put my hand on my glass. I thought about turning my tumbler to prove some point, but I didn't.

"Are you going to tell Mom?" I asked.

"Yes," he said quietly. He kept turning his glass. "I'm going to tell her in the next couple of days. Tell her what she already knows, I suppose."

I started nodding slowly for no reason at all, and then my dad started nodding, and we did this for a while, nodding and affirming nothing at all as the evening settled around us.

# Chapter 3

Three days later we got our first thunderstorm of the summer. I watched through our rear sliding glass door as the rain clouds blackened the sky and burst open and sent down huge, hard drops. My dad was at the dealership and my mother was at school teaching summer art classes, and I spent the day home alone playing video games, downloading *Lube Jobs 1–5* on my computer, and finally getting around to using the bottle of hair dye I'd had under my sink since March. I took my hair from my natural dirty blond to a deep chocolate color and then stood staring at my reflection in my bathroom mirror in nothing but my towel. The new color brought out the brown in my hazel eyes instead of the green, which I liked because it was different from before. I tried to see myself as a stranger might, to find the things about my boyish face and skinny body that might make them think I was worth talking to. Pablo had once told me that my chest looked the way Jesus' did in paintings, but he was drunk and stoned when he said it, and I don't think it meant anything.

I was stuck in this trance when my phone rang. Like magic, it was Pablo.

"Come over," he said.

"I can't," I said. "I have stuff to do."

"Like what?" he asked. "I know you don't work today. I saw on the schedule that you have it off."

"Why are you calling?" I asked.

"Come on," he said. "Why you gotta be like this? You don't have to complicate everything, Hamilton."

I stood there trying to find a way to tell him that there was no way I was going over to his house, but I couldn't. I wanted to go over there. I wondered if maybe he was right. Maybe I did complicate everything.

"What will we do if I come over?" I asked.

"What do you think?"

"I don't know," I said. "You tell me."

"Use your imagination."

I thought for a moment. "Let me get dressed. I'll be over soon."

∞

I kept my face buried in Pablo's pillow the entire time. When it was over, he stood by the bed and frowned at me. "I think I liked you better blond."

I wondered if he actually meant that or was just trying to make me feel bad. I got off the bed and crossed his basement bedroom to where I'd left my clothes in a pile on the floor. I dressed slowly, trying to ignore my wobbly knees and the hollow

31

feeling in my stomach. His cell phone rang. He let out a wet cough and picked it up. I could tell by his answers that it was his girlfriend Judy.

"Whatever," he said into the receiver as he picked at his chest hair. "Sure. . . . No. . . . No, I was just taking a nap. . . . Well, obviously. . . . Okay. Whatever."

I'd just finished dressing when he hung up the phone.

"I have to go to this thing with Judy tonight," he said.

"Jessica's party?" I said.

"Yeah."

"Well, maybe I'll see you there," I said.

"You were invited?"

"I think so," I said. "I mean, they put an invitation on the board at work. I assumed that meant anyone could come."

"Yeah. Well, I don't know if that actually means you're invited. But whatever."

"So I'll see you there?"

"You may *see* me. But you know the rules."

I wiped my sweaty palms on my jeans. My mouth was dry and sticky. Pablo's room was a mess. There were soda cans scattered around the room. Nearly every surface—the metal drafting table he used for a computer desk, the ledge under the picture window, the white wooden nightstand—was covered with a layer of dust. One of his favorite hobbies was using his mother's credit card to buy designer jeans off the Internet, and now they formed a miniature denim mountain range that stretched from the foot of his bed to his closet door. He pulled a pair of yellow plaid boxers out of a pair of discarded jeans and slipped them on before doing a few pull-ups on the bar he'd put up across the doorframe of his closet. His back muscles surged under his skin as he rose and fell.

"Did you watch the news this morning?" he asked.

"No," I said.

I sat at his computer and moved his mouse until the screen came to life. He had two windows open: SportsZone.com and some page that gave step-by-step instructions on how to make a bong out of an apple.

"They haven't found that girl who disappeared, but they did find these awesome crop circles at some farm in the western part of the state," he said. He did one last pull-up and then lowered himself to the floor. He flung himself back onto the bed. "People on the Internet are saying they're related."

"Like aliens?"

"Yeah, I guess. They're theorizing that she was kidnapped by space aliens or some shit." Pablo shook his head. "It's probably just some redneck with too much time on his hands. Crop circles are so eighties."

I considered telling him about the time I'd mowed circular shapes into my backyard when I was eleven. My father came home from work and yelled at me to get rid of them, that people in the air would think the farm was some occult compound.

"I think it's great he's expressing himself through these complex visual forms at such a young age," my mother said. My father shook his head and went out to the garage and mowed the lawn himself in his suit.

I watched Pablo scratch his belly and examine his fingernails. The spicy smell of his mother's cooking came drifting from upstairs, and right then I wanted nothing more than for him to look over at me with warmth in his eyes and ask me to stay for dinner. We hadn't really talked about what was going to happen to us after the summer. I was going to Fairmont. He and Judy were both planning on going to the University of Western Iowa. We had once talked about visiting each other, but I got the feeling that all that was off now. Ever since the Bert episode in the lunchroom, things seemed redefined, plans had changed.

"Can I talk to you about something?" I asked.

"God," he said. "What now?"

"I feel like we're not friends anymore," I said.

He screwed up his face like he didn't know what I was talking about. "Why do you say that?"

"I mean, ever since graduation we just haven't seen that much of each other."

"Well, what's so wrong with that?" he asked.

"I don't know," I said. "It's just not what I want."

"You're doing it again, Hamilton," he said.

"Doing what?"

"Complicating things."

"You keep saying that, but I don't know what it means," I said.

He let out a sigh. "It means that you need to stop asking so many questions. I mean, we're different. I'm thinking about the future, dude, and there's no place for this there."

"So what does that mean?" I said. "Is that it? Do we never see each other again after we leave for school?"

"I just feel like if we take it any further, it will mean something that I don't want it to mean."

"And what's that?"

He shot me a look. "Like what you want this to mean. Like when you said whatever about love. I want a normal life."

He'd crushed me dozens of times before, but this time the pain felt new. It stunned me and sent a cold wave through my body. I told myself not to tear up, that crying wasn't an option. For a long time we stayed like that, me at his desk and him on the bed, without speaking. Finally, he turned on his stereo and put on some hip-hop track that started out with a series of gunshots and a woman screaming.

Pretty soon his mother called us up from the top of the basement stairs in her thick accent. I silently followed him upstairs and took a seat at the kitchen table. It was just the three of us in their 1960s kitchen. Paisley wallpaper, sparkling Formica countertop, and sea green everything, even Mrs. Soto's hospital scrubs. She gave me the same cautious smile as always. Pablo glanced over at me and gave me a look like he'd forgotten I was there.

"How are you, Dade?" Mrs. Soto asked.

"I'm fine," I lied.

I was sitting in the spot where Mr. Soto had probably sat when he was still alive, back when this table was still in their old house in Arizona and before the illness that Pablo only spoke of in the most vague terms. Pablo and his mother started speaking to each other in Spanish. I filled myself with enchiladas and spaced out while they spoke, their unfamiliar language buzzing around my head like a swarm of tiny insects.

∞

When I got home I found my mother on the living room sofa with a cigarette and a glass of red wine. She was wearing the red flannel nightgown she always wore when she was sick. The lights were off except for four candles on the coffee table arranged in a square around a giant bottle of wine. Chet Baker was coming from the walls, and under his voice the central air rumbled in the guts of the house. I watched her from the foyer, watched as she stared vacantly across the room, her lips moving slowly, and I knew that my father had told her.

"Come in here," she said when she noticed me. I approached her slowly, putting my hands in my back pockets as I went. She leaned forward and looked up at me. "He said he told you." A feeling of guilt came over me, cold and heavy like a bag of ice placed on my shoulders.

"Yeah," I said. "He did."

My words had made their sound and now I just wanted to walk away and pretend they weren't mine, like they were pennies that had fallen through a hole in my pocket. She nodded to herself. She seemed strangely satisfied, like some old theory had finally been proven correct. Her face contorted into a sob, but in a flash it was gone, and though her lip still quivered, there was a disturbing calm to her face, like she had just made some vow to never be sad again.

She said, "Dade, I don't understand why you didn't tell me."

"Mom," I said. "I'm sorry. I mean, I didn't exactly want this information."

"Then give it away." She huffed out a sarcastic laugh. "Give it to me, for God's sake. You kept this from me for days, and you would have kept it from me forever had I not just asked you whether or not you knew."

Something in her face made me wonder if she'd known for a while—if she was psychic and her mind was tattooed with things I didn't want her to know about me.

"Your father didn't carry you in his womb for nine months," she went on. "I did. Your loyalties ought to lie with *me*."

"But Mom—"

"Don't 'but Mom' me," she said. She was staring at the candles, putting herself somewhere else. "Go away. Go to your room." I went upstairs and left her alone. I didn't want to stay at the house with things the way they were, but I had a feeling that the party wouldn't be much better. Pablo would be there with Judy, and none of the jocks would talk to me. I'd just move from room to room like a ghost, the way I did at every party. Sure, a few random people might say hey when they passed me by, but no one would stop to talk to me. I'd basically be scenery.

I got in the shower and scrubbed my entire body with mint shower gel, then rinsed myself and did it all over again. After the shower I stretched out on the bed and let myself cry for a few minutes in the soft flash of the purple Christmas lights that ran along the edges of the ceiling around my room. I told myself that it was okay that I was crying, that it was a necessary part of mourning, because that's what I was doing. I was mourning the end of everything that had defined my life up to this point: Pablo, my parents' marriage, this house and Cedarville and the very idea of home. My new home was in the life that was waiting somewhere on the other side of the summer. It was college and Fairmont and the great tower of adulthood that loomed before me. I stared at the lights and thought of these things until I wasn't crying anymore, until their mild flickering had coated me with a numbness that I was able to confuse with acceptance.

# Chapter 4

Jessica and Fessica lived on the outskirts of Cedarville on a residential street that had somehow been built in the industrial area of town. The recycling plant loomed at the south end of the block, and the massive cereal factory was at the north. Train tracks zigzagged across the blocks, and the trains seemed to come every five minutes, black capsule-shaped cars moving to and from unknown destinations, from what I imagined as dark, lifeless warehouses. The house itself was painted golf green and had a perfect square shape capped off with a similarly geometric triangular roof. It looked like a child's drawing of what a house should be.

People were crammed into every room on the first floor, and between the dense cloud of cigarette smoke and the din of noise, it was hard to even think. Everyone was holding red plastic cups full of beer, and some insane hip-hop track that mainly consisted of guys barking was blaring from the stereo. I didn't see Judy or Jessica anywhere, but I imagined them watching this all on closed-circuit televisions upstairs, talking about which ones of us they wanted to sleep with and which ones of us they wished would take a spill down a flight of stairs. Someone let out a meaningless scream, a wild-child howl from the highest peak of Party Island.

"Hey, Dade!" said some pimply kid I didn't recognize.

I waved awkwardly.

It was all too chaotic and there was no chance of finding Pablo in all of the insanity, so I pushed my way through to the crowded staircase and made my way upstairs. I went to the end of the hall and stood by an open window that looked out onto the street. The air from outside was warm and carried the smell of the burnt rubber from the recycling plant at the end of the block.

The next thing I knew Fessica was standing beside me. She put her hand on my shoulder, wavered back and forth like a stop sign in heavy wind. We stood there for a few moments, her looking down at the darkened yard while I watched her out of the corner of my eyes.

"I shouldn't be drinking with my medication," she said, a lazy grin spreading across her face.

I gently moved her hand off my shoulder and guided her to the wall. She leaned against it and slid slowly down to a seated position on the floor. A few people standing at the end of the hall glanced over at us. They spoke in low voices, laughed, and motioned toward Fessica and me. I knelt down in front of her.

"What kind of medication are you on?" I asked.

"Xanax." She said it dreamily, like it was the name of a boy she liked. "It's good. It relaxes me. I get kinda tense in social situations."

"Do you want me to get you some water?" I asked.

She smiled and looked into my eyes in a way that made me regret offering to do something nice for her. It was the same look she'd worn in English class when doing a presentation on *Wuthering Heights*, the face of a girl lost in a close-range haze of romanticism.

"You're sweet," she said. "And my middle toe tingles."

She reached up to touch my face, but I stood before she laid a hand on me.

"I'll be back with water," I said.

I moved down the hall, skillfully recovering from a small stumble over someone's purposefully outstretched leg.

"Where you going, Dade?" a voice called from behind me as I reached the top of the stairs. "Getting your *girlfriend* another drink?"

I didn't turn around to see who had said it. I just raised my hand and gave them the finger as I headed down the stairs. Of course, Jessica and Judy were standing right there at the bottom. They were scanning the crowd casually as if they were too cool to be there. They heard me coming down and both turned to see who it was. When they saw it was me, they each cocked a nostril and squinted at me in disgust.

"What were you doing upstairs?" Jessica said. "Upstairs is off limits."

"I'm sorry," I said slowly. "There were other people up there. And I was talking to your sister."

Judy let out a noise of disapproval and rolled her eyes dramatically. Judy was pretty enough, but her beauty was completely ruined by the fact that, like Pablo, she was always scowling unless there was some adult or authority figure that she needed to butter up. She had a pointy nose and shiny brown hair that reminded me of something from a shampoo commercial, a wave of silk in constant motion. She also had huge breasts. Pablo had once told me that sucking on them was his favorite thing in the world other than pot and football. The sight of her right then sent a pang of defeat through my chest. She had Pablo, and I didn't. I never would. For one twisted moment I wanted to be her. I wanted to get in her skin and lead her life and have all the things that she had.

"Are you my sister's friend?" Jessica asked.

"Your sister has friends?" Judy said with a smirk.

Jessica knew who I was. We'd had several classes together, and we saw each other on almost a daily basis at Food World. She was just being a bitch.

"It's Dade," Judy said. "You know. *Dade*."

"Oh," Jessica said, lowering her voice. "Pablo's Dade?"

Judy clicked her tongue. "Don't say that. It's not true."

"Oh," said Jessica. "Sorry."

"Great party," I said.

Judy moved closer to me. She smelled like vanilla perfume and the mall.

"Listen," she said in a serious tone. "I don't know why you're here, but if I catch you talking to Pablo or even *looking* at Pablo, I'll have Bert and every player on the team beat the living fuck out of you. Do you hear me? The living *fuck*."

Jessica covered her mouth in a poor attempt to hide her laughter.

"You'll be toast," Judy said, as if it was the most simple equation in the world. "Consider this your one and only warning."

Jessica smiled brightly and thrust her empty cup at me. "Dave, will you be a gentleman and get me some more beer? Keg's in the kitchen. And not a lot of head, please."

Judy and I traded death glares. I grabbed Jessica's cup and made my way to the kitchen, where I immediately tossed it on the counter in a sea of empties and half-empties. The kitchen was just as crowded as the living room. Pablo and a couple of football players were manning the keg, filling their friends' cups first, and constantly overlooking the empty cups of the kids who weren't as cool. I watched him for a bit, thought back to us in his room that afternoon. All of that seemed so far away. I stood there wondering if there was any space in his mind that was occupied by the thought of me. I thought of what Judy had said she'd do to me if I even looked at him, and averted my eyes, but after a few seconds I was staring at him again, reaching for him through the crowd with my gaze.

"Who do I have to blow to get a beer?" someone called loudly.

"Me!" Pablo yelled into the crowd. "You have to blow me, fag."

43

"Yeah!" said one of the other players standing at the keg. "Settle down. We'll get to you soon enough."

I found a coffee mug in the cupboard and filled it up with tap water for Fessica. I told myself that Pablo wasn't there, that I didn't know the guy handing out the beers. I ran into Judy and Jessica on my way back upstairs to Fessica.

"Where's my beer?" Jessica asked.

"Keg's dry," I mumbled. I brushed past them and went upstairs.

Everyone had vacated the upstairs hallway except for Fessica. I kneeled down in front of her and held out the water. Her eyes were closed.

"Hey," I said. "Drink this. You'll feel better."

She slowly opened her eyes. She looked at me, then at the mug, and then back at me. I sensed that she wanted me to put it to her lips and help her drink, but I wasn't about to do that.

"Come on," I said. "Take it."

She took the mug and downed the water in loud slurps. When it was gone, she let out a dramatic "Ah!" and handed it back to me. I set it on the floor.

"Take me to my bedroom," she said. She nodded to the door across from where she was sitting. "Right there."

I pulled her up and dragged her into her room. The pink canopy above her bed sagged in the middle, and the walls were covered with posters of horses in nature and posters from horse movies. On the far wall at the foot of the bed was a large table and a vanity mirror whose edges were decorated with pictures of Fessica riding a horse at what appeared to be various competitions. There was a white dresser across the room, and on top of this was a mirrored tray covered with bottles of drugstore nail polish and pop star concocted perfumes, fragrances with names like Forever Girl and Galactic Kiss.

She fell onto the bed with a sigh, her eyes still half closed. I turned off the light and stood in the middle of the room and watched her for a while, the low-hanging Pluto on a mobile of our solar system sometimes brushing across the top of my head. Above us were the sounds of people skidding down the roof, laughing.

"Do you want to get in with me?" she asked.

Her voice was small and narrow, the voice of someone who spent a good portion of her life trying to not draw attention to herself. I'd sensed the same thing in my own voice at times, and it occurred to me that there were people downstairs who thought I was just as sad of a case as Fessica Montana. I moved slowly across the room and lay next to her. Our shoulders touched as we stared up at the sagging canopy, at the shadows that came through the window. They shifted whenever a car passed by before finally settling back into their primary pose.

"Remember when someone wrote faggot on your locker after that thing in the lunchroom?"

"Yeah," I said. "What about it?"

"That was my sister. I heard her and Judy laughing about it on the phone."

The thought of it caused an ache in my chest that blossomed like a firework and then faded.

I let out a sigh. "Yup. That makes sense."

She turned onto her side. She was staring at me, her eyes so wide, they seemed to give off their own light.

"I heard the strangest conversation down in the kitchen," she said.

"Yeah?" I asked. "What about?"

"These two guys were saying that they were smoking pot on the golf course the other night and they saw that girl who disappeared. Jenny Moore. They said she walked out of the woods right by the seventh hole and then walked right back in. Like she was stepping out of the house to see what the temperature was like."

"Really?" I said. "And what do you think about that?"

"I don't know," she said. "People see things."

"People lie, is more like it."

"That too," she said. "I bet you never lie."

"I lie every day," I said.

"About what?"

"About everything. Sometimes I lie about the lie itself. That's where things get tricky."

"What's that mean?"

I shook my head. "Never mind. I'm being stupid."

She swallowed. It made a wet, foreboding sound.

"Dade?" she said.

"Yeah?"

"Can we try something?" she asked.

"Try what?"

Her response came in the form of her hand working on the button of my fly.

"Whoa," I said. I tried pushing her hand away, but she resisted. "Not cool."

She kept at it. She even sat up a little bit to get a better handle on it.

"Stop," I said.

I jumped off the bed, falling onto the ground in the process. I checked my fly and fixed the top button that she'd somehow managed to undo.

"What are you doing?" I said. "Are you crazy? Are you out of your mind?"

"I'm sorry." She sat up quickly and backed against the headboard as if repulsed by what some outside force had just made her do.

"Not cool," I said. "Not cool at all."

"It's just—"

"I should go."

"Please don't," she said. "I'm sorry. That was stupid of me."

"I gotta go."

I was out the door before she could respond. A girl at the end of the hall was sobbing uncontrollably while two of her friends hung on either shoulder. I stumblingly ran down the stairs into a sea of people bouncing in unison to some hip-hop track that had been popular two summers before.

"See ya later, Vagisil!" someone shouted as I made my way to the door.

When I reached the porch I was out of breath and my heart was racing. It was as if I'd just saved myself from drowning. I bounded off the porch and walked quickly down the shadowed sidewalk, my eyes on my shoes as I passed the row of darkened houses. My mind was a chorus of voices all telling different reasons why I shouldn't have come.

"Party this way?"

He caught me off guard. I looked up from my shoes and saw a boy in a sleeveless black hoodie coming toward me on the sidewalk. I noticed his arms. They were tan and toned. He stopped walking, but I kept moving past him.

"Back there," I said.

"You need anything?" he called two seconds later.

I stopped and looked back. "What?"

His hood was up. His face was all shadows.

"You need anything?" he said again. "You know. Smoke?"

He lifted his toes and balanced on his heels for a second in a pose that was decidedly aw-shucks, something to match the straight-armed way he had his hands jammed in the pockets of his black skinny jeans.

"Do you need a cigarette?" I asked, confused.

"No, no, man," he said. "Do *you* need anything?"

"Do *I* need a cigarette?"

He laughed and sauntered over toward me. He pulled his hood back as he came over. He put his hand on my shoulder and leaned in. He had perfect stubble, the kind I could never grow, and huge brown eyes that were wide and a bit wild, like he was up for anything. His hair was a mess of black triangular pieces jutting out in every direction. I couldn't stop staring at his full upper lip. He looked like the kind of guy who had a banged-up electric guitar and a sticker-coated skateboard and a lucky lighter that he never left home without. He was beautiful.

"Weed, man," he said. "Do you want. To buy. Some weed?"

"Oh." I stopped to think. There was a stirring in my pelvis, only partially due to the butterflies in my stomach. I didn't need any pot, but I definitely wanted to keep talking to him. "I think I'm cool."

The right side of his mouth stretched out into a sideways grin. It was pure charm, something he probably kept in his back pocket for frequent use.

"You sure?" he asked.

I had thirteen dollars on me. It didn't matter if I wasn't.

"I'm sure," I said.

We stood there for a few seconds, waves of something awkward and unspoken passing between us. He looked up toward the party, then back at me, and he gave a polite but curt nod good-bye.

"See you around, man," he said.

And he headed on toward the Montanas', leaving me there on the sidewalk, speechless.

# Chapter 5

My father had already left for work when I woke up the next day. I found my mother mopping the kitchen floor in her housecoat. The air reeked of bleach and Lysol. Jenny Moore's parents were on the refrigerator television. They were pleading into the camera, describing what their daughter was wearing when last seen—denim shorts, a pink T-shirt with a cartoon giraffe on it, canary-colored flip-flops. They talked about how sweet and special she was, how much she loved school, Jesus, and her new puppy Oscar. Her mother said something about how it was never too late to do the right thing. I thought of what Fessica had told me the previous night about the stoners supposedly spotting her on the golf course. Of course it wasn't true. People were messed up.

"Do you need help?" I asked my mom.

"No," she said without looking up at me. "I have it under control."

I went back upstairs and put on a Vas Deferens album and stretched out on my bed. I reached over to the drawer in my nightstand and pulled out an envelope that Fairmont had sent me the previous day. It was filled with literature about the university. The campus looked idyllic, like something from a movie about college. The dormitories all had stately names like Ford House and Butler Place. I imagined myself in one of their rooms, autumn simmering outside my window while I read Dostoevsky or Pynchon or some other author I was still too scared to touch. I even inserted a hot roommate into a fantasy, a detail that quickly led to me locking my door, turning up my music, and jerking off. Afterward I lay there on my bed in a sea of Fairmont brochures and booklets and stared up at the ceiling.

"I'm gay," I said to the ceiling fan as if it didn't already know. "I'm a fag."

I thought about what my dad would say when he found out. I'd have to tell him someday. I was sure he'd make some comment about me always having to do things the difficult way and then tell me that I'd better find a way to still have kids, as if that was the only way to save my life from being a complete waste. My mind wandered to Vicki, the woman my father had told me about at the country club.

*A poetry class*, I thought. *A fucking poetry class.*

I tried to imagine my father sitting at a table with a group of middle-aged adults while they listened to each other read their writing. What did my father write about? Did he write about me and my mother? Was his poetry praising us, or we were the root of some misery that he exorcised through awkward rhymes and bad metaphors?

I went down the hall to my father's den. I opened the door slowly, nervous about entering a space that was so singularly his. I imagined him in his office across town, looking up from some contract and sensing that someone was trespassing on his domain. The walls were lined with bookshelves that housed leather-bound volumes of classics that most likely had never been opened by anyone in this house. His giant oak desk sat facing the window that overlooked our backyard. This was the one room in the house where he was allowed to smoke his cigars, and the scent hung heavy in the air as if he'd smoked one there that morning before heading to work. I sat in his leather chair and marinated in the residue of his aura for a few moments before going through his drawers.

In the bottom drawer I found a black leather portfolio with "Ned's Poetry" embossed in gold letters on the front. I sniffed the cover, took in the leather smell. There was a photograph of a woman glued on the first page. It was an eight by ten with a waxy surface, the kind of photograph one gets taken in one of those department store portrait studios that always seem to be located down some depressingly narrow hall with scuffed floors and bright fluorescent lights. The woman in the portrait was black, probably about forty or so. She had a wide mouth and a slim face, and she wore a relaxed smile that made me think she was one of those women who always spoke in a low, controlled tone, a woman who prided herself on being a soothing presence. She wore a purple turtleneck and silver hoop earrings, and her hair came past her shoulders in wet ringlets. The backdrop behind her was a blue and white marble pattern, a weak suggestion of sky. There was a message written under the photograph in purple pen.

*For my darling Ned. In a world of danger, a safe place for your thoughts.*

*XOXOXO Vicki*

I turned the page, read the first poem in the book. It was written in my father's obsessive miniature handwriting.

*so maybe last night*
*i was not your husband*
*instead i was the burglar*
*hiding in our bathroom*
*with the lights out and his shirt off*
*attentive to only your breathing*
*in the hollow heart of our bedroom*

I read the lines over and over. I imagined my father standing in the darkness of their bathroom as my mother's breathing steadied out into sleep. Perhaps he was the same as me, someone with the word *escape* flashing in his mind like a neon sign advertising an opportunity. For a moment I felt sorry for him, but then I flipped back to the picture of Vicki and I was angry all over again. I turned the second page to read the next poem, but there was nothing else. The remaining pages were all blank.

I put the book back in the drawer. I didn't want to know anything else about my father or Vicki or his poetry. Some small part of me took pleasure in his apparent confusion, in the fact that he'd come to a fork in the road of his life and wanted to somehow take both paths. It just proved what I'd always suspected, that he didn't know anything more than anyone else.

I sat there slowly spinning in his office chair and making myself dizzy. I thought of the guy I'd seen the previous evening when I was leaving the party, the one with pretty eyes and messy hair and sexy arms. The idea of him set off a whirlpool of desire in my chest. I wanted all of him. I wanted to know his name, his birthday, his favorite color, what he liked to have for breakfast, what his favorite bands were, the size and brand of his favorite pair of jeans. I wondered if everyone felt such urgent desire for people they hardly knew, if mine was actually unremarkable. I wondered if Fessica made a mental diagram that divided me into my tastes and smells and mannerisms and possessions, all the little things visible from the outside that made me who I was.

I went to my room to get ready for work. I kept the Vas Deferens on as I showered and then dressed in the khakis and white collared work shirt that all the Food World employees were forced to wear. I smiled brightly at my reflection, and there was an unexpected moment where I somehow found myself sorta handsome. I thought of the guy I'd seen the previous evening. I wondered what he'd think of me right then, of my retro tie and my shaggy hair and the pair of expensive Italian dress pants I found buried in a bin at a thrift store downtown. Could a boy like that ever like me? Maybe.

∞

It was Saturday, and Saturdays were always busy at Food World. The parking lot was filled with the SUVs and minivans of house-wives there to throw down hundreds of dollars on their family's weekly grocery supply. I parked my car in the employee lot at the side of the building and entered through the fire door out back by the Dumpsters and bread racks. The supervisors went there to smoke throughout the day, and the door was always propped open with a cinder block. The old purple-haired woman who worked in the bakery was out there with her back against the open door, the smoke from her Capri drifting back into the store. I gave her a friendly nod when I entered. She just kept staring off into space.

I waited with the other employees in the break room for my shift to start. It was white-walled with a long boardroom-type table. The sound of the lights humming in their fixtures and the low drone of the pop machine created two dissonant notes, the perfect depressing soundtrack for waiting to clock in for work. Two freshmen were at the end of the table whispering to each other and chuckling dumbly.

I took a seat at the opposite end and flipped through one of the Food World newsletters that came out every month. As usual, it was filled with stupid crap. There were retirement announcements from employees at Food Worlds across the Midwest and breathless updates in the deli menu (*"Banana custard is being discontinued and will be replaced with hot mocha pudding as of July 1. The banana custard will not be returning to the Food World deli menu in the near future. We ask that you please inform all customers of this change so they can plan their summer menus accordingly.").* There were recipes from Food World employees, mostly the older men and women who spent their semi-retired years bagging groceries on the early-morning shift, and these all seemed to involve raisins, nuts, or okra, sometimes a lethal combination of the three. On the back page there was a produce-themed crossword puzzle.

The door to the break room swung open, and Jessica walked in. Instead of a tie she wore a hot pink rhinestone brooch at the neck of her collared shirt. She pointed at me and let out a sharp burst of laughter before walking over to the pop machine and inserting a crisp dollar.

"What's so funny?" I asked.

She looked over her shoulder as she pressed the diet soda button.

"Oh, nothing," she said. The smirk on her face suggested otherwise. "Nothing at all."

My face felt hot. It was times like these that made me wish the desire to inflict pain upon others was an inherent part of my nature, but it wasn't. I shook my head and went back to the newsletter and stared at an article about the upcoming car wash the Cedarville High cheerleading squad would be holding in the Food World parking lot to raise money for new uniforms.

Jessica took a seat directly across from me. She sipped slowly from her diet soft drink and stared at me. Her hair was a whiter shade of blond than it had been last night, and between this and the thick layer of foundation on her face, she looked especially trashy. The two freshmen at the end of the table stared at her and me like they knew something was about to happen.

"Yeah, I'm not laughing at anything," she said. "Except for the fact that you spent a good portion of my party getting busy with my sister. What's up with that, Dade? Is the whole gay thing not working out for you?"

"I don't know what you're talking about," I said. I gave a quick glance at the freshmen. They were slack-jawed. "I barely talked to your sister last night. I got her some water and helped her to her room."

"Well, that's not what she's telling everyone," Jessica said. She sat up straighter in her chair, seemingly satisfied with how well her mortification of me was going. "She told me that you fingered her for, like, three hours. That's gotta be grounds for getting your butt pirate license taken away. Or at least enough to get it suspended."

I stared at the newsletter, my anger emptying the words and images of all their meaning. I could feel Jessica and the unfamiliar freshmen watching me and waiting for my reaction. I thought about telling her how I spent the day of the party having sex with her best friend's boyfriend, but I knew that would only make things worse.

"Who did she tell this to?" I finally said.

"Just me so far," she said. "But I'm sure by the end of the day everyone will know."

"Why?"

"Because, Vagisil. Inquiring minds want to know."

I went over and grabbed my punch card from the rack on the wall and slid it into the time clock without saying anything. The freshmen snickered.

"Shut the hell up," I said to them before leaving.

I usually checked in with my supervisor at the beginning of my shift, but instead I headed directly to the movie rental department. I found Fessica behind the counter reading *Teen Diva*. Some blond starlet smirked icily from the cover. She gave me a terrified look when she saw me storming toward the counter.

"You told your sister I fingered you for three hours?" I hissed. "Are you out of your mind?"

"I didn't tell anyone that," she said, her voice cracking. "I don't know what you're talking about."

"I just saw her upstairs. She told me you told her that we hooked up."

She bit her lip and looked down at the magazine she'd set on the counter.

"Do you hate me now?" she asked.

"Um, yeah. Pretty much. My social life is complicated enough as it is. I don't need shit like this making it worse."

Her eyes were tearing up. She pulled a crumpled tissue from the pocket of her khakis and wiped her nose.

"I'm sorry," she said. "I don't know what I was thinking."

"You obviously weren't," I said. "Why would you do that? Did you really think I wouldn't find out?"

"I don't know," Fessica said. She was really crying now. "Jessica was just making fun of me all this morning. I was helping her dye her hair and she kept asking me if I got any at the party. She was just teasing me and being mean, and then she said something about you and it just went downhill from there. She started insinuating all this stuff, so it wasn't all me . . . but I really didn't try and disprove her. I didn't think she actually thought it was true. And she probably doesn't. She's just being Jessica. It was a dumb conversation. I'm sorry. I didn't think it'd get this far."

I looked down and kicked at the floor. The toe of my shoe left black scuff marks. I couldn't help but feel a little sorry for her. Her magazine was lying open on the counter at a page with a quiz called "How You Can Tell if He's Worthy of 2nd Base." And then I thought of something.

"I won't kill you in your sleep if you do something for me," I said. "There was a boy at the party last night. He was coming as I was leaving. I didn't recognize him from school. Maybe you saw him."

"Maybe. What did he look like?"

"Sleeveless black hoodie. Hip haircut." I resisted the urge to describe him as cute. "He asked me if I wanted to buy pot."

"Oh. Alex. He's my sister's friend. Well, not her friend. He sells her and all those guys weed. He went to Cedarville South."

Cedarville South couldn't even be described as a rival high school in our town. It was dubbed Slacker Academy because that's where they sent the "troubled" kids, the ones who skipped class all the time and got into fights. School days at Cedarville South started at noon and ended at three, a stoned blur for most of the student body. They offered classes with names like Meditational Collage and Modern Facts. Like everyone else at my school, I'd always regarded the kids who went to Cedarville South as losers, slackers, and burnouts, kids with switchblades in their socks and homemade tattoos on the insides of their wrists. I was a bit weirded out to discover that my crush went to school there, but at the same time there was something about this that excited me. He was already proving to be unlike everyone else I knew.

"Where can I find him?" I asked.

Fessica screwed her face up. "Why?"

I just wanted to see him one more time. He could just give me that grin again. That would've been enough.

"I just do," I said.

"Do you do drugs?"

"Yeah. I need the hookup." The phrase *the hookup* sounded insanely stupid coming out of my mouth. The only time I'd done drugs was when I'd smoked pot with Pablo.

"Do you like boys?" she asked.

I didn't know what to say. The only other person that had actually asked me if I was gay was Bert McGraw, and that was during our confrontation in the lunchroom. The one good thing about people just assuming I was a queer was that I never had to confirm or deny it, and without my input, there would always be a tiniest speck of doubt in their minds. Without me, they could never know for sure.

"What does that have to do with anything?" I said.

"I'm just curious," she said.

"Did you ever think that maybe it's not any of your business?" I asked. "Just tell me where I can find him. You owe me."

"I mean, did you not wanna do that stuff with me last night because you're gay, or did you not want to do it because you're not, like, into me?'"

"Seriously, I can't talk about that with you, Fessica. I'm sorry, but I can't."

She looked down at the magazine on the counter, at the beauty secrets yelling to be heard over each other.

"Please," I said. The desperation in my voice made her look up at me again. It was a tone that surprised even me. "Just tell me where I can find him."

# Chapter 6

She told me he worked at Taco Taco, a Mexican fast-food joint located in the parking lot of an abandoned strip mall a couple miles away from Food World. She said she was sure he was working that night, that he worked nearly every night there because he was saving up to get out of Cedarville. I drove there in my used BMW after work with my tie loosened and the top of my shirt unbuttoned. The sun was almost gone, turning the hem of the western sky a warm pink. As I drove, I thought of Fessica locked in her bedroom for the rest of the evening. I wondered if her mind went back to me the way mine sometimes went to Pablo.

I parked in the back of Taco Taco, next to one of the two massive yellow Dumpsters. I got out of my car and was immediately met with the spicy stench coming from the garbage. Beans and meat and rancid vegetables.

"I don't even know if he's gay," was the last thing Fessica had said to me before I left her in the video department that afternoon. I didn't know either. I was acting on some instinct that I didn't know I had. I'd never gone out of my way for a guy before. Even my and Pablo's first encounters were totally initiated by him. I never went out of my way to follow crushes around high school. I never approached anyone with the hopes of getting a phone number or even a name. I was afraid of giving myself away. I didn't want anyone to know. Sometimes even I didn't want to know.

I leaned against the car and shut my eyes.

*You're crazy, Dade*, I thought. *You're stalking some guy you don't even know. This won't work out.*

I walked around the side of Taco Taco to smoke a cigarette before I went inside. I needed something to calm me down. I took two drags before my stomach began to twist. Maybe it was the smell of beans and meat coming from the Dumpster around the corner or maybe it was my nerves or just the cigarette. I crouched down and puked on the ground. It came out brown and lumpy and left an acidic aftertaste in my throat. Some of it splattered onto my black work shoes.

*Good*, I thought. *I'm glad I puked on these damn shoes. I hate these things.*

There was a little blue metal newspaper dispenser near the entrance filled with copies of the *Penny Saver*, and I used one to wipe the vomit off my shoes before going inside.

Taco Taco was a pretty trashy place. I hadn't been there since third grade or something, and its appearance hadn't changed a bit. There were orange plastic booths throughout the dining area and a few plastic potted plants that still somehow managed to look like living things on the brink of death. About half of the overhead lights were burnt out, creating small dark areas throughout the restaurant. There was no one there except for a tall black guy with dreadlocks behind the counter. He was chewing on something and casting a vacant stare in my direction. He was about my age, attractive, with a narrow face and thin mustache. Flamenco music cracked from blown speakers in the ceiling, a man howling sadly in Spanish along to an acoustic guitar. I went up to the counter.

"Welcome to Taco Taco. Would you like to try the Deus Ex Mexicana?" His words came out in an empty, rehearsed stream. The tag on his shirt said his name was Jay.

I reached into my pocket, felt for money. I wasn't hungry, but I felt like I should order something. I at least needed something to drink to get the vomit taste out of my mouth. There was a square window behind Jay that revealed a surprisingly clean metallic kitchen. I could hear someone else moving around back there, but I couldn't see who it was.

"What's the Deus Ex Mexicana?" I asked.

"It's this month's special burrito. Ground beef, chicken, steak, black beans, red beans, pinto beans, hot sauce, chipotle sour cream, and fiery guacamole. Five ninety-nine, plus tax. Comes with an orange soda and a shot of Pepto-Bismol."

"Do you guys just have like quesadillas or something?"

He gave an exaggerated eye roll and let out a loud sigh.

64

"Alex," he called into the kitchen. "Do we have quesadillas tonight?"

A voice called out, "Nope. No quesadillas tonight. Try back tomorrow."

"No quesadillas," Jay said. "I think we got tacos, though."

My pulse raced, and the sick feeling in my stomach came back. That had to be him back there. I stood on my tiptoes to try and get a better glimpse of the kitchen. From somewhere in back was the sound of a faucet being turned on.

"Is Alex back there?" I asked.

"You one of Alex's friends?"

"Sorta."

"What's all over your pants?" Jay asked.

I looked down. I thought I'd only gotten puke on my shoes, but there were little chunks of vomit all over the front of my khakis as well.

"Damn, man," he said. "You sure you need Mexican food right now?"

"I got sick. I'm sorry. It just happened."

"You want some Pepto-Bismol?" He pulled a bottle of the stuff from under the counter and placed it in front of me. The bottle was covered with grime, like it had been rescued from the bottom of the Dumpster out back. He called out over his shoulder, "Yo, Kincaid! One of your white junkie friends is here. He's got puke all over his pants."

"I'm not a junkie, dude," I said.

"I'm finishing this drive-through order," the voice called

from the kitchen. "Can you tell them to wait outside?"

Jay nodded, turned back to me. "He said to wait outside. He'll be right out."

"I'm not a junkie," I repeated.

"Denial's not just a river in Egypt, son."

"Can I get something to drink at least?" I asked.

He rolled his eyes and filled up a cup of soda from the fountain. "Here. On the house. Now go wait outside."

I left and sat on the curb several feet away from where I'd puked. From the unseen everywhere came the intermittent rush of cars passing by. I forced myself to stop staring at my vomit and looked out across the empty parking lot at the vacant strip mall whose trim still bore the discolored outlines of old store signs. I remembered shopping there a few years back. There'd been a discount shoe store that my mother loved called Sole Mates and a beauty supply store staffed by girls with neon eye shadow and trailer park hair. Now everything was closed. I wondered where those neon-eyed girls were now, if maybe they'd escaped Cedarville just like I was about to.

A voice behind me said, "Hey."

I turned around. His hair was different than it had been last night. Now it was combed down so that it hung right above his eyes. He was wearing baggy black trousers and a purple collared shirt with "Taco Taco" embroidered in yellow stitching above the right breast pocket. He gave off the impression that he was overwhelmingly bored and maybe a little stoned. I liked the fact that he seemed like someone who didn't care too much about anything. I was beginning to think that caring too much was what got people into trouble.

"I didn't hear you come out," I said.

"Came out around back. From the kitchen." He looked me up and down like he was trying to place where I was from.

"You don't know me," I said. "I met you outside of the party last night. My name's Dade."

He pulled back a bit. "Yeah? And?"

"Well, you asked me if I wanted to buy some pot, and I didn't. Not then. But now I do. Something came up."

He nodded slowly and kept staring at me, studying me. The charm from the previous night had been dulled with doubt and suspicion. Something about his smoldering gaze made him look like one of the mechanics in *Lube Jobs 4*.

He glanced around the lot. "You caught me at a funny time. I'm dry at the moment. Gotta meet my guy after work, so I won't be able to hook you up for another couple of hours."

He looked back at me and waited for my reply. I'd never actually bought drugs before. I always just smoked Pablo's weed. I wasn't sure how drug deals worked, what the rules of conduct were. Should I say I'd leave and come back? Tell him I'd call him tomorrow? Or just say yeah, and wait around? I looked down at my feet and kicked the grimy toe of my dress shoe at the ground.

"Who did you say you knew at the party?" he asked, not entirely convinced of something.

"Jessica and Fessica. I work with them," I said. "And went to school with them."

That charming grin finally made an appearance.

"Ah, Jessica and Depressica," he said. "My two favorite pop tarts."

I wanted to ask what that meant, but I didn't. He looked down and got lost in some private thought and shook his head and laughed before looking back up at me and getting back to business.

"I'm Alex," he said, extending his hand.

"Dade."

"Right. So I need like forty-five minutes before I can leave," he said.

"Okay."

"So . . . you can wait out here if you want. Or you can go. Or whatever. Happy to help you out, though. Any friend of those girls is a friend of mine. Not that either of them have what you could really consider friends."

I laughed. "I hear that. I mean, I'll just stay and wait. If that's cool with you."

"Sure," he said. "Whatever. If you've got nowhere else to go."

"I don't," I said.

"Okay," he said. "Be out soon."

He gave a halfhearted wave good-bye and went back inside to close the place. He wasn't gone for thirty seconds before I began to tell myself that I was being stupid, that waiting was a dumb idea. It made me look weird. I considered just leaving. I could swing by Pablo's house and see if he was awake. It'd been a long time since I'd snuck up to the little window of his basement bedroom to see if he wanted to fool around. I pulled out my cell phone to call him, but when I saw his name on the screen it looked awful. I thought about him playing keg commando at the party the previous night. I scrolled up and called my mother instead.

"I'll be home late," I told her.

"That's fine," she said. "Pablo came looking for you. Is he okay? He seemed anxious."

She sounded tired beyond the point of being angry at anyone or anything. I imagined her wandering through that house she never wanted, touching all the appliances and flipping through the hundreds of stations on the huge flat-screen television in the family room. I knew how lonely our house could feel when there was no one else in it, and for a moment I wished I was at home so she could feel me sleeping on the other side of the wall that divided our bedrooms.

"Yeah," I said. "He's fine. I'm with him now. I'll be out with him pretty late. I should go, though."

"Thanks for calling," she said numbly. "Be safe."

I hung up and waited on the curb. The neon sign blinked off, making the tall lamps that dotted the lot the primary sources of light. I waited. Eventually I stood up and leaned against the side of the building near the glass entryway and watched as Alex and Jay went about cleaning the restaurant. They turned off the Latin music and turned on some New Wave eighties music at full blast. They went around lazily picking up chairs and putting them on tabletops, and sometimes they would stop to play air drums along to a song or blindly bounce around. I watched as they mopped the floors and wiped down the tables and the front counter. There were parts of Alex's movements—the lazy U-turns he made when mopping, the way he sometimes couldn't figure out the proper way to brush his hair out of his eyes—that made him seem young and careless, but then he'd get all stiff-backed and shoot Jay a glare for doing more dancing than cleaning and reveal an unexpected sliver of responsibility.

I met them outside the rear entrance after their shift ended. They made plans to go to a party the next night, while I stood off to the side in silence with my hands stuffed in my pockets. They spoke for a few minutes and then Jay left, giving a nod and wave as he walked away. Alex turned to me, rubbing his eyes and letting out a yawn. His Taco Taco shirt was unbuttoned to reveal a white wife beater. There was a bit of chest hair visible in the valley of the shirt's collar. I caught myself staring at for it a few seconds too long and thought to myself, *Look at you. You're memorizing him already.*

"Having a job blows," he said. "You ready to go?"

I nodded. "Yeah. Sure. Totally."

He gave me a look, something studious and unsure. Had he noticed me staring? A jolt of worry shot through me. I followed him over to a black Chevy Citation parked in the corner of the lot. There were patches of rust on the doors and hood, and a dark red pinstripe running around the body of the car. The interior smelled like cigarettes and watermelon air freshener. The backseat was a mini landfill composed of fast-food wrappers, tattered skateboarding magazines, empty soda cans, and other assorted trash. He turned on the car. "Working Overtime at the Clarity Foundation" poured out of the speakers at full blast. He quickly reached for the volume knob and turned it down.

"Sorry about that," he said. "I always rock out before work. Gets me psyched."

"Oh my God. I love the Vas Deferens. *Vasectomy* is, like, my favorite album."

"Yeah, everybody loves the Vas Deferens after they used their song in that stupid car commercial," he muttered before pulling out of his parking spot. "And *Vasectomy* is good, but *Emotional Aviary Death Watch* is way better. At least in my opinion."

"As an album, *Emotional Aviary Death Watch* is definitely better," I said, suddenly convinced.

We drove through town past the darkened doctors' offices and the brightly lit car dealerships.

"So, do you go to school?" I asked, trying to sound casual.

"No. I don't go to school. I sell weed."

"And you work at Taco Taco."

"And I work at Taco Taco," he said with a slow nod. "I sell weed and I work at Taco freaking Taco." He raised his hands, gestured up at the gray upholstery that sagged from the ceiling of the car. "This is my life. So my dealer just lives a bit outside of town. You got time, right?"

"Yeah," I said. "I've got time."

I slouched in my seat and tried to look relaxed, when in reality I just kept wondering what I'd gotten myself into. I didn't know this guy. He could take me anywhere.

We were passing the Gas-N-Go when I caught a glimpse of Pablo and a few of the other football players hanging out in the parking lot. They were all draped over the hood of Bert McGraw's lime green Camaro, paper-cupped drinks in their hands. It all moved by so fast, something wildly out of my control. Part of me wanted nothing more than to make Alex stop the car so I could walk up to them and scream, just loud rage flying in their faces. It would've told my story better than words ever could. They were several blocks behind us before I became aware of how fast my heart was beating, how clenched my jaw was.

"You okay?" Alex asked.

"Yeah," I lied. "I'm fine."

We got on the interstate and took it north past the city limits. About ten miles later he took an exit that took us west over the interstate onto a two-lane road. Soon the lights around the exit ramp faded out and there was nothing but flat farmland all around. He cracked his window a bit to let in a stream of cool evening air.

"Do you want to see something awesome?" he said.

The light from the dashboard made his face look green. He reached down and clicked a button under the steering wheel and the green light went out along with the headlights, and the car was thrown into darkness. The moon lit up the road in front of us. I grabbed on to the door handle.

"Dude, turn 'em back on," I said. "This is so not safe."

"You're missing it. Look."

"But we could hit—"

"Jesus." He leaned over and pointed out my window. "Just shut up and look."

I looked out at the pasture. There were thousands of lightning bugs swirling in the air over the field. It was as if a million tiny stars had descended to the earth and were all lightly flashing out of sync. I told myself that it was okay to be driving in the darkness with this guy, that I should enjoy the moment.

"It's been like that for the past week or so," Alex said. "I think it's mating season or something."

"It's beautiful," I said. I don't know why, but I was surprised he was so into this, surprised at his hushed tone of voice. He flicked the headlights back on.

"I've tried to explain to people what it looked like," he said. "But you kinda have to see it for yourself."

After about a mile he turned the car down a gravel road and pulled over to the side. He shut off the car and killed the headlights.

"We have to walk a bit," he said. "Parking right in front makes me paranoid."

The sounds of the engine and radio were gone and there was nothing but the heavy quiet of the outdoors. We got out of the car and I followed him toward a cornfield.

"We gotta walk through here," he said.

I followed him over the barbed wire fence. The cornstalks loomed in tall rows on both sides of us. Above us the clouds slid slowly across the starry sky.

"I used to do this all the time," I said.

"Do what?" he said.

"Wander through the cornfields," I said. "I lived on a farm when I was younger."

"Did you milk a lot of pigs?"

"Um . . . no."

"No? Why not?"

"No. My parents weren't farmers or anything."

"So you didn't get to, like, artificially inseminate any horses or anything?"

I didn't respond.

"That was a joke, dude," he said.

"I know."

"You got all quiet on me."

"No, I didn't."

"Yeah, you did." He was far ahead of me, just a shadow rustling a few yards away. "You could have laughed. Artificially inseminating horses is funny. I saw it on television once. Laughed my ass off."

I laughed softly at this, and when he heard me he started laughing too.

"And you don't have to agree with me, you know," he went on. "Just because I think *Emotional Aviary Death Watch* is the Deferens' best doesn't mean you have to."

"Oh," I said, embarrassed and blushing in the dark. "Right. I mean, it's hard to pick a favorite."

"If *Vasectomy* is your album, then it's your album," he went on. "Don't let me take that away from you."

There was nothing mean about the way he was saying it, but it still felt awkward to be called out. We didn't say anything else for the rest of the walk. When we came out of the other side of the cornfield, we were standing in the backyard of a weathered little house. Its sunny yellow paint was peeling, and the windows were cracked and dirty. Beyond it was a dirt road and on the other side of that were more cornfields, always more.

Alex walked up the porch steps and slapped his open hand hard on the back door. We waited. Around us the night moved. Wind rustled the corn, and the chirps of crickets pinballed around us, first here, then there, then over there. Then came the sound of heavy footsteps from inside the house. I thought *Fee-fi-fo-fum* and the door swung open.

The guy who answered was taller than Alex by at least three inches. He had long, stringy black hair and a flat nose and a bushy black mustache so fake-looking that it had to be real. He had the carved-from-stone physique that led me to believe he worked out constantly. His blue jeans were caked with mud and his pectorals pushed aggressively against the old Guns N' Roses T-shirt he was wearing. He glared at us.

"Fuck do you want?"

At first I thought the guy didn't know who Alex was, that there'd been some terrible confusion that was going to lead to us getting beaten up, but then the guy flashed a yellow grin and slapped Alex on the shoulder.

"Just kiddin'," he said. "Get inside." He quickly took me in from head to toe and back again. "Who's your friend?"

"This is Dade," Alex said, stepping inside. "Dade, this is Dingo."

I nodded and extended my hand. Dingo looked at it like I was holding a Bible tract. He gave me an intense glare before giving me a firm handshake. The skin on his fingers and palms was cold and rough with a gritty texture, like he'd been playing with dirt recently.

"Come on in, kids."

He led us into a dark little kitchen. Every inch of the kitchen counter was covered with empty bottles of Bud Light. The doors of the cupboards had been taken off to reveal empty shelves, and the small kitchen table in the corner of the room had been cut in half.

"What happened to the table?" Alex asked

"It got broken during the filming of our first music video," Dingo said, leading us into the next room.

"You guys made a music video?" Alex laughed.

"We did."

The living room of the cottage was small. It was barely big enough to fit the sofa, coffee table, and television that it held. The lights were off. There were two guys around my age sitting shoulder to shoulder on the couch watching the television. One was skinny with red hair and a long pale-skinned face. He held his chin close to his chest and looked up at me in a manner that was strangely demure. The other was blond and jockish. He sat with his legs apart and his arm up on the back of the couch and sneered benignly at the television. When we came in they moved apart so Dingo could sit between them.

"Have a seat," Dingo said, motioning to the floor in front of the couch.

I looked at Alex for permission, but he didn't notice. He just plopped down in the narrow space between the television and the coffee table and stared at the TV. I maneuvered myself down beside him. *Dawn of 1,000 Werewolves* was on. It was the sequel to Johnny Morgan's first film, *Night of 1,000 Werewolves*, the starting point of my crush on him. I'd always found it inferior to the first one for many reasons, the main one being that Johnny Morgan wasn't in it. Johnny had gone on to bigger and better things and the role of preppy werewolf slayer Kip Tracer was taken over by a shiny-faced actor named Jack Jackson who looked at least forty but was still somehow playing a college freshman on a campus full of werewolves. He looked like Johnny only in the vaguest sense.

"What are we watching?" Alex asked.

"*Dawn of 1,000 Werewolves*," I said.

"You know it?" Dingo asked.

"Totally," I said.

"It's, like, the best bad movie ever," the redhead on the couch said excitedly.

"My favorite part is the toga party with the keg filled with blood," the other one said. He moved his mouth as little as possible, maybe to keep his sneer intact

"Oh my God," said the first kid. "Totally. I love that suddenly there's a vampire in this movie about werewolves. So random."

"Yeah," his friend said. "But it totally works. I mean, college is, like, full of surprises."

"This is Thomas," Dingo said, nodding toward the redhead. "And this is Louie. You guys know Alex. This is his friend Dave."

"Dade," I said.

"Sorry. Dade."

On the screen Jack Jackson sprinted across the quad, a preppy pink sweater tied around his neck and a legion of snarling werewolves on his tail. It felt weird to be watching the movie in this creepy little house when I'd seen it so many times in the comfort of the family room. The idea drew an invisible line between this strange, dark moment and the rest of my life.

"So what can I get for you boys?" Dingo asked.

"Just some good old-fashioned marijuana," Alex said. "Same as always."

"I think I can do that. Follow me."

He led the four of us back into the kitchen, where we took the stairs down to the basement. There was a turquoise-colored washing machine with a matching dryer against the wall, a weight bench, and a circle of metal folding chairs around a large wooden crate. In the corner was a drum kit, two huge amplifiers, and two beat-up guitars that looked like they'd been tossed to the concrete floor in a fit of punk rock indifference. The floor was littered with cigarettes and ash.

"You guys in a band?" I asked.

"We are," said Dingo. "We're called Death Grip."

"I still don't like that name," Louie said.

"I like it," said Thomas.

"That's because you like things that are dumb."

"Alex is our manager," Dingo said.

"What he means is sometimes I hang out and watch them play and tell them what songs suck, which is all of them," Alex said.

"Har har," Dingo muttered.

We each took a seat around a crate. Dingo opened it up and pulled out a cigar box filled with little bags of weed.

"You guys want to smoke some before we transact?" Dingo asked.

"Let's do it," said Alex.

Alex and Dingo both looked over at me.

"Just a little," I said. "I don't wanna get too stoned or whatever."

"Suit yourself," Dingo said. He pulled a joint from the box, lit it, and took a hit. "Here, kid," he said, passing it to me while still holding smoke in his lungs.

I took a medium-size hit. The smoke was sweet and liquidy, like sugar water rolling around in my mouth. I sucked it down into my lungs, and told myself not to cough, that I didn't want to look like an amateur in front of these guys. I exhaled a large cloud of smoke toward Thomas and Louie and then handed the joint to Alex.

The pot haze came quickly, like a blanket dropped around my head. My heartbeat sped up, and I crossed my legs slowly like I was moving through melted caramel. I wondered how much longer we were going to be there. I thought of my mother lying in bed, fading in and out of a dreamless sleep. And where was my father? With Vicki, of course, in a motel room that my mind created at that very moment, someplace with brown sheets and a tattered Bible in the nightstand, red velvet wallpaper and a bathtub with a clogged drain.

"You guys hear about that girl in town who got kidnapped?" Louie asked after taking his hit.

"Yeah," Thomas said. "She's been gone for like a week or something."

"I think it's only been a few days," I said.

"But still," Thomas said.

"A week, a few days," Dingo said. "What's the difference? She's dead. Gotta be."

"They could find her," Alex said.

"She's artistic, right?" Louie said. "My step-cousin is artistic. She wanders off all the time."

"It's autistic, moron," Dingo said.

"Oh."

"They'll never find her," Thomas mumbled.

"People on TV keep talking about her in the present tense like that's what's gonna keep her alive," I said. "So weird."

Everyone looked over at me as if it was the smartest thing they'd heard all day. Dingo nodded slowly in resigned agreement, the others kept quiet. The topic had dimmed everyone into themselves. The joint had burned down to a roach. Dingo tossed it onto the floor and grinded it with the sole of his boot. He then opened the cigar box that was still sitting on top of the crate.

"How much do you want?" he asked.

"Just like an ounce," Alex said. "All I need for now."

Dingo flipped through the bags.

"There's exactly an ounce in this box," he said.

Alex jokingly asked if he took checks, but nobody laughed. He reached into his pocket and tossed him a wad of cash. Dingo handed the cigar box to Alex.

"Don't smoke it all in one place," he said, flipping through the money.

I was ready to leave. The house was depressing, and the mere thought of all the lonesome farmland just outside was depressing as well. Strangely enough, I found myself longing for the sterile safety of my subdivision, for the brightness of our foyer and the way every room in our house was perfumed with a candle that my mother had bought at the Crafty Candle Company at the Cedarville Mall.

"You ready to go?" Alex asked. "We should be getting back."

I nodded slowly and stood, and we all headed upstairs. My body felt so tired and wobbly that for a moment I was scared I wouldn't make it up. Alex was in front of me, and without thinking I put my hand on his back to steady myself.

81

"Whoa, partner," Alex said. "You okay?"

"Yeah," I said, quickly pulling my hand back. "Sorry. Dizzy spell."

Up in the kitchen I stood off to the side as the four of them said their good-byes. I was trying to make myself less high by breathing in and out, but it wasn't working. I stared out the window over the kitchen sink to where the corn waved under the night sky like a jagged black ocean. I tried to imagine what it would be like to dive into an ink-black body of water, and then I thought to myself, *All you do is look for places to get lost.*

"You ready?" Alex asked.

I snapped out of my trance and brought myself back into the house.

"Yeah," I said. "I'm ready."

"Nice meeting you, Dade," Dingo said.

Louie and Thomas were back in the living room watching TV.

"Nice meeting you too, man," I said. The words fell from my mouth like lumps of wet clay. The two of them looked at each other and laughed.

"Okay, kiddo," Alex said, slapping me on the back. "Let's get you back home to Mommy and Daddy."

I was too messed up to find his comment patronizing. In fact, going home was exactly what I wanted. We stepped out of the house and into the warm night. The yard was dotted with fireflies, nothing like we'd seen on the way out, but enough to make me smile dumbly to myself at the beauty of summer, of the world in general. Alex and I walked silently into the corn-field. The night teetered in my vision. Alex took my hand as if he could sense this.

"You okay there, partner?" he asked. "You're kind of wob-bling back and forth."

"I am?" I asked. "I didn't notice."

He laughed. "You are."

"I'm stoned," I said in an apologetic tone.

"Don't worry," he said. "I'll take care of you."

It's hard to imagine a more perfect thing for him to say. We ambled through the field, not in any sort of rush. I suddenly felt so happy and relaxed and free that I began laughing out loud. I hooted and hollered at the night sky. I let out an especially severe yell and a flock of birds sprang from where they were roosting and spread out in a black swarm over our heads. Alex just laughed and shook his head.

"Captain Crazy Person over there," he said. He was walking down the row next to me, a companion so shadowy, he may as well have been imaginary.

"I'm sorry," I said. Little bits of laughter kept tumbling from my mouth. "I'll be quiet now."

"No, no," he said quickly. "By all means, let it out. It'd be a shame to let all this space go to waste."

We came out on the other side of the field and he suggested we sit on the roof of his car and share a cigarette before going anywhere. We sat there sharing a smoke in silence. I kept look-ing over at him. I wanted to kiss him. Pablo was the only guy I'd ever kissed, and those kisses only came about in the heat of the moment when he was so messed up that he forgot to push me away.

"We should hang out again," he said. "Unless you're scared of me."

I wasn't expecting him to say that. But he was right. I was scared of him. Just a little bit. But I wasn't scared of what he would do to me; I was scared of what being around someone like him could make *me* do. I felt different around him, unpredictable to even myself.

"No," I said. "I'd like that."

We each pulled out our cell phones and exchanged numbers. My hands shook as I typed out his name. A-L-E-X. A magic word.

# Chapter 7

The next day I came downstairs in my boxer shorts and found my mother drinking a cup of coffee and reading the newspaper at the kitchen table.

"Good morning," she said. "Do you want coffee?"

She never offered me coffee. Juice or milk, but never coffee. Ever since I could remember, she'd told me that coffee would stunt my growth and there was no way she would allow me to drink it, not in her house. I looked around the kitchen. Everything was immaculately clean. The television on the fridge was playing some morning news show on mute. The scent of the coffee mingled with a warm floral scent that was probably coming from some new electric air-freshener.

"Coffee would be good," I said.

I moved toward the coffeemaker, but she sprung up from her seat.

"Let me get it," she said. She smiled at me when she passed by. "You sit down. Let's talk."

I sat at the kitchen table and watched as she prepared my coffee. She didn't ask if I took cream or sugar. She just added liberal portions of each.

"Since when can I drink coffee?" I asked. "I usually have to sneak coffee to my room in the morning."

"Well," she said, coming back to the table. She placed the coffee in front of me and sat down. "I think it's time that there were some changes around here."

*Great*, I thought. *More changes.*

She smiled and watched as I sipped the coffee.

"So, you seem to be in a good mood," I said. "Did you and Dad work things out?"

"No," she said. "I actually haven't seen your father since he left for work yesterday morning. He didn't come home last night."

"So where is he?"

She shrugged casually. "I really don't know."

"And that's . . . okay?"

She furrowed her brow and squinted one eye toward the ceiling. She was one of those people who wanted you to know when her brain was working. I took this as my cue to wait.

"The reality of this is that you're not going to be here in two months," she finally said. "I don't see any reason for your father and me to create some big mess out of your last weeks at home. Seems like a waste of time."

"So you're just not going to do anything?" I asked.

"I wouldn't say *nothing*," she said. "But I would say that I plan on doing as little as possible."

"Why don't you leave him?" I asked. "Why don't you tell him to stop seeing that woman or else?"

"Or else what?" she said with a little laugh. "Dade, your father is going to do whatever he wants to do. I'm not giving him any ultimatums. I think that's best for everyone. And I'm not holding anything against you, Dade. Your father put you in a terrible, terrible position. I need to recognize it and place the blame in the appropriate box."

The appropriate box? This was obviously crap she'd picked up from some self-help book.

"Aren't you mad at him?" I asked. "Don't you want to strangle him? I mean, he's got a picture of her in his study. It's in some book that she gave to him."

A cloud passed over her face, not one strong enough to completely wipe away her happy façade, but enough to reveal that underneath it all she was still hurting.

"I hate this," I said. "I hate the fact that he's off doing whatever he wants and we're here being miserable about it."

"A picture?" she said.

"Yeah," I said. "Up in his study. In some book for his dumb poetry."

She looked away for a second, but then brought her eyes back to me, and the smile returned, as empty as ever.

"Like I said, your father is going to do whatever he wants to do. But that being said, so are we." She paused. That mildly triumphant statement hung over our heads, a banner announcing the summer's theme. "I know we've been talking about going out and getting you things for school. Should we do that today?"

"Um . . . sure. Like, what are we gonna get?"

"Well, you'll need a new backpack. A refrigerator for your dorm room."

"What about the backpack I have now? It's fine."

"Somebody wrote *vas deferens* on it."

"I wrote that. The Vas Deferens are my favorite band."

"Are you serious?" she said, making a face. It was like she'd never heard me mention them before. "That name makes me ill. Please. Let me buy you a new one."

"Why does it make you ill?"

"Dade . . ."

"Seriously. Why?"

"You're getting a new backpack."

"Fine. New backpack. Whatever."

"You're going to need all sorts of things. Maybe we can even find a little dorm refrigerator with a built-in television. That would be fun, right?"

"That would be beyond ridiculous."

She widened her smile. "Well, why don't you go upstairs and shower and get dressed and we'll go?"

∞

She took me to the Cedarville Mall. We wandered from store to store in silence, me with my hands in my pockets and a look of boredom on my face, and her straight-backed and smiling sleepily at every salesgirl. We moved sluggishly from one store to the next until she'd bought me five pairs of jeans, two pairs of shoes, eight shirts, and all the socks and underwear in the world. In the end I wound up with this plus a toaster, a small refrigerator, a TV/DVD player, an electric toothbrush, a mini tape recorder for recording my lectures, an iron, a blow dryer, a coffeemaker, a coffee grinder, a microwave, a rice cooker, a set of silverware and plates, and a set of beer mugs.

"I think we did pretty well today," my mother said on the drive home. The back of her SUV was loaded with stuff. It was impossible to see anything out the back window. "Of course, if there's anything we forgot, we can go back and get it, but I think we got everything."

She flashed me a smile that I couldn't bear to respond to. I turned away and looked out the passenger window at the new Benny's Burger Barn that had popped up overnight on the corner of First Avenue and Collins Road. The parking lot was full of SUVs and luxury sedans. Even from a distance I could spot the tiny Hamilton Luxury Motors decal on the trunks of a few of them. I thought of my father and the fact that all we really knew of his whereabouts was that they most likely involved another woman, a woman who was not my mother.

*Screw him*, I thought.

∞

When we got home I put the stuff in a pile in the corner of my room. It occurred to me that these things made of plastic, glass, and metal would become the foundation for my new life. I thought of our house in Cedarview Estates and how at one point in time it was supposed to be the foundation for my parents and their new life. I wondered what it meant that people were so intent on building something better out of things, if I'd be able to make it work in a way that they hadn't, or if all this new stuff would give way and become worthless under the weight of all that spread before me.

I reached under my bed and pulled out the pile of literature from Fairmont College. The catalogs and brochure featured pictures of smiling kids of various races. There was one picture of a bunch of kids sitting on the steps of some old distinguished-looking building. One of the kids in the photo had spiky blond hair and a show-choir grin. The token fag. He was sitting between an Asian girl and a black dude. They were all cutouts, walking smiles. For the first time I felt like I wasn't ready for Fairmont. I thought of Alex and my time with him the previous night. Any wish to transport myself to the end of August was also a wish to leap over the unfolding story of us.

I shoved all the stuff back under my bed and changed into my swimming trunks and went down to the pool. My mother was working in the small vegetable garden in the backyard. She was wearing her yellow gardening gloves, a wide-brimmed hat, and ignoring me behind her large red-framed sunglasses. I took off my T-shirt and lay on one of the chaise longues and watched as she pulled weeds, hummed to herself, plucked cherry tomatoes from their vines and put them in her mouth. She dug holes with a miniature shovel and poured pouches of seeds into the earth.

I thought of Alex, of my hand on his back as we walked up

the stairs, the world of skin under his shirt, and his words as we headed into the cornfield.

*I'll take care of you.*

My mother was humming in the corner of the yard. I faded in and out of sleep in the warmth of the sun. The day glowed bright red on the other side of my eyelids, and I pictured my heartbeat as a fantastic throbbing lightbulb in my chest.

"Dade."

I woke up to my mother standing over me. The sun was radiating over her shoulder. She was still wearing her sunglasses, and a light breeze tossed her hair gently about her head.

"Dade, wake up," she said.

"What is it?" I mumbled, sitting up.

"We're going to a barbeque at the Savages'. I just talked to your father and he's coming with us. So you need to get up and shower. And if you could take out the trash, that'd be peachy."

She turned and went inside. A cloud slid across the sky and blocked the sun. My body felt heavy with sleep, my chest and arms warm with sun. It felt like I'd only been asleep for a few minutes, but when I checked my watch I saw I'd been out for almost an hour.

My mother chose my outfit for the Savages' barbeque by vetoing everything I came downstairs in. Everything was too casual, too dressy. Was that a stain? When did those jeans get so many holes? Didn't I have something less *edgy*? We finally settled on a preppyish pair of blue and red striped shorts and a crisp white T-shirt, both purchases from that day. Either she didn't notice my canvas slip-ons with the skulls and crossbones on them, or she didn't care.

I waited on the living room sofa for my father to arrive home. I sat there with a pen and a notebook with the intention of writing a poem, but I couldn't get a single line down. I just gazed out the picture window onto the neighborhood. I wondered if something similar had happened to our father when he tried writing in the book Vicki had given him. Maybe he got so stuck staring at his life that he forgot to write anything down.

Families from down the block were making their way to the Savages'. The parents held containers of food, their children's hands. One father guided his young son by the shoulder around a small dead bird that had been flattened into a morbid pancake in the middle of the road. My mother hummed in the kitchen as she prepared the salad she was bringing over to the Savages'. A newscaster on the refrigerator television was going on about Jenny Moore, about abductions in America, about the kids who were found and the kids who were lost forever.

My father pulled into our driveway at around six, the Audi gleaming from a recent washing. He took his time pulling things from his car. His briefcase, a sweatshirt, a coffee mug I could tell was empty by the casual way he held the handle with his pinky. He moved slowly up the path to our door with these things. He raised his hand in greeting at some unseen person down the block, someone who probably thought his slow, plodding steps up the porch were due to a long day at work instead of a quiet dread of having to interact with the people inside.

When he walked in, our eyes met and there was a moment where it was like he was considering turning around and leaving, getting back in the car. Instead he walked over to me and squeezed my shoulder. His mouth was set in a sort of grimace of approval, like it was okay with him that I was here waiting for him. It was condescending and bumped my annoyance with him up another level.

"New clothes?" he asked.

I nodded.

"I heard," he said. "The credit card company called me at work to make sure my card wasn't stolen. You guys must have done some damage, as they say."

My mother came into the room with a salad in a big plastic Tupperware bowl. She gave my father a look that acknowledged his presence but also warned him not to say a thing to her.

"Ready to go?" she said to me.

At the Savage residence, two lines of kids were playing a game of red rover in the front yard. The air was tainted with the smoky smell of the barbeque. We followed the sound of the Top 40 music into the backyard, where about eighty people were congregated. There were a few kids around my age there, but they were all a grade or two behind me. I didn't know their names, and I was guessing that if they knew mine it was only because of some incident or rumor I'd rather not be known for.

Dana Savage peeled herself away from a crowd of women drinking pink wine out of clear plastic cups. She was wearing turquoise stretch pants and a flowery tank top. The skin sagging from her upper arm reminded me of pizza dough. She painted her nails terrible shades of orange, and my father once said she considered a foreign film anything that starred Hugh Grant. My mother told him that wasn't funny, but she had to turn away to hide her laughter when she said it.

"Ned, Peggy," she chirped as she came over. "How are you? So glad you could come."

My mother offered up the salad. "This is for everyone."

"Hello, Dana," my father said. He said it in the overly cheery tone he reserved for people he didn't like. "Great party."

"Hank is over by the grill with the other hubbies. Feel free to grab a Bud Light and join in. They're staring at the coals. Real man work, if you know what I mean." My father walked off and Dana turned to me. "And how are you, young man? You high school graduate, you. Did you have a graduation party? Because if you did, I didn't get an invite and there's a rule somewhere that says it's not a party unless I'm there."

"I didn't have a graduation party," I said.

"That's right," Dana said. "Like I said, how could it be a party if I wasn't there?"

My mother laughed good-naturedly. "No, he really didn't. Dade wanted to keep it low-key. We had a nice dinner at the country club and that was it."

"Oooo, the country club," Dana said. "I have naughty dreams about their seared tuna. I have similar dreams about the new chef, the one from Miami, but don't tell Hank that. *Muy caliente*, if you catch my drift."

I didn't like Dana, but whenever I thought about how much I disliked her, I remembered that their daughter had died in a car accident. It was a long time ago, before we knew the Savages, before our neighborhood even existed. Her picture still decorated their house, photographs that they took off the wall of one home and hung in another long after the blond girl in them was dead. I thought of Jenny Moore and her parents and how grief seemed like a club we'd all join eventually whether we liked it or not.

"How's your summer so far?" my mother asked.

"Well, my niece is staying with us for a while," Dana said. "She's from Los Angeles. Was having a bit of trouble and her parents thought some time away might be good, so they sent her to Aunt Dana."

"What kind of trouble?" my mother asked.

"Drugs," said Dana, drawing out the word as if lengthening the sounds could reveal greater wrongs. "Mostly marijuana. But other things too, I'm sure. Marijuana alone doesn't make girls do the things she was doing. She's a good kid, though. A little lost, but not too far gone. She's sweet at the core. You can't say that about everyone."

Dana Savage nodded over to the back of the yard. There was a tire hanging from a tree, and three little boys were climbing all over it like monkeys, pushing it back and forth, falling harmlessly into the patch of dust that had formed under the tire and then climbing back onto it again. There was a girl standing against the tree. She was calmly watching the boys and sipping something from a red plastic cup. Her hair was a dirty blond with a subtle rust-colored tint and styled in a pixie cut. She wore a white skirt and a gauzy white top, cloud remnants clinging to her skinny body.

"I'm sure she'd like some friends," Dana said. "She doesn't know anyone."

"Go say hi, Dade," my mother said with a gentle push on my shoulder. "Introduce yourself. She's pretty."

I hated that my mother sometimes tried to push me toward girls, but I also knew it was nobody's fault but my own, so I walked off without a word. The girl didn't notice me until I was two feet away. The kids on the tire gave me a wary glance before going back to their rambunctious game. For some reason the first thing I thought to say was, "What are you drinking?"

"Did my aunt send you over here to ask me that? Because if she did the answer is Diet Coke."

"She sent me over, but not to see what was in your cup."

"Are you a tattletale?" she asked.

"God no."

"Good. It's a rum and Diet Coke with three limes. My signature drink."

"I don't know what my signature drink is," I said. "My name's Dade. I live a couple of doors down."

"I'm Lucy." She smiled and put out her hand. It was small and soft.

"You really should get a signature drink," she said.

"Can I have a sip?"

"Sure." She held out her cup. "Knock yourself out."

I took a swig. A liquory burn blossomed in my chest. It was strong. I took another swig and handed it back to her.

"Can you get me one?" I asked.

"Come with me. The liquor cabinet's inside. All they have out here is beer and shitty wine. My aunt is drinking white zin. Talk about a gagfest."

I followed Lucy up to the house. She walked with a burdened gait. I guessed that Lucy was the kind of kid who often rolled her eyes at adults and sometimes just flat-out ignored their attempts to strike up an innocent conversation. Dana and my mother noticed us heading inside and waved. I waved back, but Lucy went on, pretending like she didn't see.

Hank Savage had basically converted the basement into a sports bar. Flags bearing the logos of multiple football teams hung everywhere. A glass case of ceramic sport figurines took up an entire wall. An insanely large flat-screen television dominated the corner of the room. A small bar area took up one side of the room, and under the counter was a tiny beer refrigerator. The glass cabinets above were stocked with shitty liquors, cheap vodkas and rums with names I'd never heard before. There was a football-shaped cookie jar. Lucy got plastic cups from the cupboard and ice from a small compartment in the fridge.

"Classy joint, right?" Lucy said, gesturing around the room. "Flags and figurines and all that shit. God, sports are lame."

I laughed. "Yeah, they are."

"Glad you agree," she said, putting ice into the cup.

"Dana said you're from California."

"I am," she said. "Los Angeles. My parents are both in the industry. Before you ask, they're no one famous. And I'm not one of those kids who skip class and spend the day doing coke in the dressing rooms at Fred Siegel or anything."

"What's Fred Siegel?"

"It's where Satanists shop." She laughed at some private joke. She poured a liberal amount of rum into the cup, followed by a splash of soda. "This kid from my high school used to tell people he was a Satanist. He was always talking about how the devil was his biological father. It was so ridiculous. Meanwhile, his parents were super religious. His dad, like, wrote books about how to have a Christian marriage. People are so weird. Should we see what brand of moron they're showing on MTV?"

We took our drinks and sat on the floor in front of the television. Lucy fooled around with the remote control for a few seconds, trying in vain to turn the thing on. The television was so big that I felt like it was looking back at me.

"So you're gay, right?" she said distractedly.

I almost spit out my drink. Her bluntness caught me off guard. She just went on fooling with the remote control. How did she know? I didn't know how to respond. She finally figured out how to turn the television on and promptly turned it to MTV. Girls in bikinis on a beach having a conversation about a boy they all liked. Lucy looked over at me and laughed.

"What? What's up with the look of shock? Are you not out yet?" A look of genuine concern crossed her face. "Oh my God. Do you not even know it yet? Do you have a girlfriend? Am I, like, rocking your world right now?"

"Jesus God, no. I know that I'm—"

"Gay?" she finished. "Well, that's good."

"Yeah. I just . . . I just never have talked about it because there was never really anyone to talk about it with."

"Really?" she asked.

I nodded slowly. It occurred to me then just how much of my life was lived inside my head, invisible to the outside world.

"Well, if it makes you feel better, I'm a lesbian." She seemed more into what was happening on the screen than the subject at hand. "It's not a big deal. Not to me, at least."

"You are?"

"Yeah. That's why I'm here. My parents aren't cool with it. I had to convince them to not to send me to this camp where they brainwash the gay out of you. They sent me here instead."

"I've seen stuff about those places on TV," I said. "They scare me."

"Do your parents know about you?" she asked.

"No," I said. "I'll tell them after I'm out of the house. I don't want to have to be around them after I tell them. I don't think they'd ever send me to a camp or anything, but I'm sure it'll be awkward."

"Totally terrifying," she agreed. "You got an escape plan?"

"Yeah. Going to Fairmont College in the fall. It's in Michigan."

"I know where Fairmont is. That's a good school."

"I guess," I said.

"You smart?"

"I don't know."

"That's a yes," she said. "I've got another year of high school. Then I'm taking off. Getting away from my parents, from California. I don't wanna end up giving stress tests to people outside the Beverly Center like some zombie, like some people I know."

The girls on the show were now at a party in a glass mansion that looked out over the ocean. Guys in Abercrombie shirts and backward baseball caps trolled around the pool. The camera kept panning to the girls' panicked and insecure faces. The girls kept talking about a boy named Cross, about how hot he was. The boys took their shirts off and started throwing each other into the pool. A helium-voiced girl sang along to a rock track in the background, and whatever canned beverage the girls were drinking was scrambled by some post-production visual effect. Cross grabbed the prettiest girl by the waist and pulled her close. She giggled as he whispered something in her ear, and the soundtrack soared.

"I've slept with girls like that," Lucy said. "They always taste like spearmint gum. You got a boyfriend?"

"There was a guy named Pablo, but that's over now."

"Why is it over?" she asked.

I thought about it for a few seconds before I spoke. "I guess you could say that he just couldn't handle it."

"You just fool around buddy-style, right? God, been there, done that. Ninth grade. Vanessa Shimmer. She was a violin prodigy. Played with symphonies all over the world. I was so obsessed. Now she lives in Rome and bones the sons of shipping moguls. Do you do him or does he do you?"

I took a drink. "Um . . . he does me."

She smiled. "I figured."

"Why do you say that?"

"Nothing. Just did."

I didn't know whether I should be offended.

"Do you really think you'll be giving stress tests outside of that center?" I said during the commercial.

"I was being silly," she said. "I don't think that'll happen. What about this Pablo guy? What's his story?"

"Well, he's got a girlfriend. And it was never really about love. I just realized that recently. And I want to be in love with someone."

I thought of driving through the countryside with Alex, of the songs on his stereo and the fireflies out the window. I pulled out my phone to see if he'd called or sent me a text. But there was nothing.

"Well," she said in a quiet voice, "that's a good thing to figure out. Some people run into that problem and don't get that until it's too late."

"It was too late a while ago." A smile crept up on my face. "There is this boy that I really like. He's really cute."

"Oh yeah? What's his name?"

"Alex Kincaid."

"Sounds like a doctor from a soap opera. Does he do brain transplants? Does he have an evil twin? Or is *he* the evil twin?"

"He works at a taco joint."

She gave me a stern look. "From now on you should tell people he's a restaurateur or something like that. A taco joint doesn't cut it."

I laughed.

The boys on television were wrestling by the side of the pool. A little window popped up in the corner of the screen and one of the girls started talking about which guy she thought had the best body.

"Oh my God," said Lucy. "I think I went to preschool with that girl. She used to eat crayons."

We stayed like that for almost an hour. We laughed at a commercial that featured a hapless twentysomething guy fleeing from a horde of women gone mad by the scent of his $3.99 shower gel and joked about ordering an eight-disc best-of grunge box set. I even took out my phone and made like I was going to call. I wanted to make her laugh, and I did. Every so often Dana called our names from the top of the stairs. I was more than a little tipsy and looking around the Savages' basement when I noticed the picture on the mantel amongst the plastic figurines of famous athletes. It was a gold-framed eight-by-ten picture of the Savages' deceased daughter. It looked like it was probably a high school picture. She was blond and wide-eyed and smiling hugely. I could almost hear her voice echoing off the walls of my brain, boys' names and weekend plans.

"Did you know her?" I asked.

Lucy followed my gaze up to the picture. "Lindsay? Of course. She was my cousin."

"What was it like?" I asked.

She turned and looked at me. "What was what like?"

I found myself wishing I hadn't brought it up. "No one close to me has ever died. And all that stuff about that girl who disappeared has me thinking about it. It's just that it's everywhere. It's only a matter of time."

"Only a matter of time until what?"

I thought for a moment. "Until I experience it, I guess."

"Well, you're lucky if no one you've known has ever died," she said. "I've known a few people who've died. It's more weird than anything. Suddenly someone just isn't there anymore. We have these ideas of heaven and hell and all that, but what is that? What *is* that? That's why people like my parents get involved in crazy religions and start becoming other people. We're all trying to avoid it. Or to at least make it not so bad. But no one's ever going to come up with anything big enough to smother death. It's stupid to even try."

"I'm sorry."

"I remember when my parents weren't the way they are now," she said, staring blankly at the television. "They got involved with this crazy church about three years ago and now they've totally changed."

"I think that same thing about my parents. I remember when they were different."

She looked over at me. "What's the matter with your parents?"

"I can't even describe it," I said. "I think maybe they're just sad. But I'm not sure. There's more to it than that. I don't quite understand it, but I know there's more."

"Story of the world," she said.

A voice called our names from the top of the stairs. This time it was my mother.

"Let's go," Lucy said, standing up. "We can't stay down here forever."

We dumped what was left of our drinks down the sink of the Savages' bar and went upstairs. My mother and Dana were in the kitchen amongst a gaggle of other housewives. My mother handed me a tray of deviled eggs and I took them outside, leaving Lucy to help her aunt with the condiments. I sat the tray on a picnic table where several younger kids were sitting around eating marshmallows from a bag. They eyed me suspiciously, waiting to see if I was the adult they were expecting to come out and tell them to knock it off.

"How are them marshmallows?" I asked.

They all stared at me. One little girl finally nodded, her mouth full of goo. My father was across the yard standing separate from the group of men taking the meat off the grill. He was holding a Heineken. He looked like a guy who'd just cleaned up after several dirty years outside of society, a recently released prisoner or someone just rescued off a deserted island. I felt a little spike of sympathy cut through all the anger I felt toward him. When he saw me, he slowly raised his hand and gave a little wave. From across the distance, I waved back.

∞

I woke up that night to the sound of my phone ringing. I crawled out from under some dream whose details vanished the moment I woke up, and grabbed my phone off the nightstand. It was Pablo.

"You sleeping?" he said.

"It's three a.m.," I said. "What do you think?"

"I'm outside your house."

"Why?" I asked. "What are you doing?"

"Just come outside," he said. "I need to see you."

I sat up and rubbed my eyes. I didn't say anything for a long time. Light from a streetlamp outside was coming through my window. I'd forgotten to close my blinds. I imagined him slouched in his little pickup under that same light, his phone up to his ear while his other arm dangled out the open window.

"I don't want to see you," I said. "I feel like there's nothing left to say."

"Come on, dude. Don't be like that. If you don't come down I'll ring your doorbell over and over until you do."

"You wouldn't," I said.

"Try me."

"You're a jerk," I said. "I'm coming down."

There was a small part of me that expected to open the front door and find he wasn't there, to get a giggling call back from him and Judy and God knows who else saying that it was all a joke and that I should go to hell. But he was there, parked in his little gray pickup truck down a bit on a darker stretch of the block between the glow of two streetlights. The chrome on the grille and around the headlights glinted in the night and made his truck look like some dangerous reptile biding its time in the shadows.

The passenger door was unlocked. Pablo was slouched in almost exactly the same pose I'd imagined in my room. Some generic modern rock track was playing softly on the stereo. His eyes were fixed straight ahead and far off into the distance. He didn't even blink as I slid in the cab and shut the door behind me.

"You have three minutes," I said, crossing my arms.

"Good to see you too," he said. He still didn't look over at me. "Just wanted to say hi. See what's up."

"You woke me up, man."

"Sorry," he said. "Go inside and go back to bed if it's that goddamn big of a deal."

"Fine," I said, opening the door.

He grabbed my arm. "Wait."

I saw a flash of something vulnerable in his face.

"What do you want?" I asked. "Seriously."

"I just want to figure out if there's maybe some way to make things work," he said blankly. He stared out the windshield again. "I don't see where there's a problem."

"Judy," I said. "The fact that you have a girlfriend is a problem. The fact that you've never acknowledged the significance of all the things that have happened between us is a problem. You're constantly acting like I don't really exist and it makes me feel like the last two years have meant nothing to you. And they meant a lot to me, man."

"I stuck up for you," he said. "That day in the lunchroom. I fucking punched one of my best friends for you. What do you think that was?"

"And then you were hanging out with him again two weeks later," I said. "And where was I?"

"You came over that one day. The day my mom made us enchiladas."

"You mean the day you said you'd never love me?" I said. "Is that the day you're talking about?"

He spoke with forced calm. "Like I said, I just want to see if there is maybe some way we could make it work. Things were fine junior year. There was Judy and there was you and we made it work and—"

"But that's the problem," I said. "There was Judy and there was me and there was all this complicated bullshit because of that. I let you have it both ways for a long time, but it can't be like that anymore. You always say that I complicate things. Well, this is me simplifying them."

He didn't say anything. I wanted him to say that he'd never said anything bad about me and that he never would. I wanted him to say that he always stuck up for me, even during the little moments, the ones where the entire lunchroom wasn't watching, the ones where people showed you what they were really made of.

"I've always been shit to you," I went on. "I used to think that would change over time, but after that day I came over to your house and you *slapped* me, I started to realize I was wrong."

My mind went to Alex. All I wanted was to talk to him again, to be close to him again. I thought of how it felt to sit next to him in his car and how different that was from sitting next to Pablo. I wondered if I was finally able to say all this to Pablo because I had somewhere else to go and that somewhere else was Alex.

"Are we done here?" I asked, my hand on the door handle "Do you have anything else to say?"

He stared at his lap and shook his head. I got out of the car and slammed the door behind me. I felt brave and in control of the situation for the first time. I didn't let myself look back as I walked up to my house. I stood there in the coolness of our foyer with my back pressed against our front door as if I were keeping the whole world from breaking in. It was then that I heard his truck come to life, the engine noisy and sick like a broken toy. I stood there in the shadows and listened to the sound of him fading down the block.

# Chapter 8

Almost two weeks passed and Alex hadn't called. Hadn't he said he wanted to hang out? He probably said that to everyone. My crush had made it impossible for me to picture what he looked like. His face only came clearly when I wasn't expecting it. I'd be stocking the milk cooler at Food World or standing in the shower and he would suddenly appear in my mind. His long dark hair, his narrow and perfect face. Everything became clear for a few rounded moments and then I'd lose the image again and the frustration would return, familiar and physical, something quivering right under the skin on my arms.

I'd started hanging out with Lucy on a regular basis. We went downtown and watched fireworks from the top of a parking garage on the Fourth of July. We scoured every thrift store in town for the perfect pair of pants, T-shirt, or ashtray. Sometimes we met at the twenty-four-hour diner by the interstate to talk over coffee and French silk pie. I'd bring along a poem or story that I'd written and Lucy would read it right there and tell me what she thought. I never felt shy sharing my stuff with her. She was the least judgmental person I'd ever met.

She once said, "Sometimes it's a bit too clear that the guy in the story is actually you." She was sitting across from me in a booth at the diner, slowly flipping through the pages of a story of mine she'd read. "I think you need to not do that. Make it more universal."

Even when she was talking about some line I'd written that was so personal it made me blush, she'd speak with the casual yet warm distance of a doctor. I was a year older than her, but I looked at her as the smarter, more worldly of the two of us, and because of this I valued her opinion of me, my writing, and my life more than almost anyone else I'd met before.

In the meantime, a strange calm had settled over our household. My mother started painting outside. Every day she woke up at six a.m. and spent the entire morning and a good part of the afternoon painting pictures of our backyard. She painted the pool and the garden, the sky and the clouds. Sometimes I would take a swim while she worked and she would insert me into her painting. I would be there, a blurry-edged outline of a boy swimming underwater.

"I'm trying to create sort of a visual diary of this summer," I heard her say to her sister over the phone. "I feel like eventually these pictures will become important, like someday I'll be able to look at them and find the answers that I can't find now."

My father was around more. I wasn't sure if he'd stopped seeing Vicki or not, but after the night of the Savages' barbeque, he was always home for dinner. He seemed to be taking a cue from my mother, moving through our house with a medicated sense of calm. His peace seemed organically psychological, the product of self-reflection and maybe even resignation. It was as if they were both operating under the understanding that as soon as I left for college, they could do whatever they wanted. They could get a divorce and sell the house or hurl insults like bricks and decorate the walls with each other's blood. All they had to do was wait for me to leave.

One night I came home from work to find my father out by the pool. He was sitting on a chaise longue smoking a cigar and holding a tumbler of something, probably scotch. The glow coming up from the bottom of the pool cast him in a trembling blue light. I grabbed a can of ginger ale from the refrigerator and started to head upstairs, but I stopped on the first step. He knew I was home and I knew he was out there. I went back through the kitchen and into the backyard.

"Yo," I said flatly as I approached.

"You're home," he said, not looking at me.

I took a seat on the chair beside him. "I am. Worked late."

"And how's work?"

"Good. Ready not to work there anymore, though."

"That's understandable," he said. "I thought you might be out with the Savages' niece, that Lucy girl. She seems nice. Pretty."

I knew my father well enough to know he was trying to see if there was any possibility that Lucy and I were an item. As always, my mind raced for a way to switch the subject.

"We have a lot in common," I said.

We fell into one of our awkward silences. Over our fence came the sound of the sprinkler system hissing in the yard of the house behind ours. Somewhere someone's dog let out a series of barks.

"I saw your mother's pool paintings," my dad said. "They're good. I like how you're in some of them."

"Yeah, I like them."

"I do too. I told her that. I think she thought I was being a jerk. She misunderstands sometimes."

I wanted to say something here, maybe mention the fact that he usually was a jerk.

"I wonder what she sees out here," he said. "I wonder what any of us see when we're in the same place for so long."

He paused here like he was waiting for an answer. Every once in a while my father would ask me these big questions. It was like he was testing me on some material or lecture he'd given me before, but as far as I could tell, he hadn't bestowed any wisdom upon me that would help answer anything.

He went on. "Someday we'll look at pictures of this house and think of this point in our lives and it will all feel like it happened to somebody else. It's all history, isn't it? All this stuff. You'll be gone soon. College. So much change. You'll love it. I promise. I love you, son."

"Um . . . I love you too."

He reached over and gave me a few fatherly slaps on the knee. He teetered a bit in his chair as he did this and I realized that he was tipsy. All of a sudden we'd fallen into some messed-up version of *Leave It to Beaver*.

"What if I don't?" I said.

"What if you don't what?"

"Love college," I said. "I mean, what if I go there and it's just as boring as here?"

"Cedarville's not *that* boring," he said.

"Yeah, it is, Dad," I said. "For an eighteen-year-old it is. I mean, you can't tell me that you don't get bored with this place sometimes."

"Getting older isn't always about having fun," he said. "In fact, in many ways it's about being bored. It's good if you can find a way to be entertained by your boredom. As for college, you'll be fine. Just let go of everything and fall in. You'll be fine."

We went quiet again. I popped open my can of ginger ale and took a sip. He held out his cigar, but I waved it away. He put it back in his mouth and sucked. The orange tip flared.

"Have you ever been in love, Dade?"

"Why?"

"Because everyone should fall in love." He took a gulp of his drink. "Don't you think? Let's talk about this like men. Answer only the questions that you want to answer. Have you ever been in love?"

The way he was gesturing with his hands made me think he was drunker than I thought.

"I don't know if I've been in love," I said.

"Have you been close to something like love?"

"Maybe. The general vicinity. Close would be too generous."

My father inhaled the night air and let it out. He slapped my knee again.

"That makes me happy," he said. "That's good to hear. It's better than nothing."

I let out a little laugh. "Is it?"

"Yeah. It is."

I suddenly had the urge to tell him everything. I wanted to dump it all over his head like a bucket of cold water. I wanted to tell him about meeting Alex. I wanted to tell him about Pablo. I wanted to tell him about the nights I stared up at the ceiling fan and told it I was gay. I wanted to do all this to test him, to see if he really loved me. But then the urge lifted as suddenly as it had appeared, and I pulled all these things away from the precipice of telling and hid them away again.

"You want to know what I've always wanted to do?" he said. "Here. Hold this."

He handed me the cigar and slipped off his sandals. He pulled his cell phone, his wallet, and some loose change out of his pocket and tossed it all onto the chair he'd just been sitting on. He walked over to the edge of the pool. He was still wearing khaki shorts and one of his blue polos with "Hamilton Luxury Motors" embroidered on the breast pocket. He looked over his shoulder and gave me a weird grin and then fell face-first into the pool. The splash was a liquid explosion in the quiet suburban night. He swam underwater to the other side and came up for a quick gulp of air before going under again and heading back toward me. I stood by the edge, looking down at him as he came to a halt at my feet. I thought of all the times my mother had referred to my father as immature. Right then he reminded me of a child who broke rules simply for the sake of breaking them.

"Get in," he said. It came out like a command.

"I don't want to," I said.

"Come on," he pressured. "Get in. Clothes and all."

"I can't, Dad."

"Why not?"

"That won't fix anything."

He shook his head, disappointed, and at that moment I wanted to be anyone else but who I was. I wanted to be the boy who would've jumped in.

∞

That night I dreamt of Alex. We were walking down a highway in the middle of the desert. It was warm and there were white flakes falling from the sky. Alex walked a few feet in front of me. I knew he was leading me somewhere, but I didn't know where, and I hadn't asked because I knew he wouldn't tell me. The rule in the dream was that I could ask about anything except where we were going.

"How is it snowing in the desert?" I asked.

"It's not snow, dude. It's ash."

I sensed that someone was behind me. I tried to turn around, but my neck went stiff and I could only move it a few degrees right or left, not enough to see who was there. The person starting humming the chorus of Debbie Loser's "I Only Want You Because You're Worthless." I reached behind my back and wiggled my fingers.

"Touch me," I said. "Touch my fingers and tell me who you are."

I felt a hand on mine.

I snapped awake to the sound of my Debbie Loser ringtone. I grabbed it off the nightstand in a groggy panic and answered it without checking to see who was calling.

"Sleeping?" the voice asked.

Was it Alex? I blinked my eyes rapidly in an attempt to fully wake myself up. No, it wasn't Alex. It was a girl's voice. Lucy. Even in my muddled consciousness there was a pang of disappointment in my chest. The longing ran under everything.

"Yeah," I said. "Dreaming."

"Meet me on your porch in ten minutes. We're going somewhere."

"Where are we going?"

"It's a surprise. Wear your ratty red T-shirt and some hot jeans. And boots. Gotta wear your boots. No sneakers. Look hot."

"Am I gonna like this?"

"Yes. I promise. See you in ten."

I found the T-shirt Lucy had mentioned (red with a hole on the left shoulder, a thrift store purchase advertising a pizza joint in Lansing, Michigan) and put it on inside out. I put on one of the new pairs of jeans I had bought along with a pair of black boots that I hadn't worn since my punk phase two winters ago, the one that ended two days before Christmas when my father told me to get my hair back to its normal color or I was going to spend Christmas wandering the streets of downtown Cedarville, a barefoot blue-haired boy in a Sex Pistols shirt asking strangers for change.

Lucy was already waiting for me on the porch when I went down. June bugs spun around the porch light like little manifestations of panic. Whenever we met again I was struck by how pretty she was. That night she was wearing pastel-colored barrettes that she'd bought at the drugstore and light blue eyeliner, both sarcastic nods to the institutions of femininity that she often declared pointless and disposable.

"We're going to Cherry's," was the first thing she said.

"What's Cherry's?"

She bounced excitedly up and down on her toes. "It's a gay bar."

"You're shitting me. Where?"

"Here in town," she said.

"There aren't any gay bars in Cedarville."

"Yeah, there are," she said. "And we're going."

The idea of going to a gay bar made me nervous. I pictured the bar as being filled with insanely attractive men, all taller and more muscular and more confident than me. Being rejected by people I had nothing in common with was bad enough, but I wasn't sure if I was ready to be rejected by the very group to which I thought I belonged.

"How are we getting in?" I asked. "I'm assuming you took into consideration the fact that neither of us are twenty-one?"

"Of course. I'm not an idiot."

She pulled two licenses from her back pocket. Both were California state. Hers was Esther Rodriguez and the other belonged to someone named Teddy Baron. The photo on Lucy's ID was actually her, but the picture on the other one was of a blank-faced skinhead with a constellation of zits on each cheek. His lips were slightly opened, as if he was about to ask a desperately moronic question, the kind of question you can only answer with baffled silence.

"Who is this tool?" I asked.

"That tool is you. Teddy's the floater ID from my group of friends back in California. We all have our own, but there's always that out-of-towner or random someone who needs one. I had a friend mail it out to me. It just arrived. I noticed the envelope on the kitchen counter and I called you immediately. I couldn't wait. Your first visit to a gay bar is a major rite of passage, my friend. Maybe we'll get lucky and you'll get drunk and dance on a box with some hot go-go boy."

"Um, I think your definition of lucky differs from mine."

She laughed. "Well, see where the night takes us. Oh, and by the way, this one is boys only, so my chances of meeting anyone are pretty much nada, so expect a visit to the Kitty Klub over in Warwick County before the summer is done whether you like it or not."

We drove there with the windows down, the AC on. She

plugged her MP3 player into my stereo and put on some psychedelic pop by some Swedish band with a name I didn't catch any of the four times she said it. I laughed as she attempted to sing along with the nonsense lyrics. I ran a red light and didn't notice until Lucy pointed it out, but there were no other cars on First Avenue so it didn't matter. We passed First Cedarville Bank on Trust with its scrolling that alternated between the time, temperature, and lame jokes.

*... 12:41 a.m. ... Why did the pair of suspenders get arrested? ... 80° F ... For holding up a pair of pants! ... 12:41 a.m. ... How do you kill a circus? ... 79° F ...*

I couldn't help but look over my shoulder as we drove by.

*... Go for the juggler! ...*

"Eyes on the road, Teddy," she said. "You're going to get us both killed."

A few minutes later we came around a bend in the road and the Hamilton Luxury Motors sign came into view.

"Hey, we're coming up on my dad's dealership."

"Awesome," she said. "Will he give me a Porsche?"

"I'm sure he could. I'll call and ask him now."

"Look at all those cars," she said as we passed. "And look at that guy."

The lot was flooded with light and the cars all shined like big pieces of expensive candy. It took me a second to notice the homeless man standing on the sidewalk staring at the sea of vehicles. He stood there motionless in a ragged overcoat. In the blur of passing, I thought I noticed his mouth hanging open in awe. I glanced in the rearview mirror, half expecting him to have disappeared, but he was still standing there, as motionless as a statue.

"That was weird," she said.

"Totally," I said.

∞

When Lucy told me that Cherry's was located in downtown Cedarville, I almost didn't believe her. Downtown Cedarville was deserted at night. Every now and then a taxi or police car would creep down the street, but even that was rare. For the most part, downtown became a ghost town after nine p.m. Lucy had me stop the car at the mouth of an alley located between a jewelry store and a used bookshop.

"I think it's down there," she said.

The steam in the alley looked like a cumulus cloud hiding in a maze of buildings. From somewhere farther down the alley, a golden streetlight illuminated the steam cloud's lethargic ascent to the sky. I pulled the car into a parking spot in front of the bank and then shut off the engine. Lucy checked her makeup in the visor mirror while I scrounged for a piece of gum in the glove compartment. I finally found one at the very bottom. God knows how long it had been there.

"Are you nervous?" Lucy asked.

"I forgot to brush my teeth," I said, working on chewing the tough old piece of gum to a manageable wad. "But yeah, a little. What if they realize our IDs are fake and they call the cops?"

"They won't do that."

"You don't know that."

"Yes I do," she said. "I know everything. And besides, we can't bail now. We've come too far. So let's go. Rite of passage. Just keep saying that in your head."

We got out and walked into the alley. About fifty feet on we came to a black door with a neon cherry over it. A man in a green track jacket was leaning against the building and talking softly into his cell phone. He was dark and balding, maybe my dad's age. Lucy opened the door to the bar, letting out a rush of hyper dance music. I followed her, but not before letting my gaze linger on the man for a second. He wasn't all that attractive, but I couldn't stop staring at him for some reason. I wanted to know who he was talking to, what he was talking about. It was like knowing these things might help me figure out how to be more myself. He noticed me looking and gave me a friendly smile and a wink. I gave a tight smile and a little wave and then hurried into the bar behind Lucy.

The place was a perfect square with a circular bar in the middle of the room and a bunch of small booths on the darker perimeter of the room. About a dozen men were sitting at the bar, all spotlit almost to the point of being washed out by the bright light coming from fixtures over their heads. The men there were nothing like I thought they'd be. There were no supermodels or Johnny Morgan look-alikes. They were all just regular guys in their thirties and forties. There was an Asian guy in an expensive-looking suit sitting at the bar and drinking a yellow liquid out of a martini glass, but everyone else was just wearing boring T-shirts and khakis that they'd probably purchased at some lame store at the Cedarville Mall that I refused to step foot in. The beautiful, well-dressed men that I thought would be here turned out to only exist in the gay bar of my imagination.

Almost everyone looked up at us as we walked in and I suddenly wanted to disappear. Lucy, however, didn't seem to mind or notice. She just looked around, trying to figure out where we should sit. There was a plump redheaded woman tending bar. She was wearing thick green eye shadow and chewing gum.

"You two'd better show me your IDs before you even think about taking a seat," she said.

We walked over to the bar and handed her our false documents. Her eyes bounced between our faces and Teddy's and Esther's photos. I looked down to avoid her glare. There were peanut shells strewn about the hardwood floor, and in the corner of my eye I spotted a shimmering green needle of glass from some probably long-ago broken bottle.

"Sit in the back," the woman said when she laid the cards down on the bar. "No hard stuff. Just beer. And I can kick you out whenever I feel like it."

"O-kay." Lucy drew out the syllables as if she was confused by the response. "Two beers then. Teddy, go grab us a table."

I took a seat at a circular table in the rear corner of the bar. The table wobbled horribly when I rested my elbows on it, and the banged-up tin ashtray in the center looked like it'd seen an entire cancer case worth of cigarettes. There was a jukebox a few feet to my left, where a man in cowboy boots and a cowboy hat stood flipping through the selections at a slow, almost disabled pace. Right next to him was a hallway leading back to the restrooms. A few of the men around the bar were looking back over their shoulders at me. I was scared to return their glances, so I looked up at the rafters as if I were an architect planning on rebuilding this place the next day by memory.

"That was cool of her to let us stay," I said when Lucy sat down.

"Are you kidding? She was totally hostile. She probably just wants the tips." She took a swig of Corona and looked around the bar. "Not a huge selection of men, but better than nothing. It must feel nice to know there are at least"—she took a quick count—"eleven other gay men in Cedarville, right?"

"The Asian guy looks like he's here on a business trip."

"Fine. Ten. Well, eleven still. That's including you."

We went quiet for a bit. I wondered what was supposed to happen next. Would someone talk to me? Should I approach one of them? I thought of Alex with his shaggy hair and dirty boots, his overall aura of danger. There was no one like that here.

"When did you know you were a lesbian?"

"I don't know. For forever. I remember I wanted to marry my friend Teresa when I was seven. I wanted to have a wedding and everything, but Teresa's mom said no way. It was only going to be a pretend wedding in my backyard with a few stuffed animals making up the wedding party. I don't see what the big deal was, even now. But we did it anyway, in secret. We had a pretend wedding in my garage. Tina the Blue Rabbit was my maid of honor."

"What happened to her?"

"Tina the Blue Rabbit? She's back in California. She is now my mother's dog's chew toy. She's seen better days."

I laughed. "No. To Teresa."

"Oh God, I don't know. I haven't thought about her in years. She moved just after that. I probably wouldn't even recognize her if I passed her on the street. It was so long ago."

A twangy country ballad came on the jukebox and shocked the bar out of its dance music daze, some sad-voiced woman singing against a backdrop of steel guitar and trotting upright bass. The guy in the boots and hat swayed across the bar, lip-synching the lyrics into the neck of his Bud Light. He went up to the Asian businessman and pulled him by the arm. The businessman looked down at his lap and tried to wave him away, but the cowboy wasn't giving up. The bartender let out a high-pitched whistle and the businessman let the cowboy pull him from his stool. They danced slowly into the middle of the bar and then anchored themselves there.

"This is hysterical," Lucy said.

It only took a few seconds for the businessman's awkward-ness to subside, for his body to relax and succumb to the cow-boy's lead, and suddenly they seemed like the most natural pair in the world. The bartender reached under the bar and flipped a switch, and a disco ball that had been hibernating in the darkness up near the ceiling came to life and sent a thousand little points of light gliding around the room. A guy in stonewashed jeans and a flannel shirt sang along drunkenly from his barstool.

Lucy said, "If you would've told that guy this morning that by the end of the day he'd be dancing with a cowboy in a gay bar in Iowa, he probably would've looked at you like you lost your mind."

We watched them dance until the song ended and something else came on, some synthesizer-heavy dance number from the eighties. The cowboy left the businessman to his loneliness and his yellow martini. There was scattered applause. I clapped along, weirdly honored that I was there to witness it. The cowboy gave his reluctant dance partner a slap on the back and then took his place a few stools down.

"Are you having fun?" Lucy asked.

"Yeah. I'm having a real good time."

The door to the bar swung open and like everyone else I looked up. An athletic guy in a long-sleeved black shirt and an olive green baseball cap walked in. All the other patrons went back to their drinks after a momentary glance, but I kept watching. There was something about the way the guy sauntered slowly over to the bar that made me think I knew him from somewhere. He leaned into the light to order a drink and everything clicked into place.

"Oh my fucking God."

It was Pablo. I hadn't seen him since that night in his truck outside my house. I hadn't really even thought of him. He took a stool at the bar and said something to the bartender, but she didn't move. She just went on staring intently at the television above the bar. The nightly news was showing footage from Jenny Moore's ninth birthday party for the ten thousandth time. Finally the bartender reached absently into the cooler for a Rolling Rock and slid it over to him. She kept her eyes on the television for another few moments and then turned and said something to him. Then they both looked back up at the screen. The bartender shook her head sadly.

"Who's that?" Lucy asked.

"That's Pablo."

"*That's* Pablo? Your ex-not-boyfriend?"

"Yeah." I couldn't stop staring at him. I was having problems breathing and speaking at the same time. It was like all the air had been sucked out of the room. "That Pablo."

Even though he was wearing a hat, I could tell his hair was longer than it'd ever been. Thick black waves crept out from under the edges of his cap, the beginnings of bigger curls that would come if he kept letting it grow. He took a big drink of his beer and looked around the room. He had his lips arranged in the slightest beginnings of a smile, like he was ready to spring a full one for anyone who might suddenly appear in front him. He adjusted the brim of his cap, pulled it down a little lower, and took another drink of his beer.

"Look at him," I said. "He's so nervous."

"Where's his so-called girlfriend?" Lucy asked.

"Probably at the mall drinking the blood of an incoming freshman."

"Are you gonna say something?" she asked.

"Should I?" I asked.

"He sounded like he has some issues."

"It'd be awkward not to," I reasoned.

"I think any way you play this, awkward is pretty much unavoidable at this point."

I thought back to a night two springs ago. He'd picked me up and we cruised around town. He was in a weirdly good mood that night. He let me pick out what music we listened to. He kept cracking lame jokes, and even though most of them weren't funny, I laughed anyway. He drove me to the deserted Cedarville High parking lot and attempted to teach me how to drive stick. The lesson ended with us parked in the back row with our shirts off and us taking turns kissing over each other's stomachs, the smell of the day's rain filling the car.

"I'm going to say hi."

"Do you want me to go with you?" she asked.

"It'll be fine," I said. "We're at a bar. It's cool. I'll be right back."

I grabbed my beer and went over. He did a double take as I approached. His eyes grew wide and he opened his mouth to say something, but nothing came out. He grabbed his beer and took a swig. He gave a quick glance to the left and then the right, and finding nothing to rest his eyes on, his shocked gaze settled on me.

I motioned to the empty stool beside him. "Can I sit?"

"Sit, don't sit. Do whatever you want."

I climbed up on the seat. On the television a hot blond guy was surfing on a tidal wave of orange soda. We sat there drinking our beers in silence until the commercial break ended and the news came back on. It was the weatherman's turn.

"Rain on Thursday," Pablo said. He was trying to act all nonchalant, but I could tell he was nervous, terrified even. "Sucks. I was gonna hit the links."

"Hit the links?"

"Go golfing."

"You golf?" I asked.

"Yup," he said, not taking his eyes off the screen. "Been goin' with Bert and the guys out at the country club. Good thing to learn before you get into the business world. Some of the biggest deals are made during a game of golf."

I thought back to all the times I'd hung out with him and Bert and the rest of the popular jocks. They would all go out of their way to ignore me. I'd be driving home afterward, feeling empty and on the verge of tears, and I'd get a text from Pablo asking me if I wanted to come over and fool around. I'd turn around in the nearest driveway, hating myself the entire time.

I rolled my eyes. "Golf is frickin' boring."

He gave me a sideways glance. "I don't remember asking you."

"Well, it is."

"If Johnny freakin' Morgan played golf, you'd be all about it."

"How's that beer?" I asked. I tried to give it sort of an edge, but there was nothing I could do to turn a line like that into a comeback. It just ended up sounding lame. Pablo didn't reply. He just kept on watching the TV.

"Where's Judy?" I asked

He turned to me. "Why? You got something to say to her?"

"I'm not gonna tell your stupid girlfriend I saw you here or anything."

"Don't talk about my girlfriend," he said. He took a drink of his beer and leaned toward me. "Do you want an apology? Is that what you want?"

"I don't want anything from you."

"Well, why did you come over here if you don't want anything from me?" he asked. "What do you need me to do?"

"I don't need you to do anything," I said. "I saw you over here and thought I'd come talk to you since a couple of weeks ago you came over in the middle of the night and basically asked me to get back together with you. I'm just trying to be nice."

"Well, don't do me any favors."

"Fine," I said. "I guess I'll leave you alone."

"You know, man," he said. "This is really giving me a headache."

I should've walked away then, but I didn't. We watched the weather and sports on mute. The bartender brought us two more beers without us having to ask, and when Pablo put down just enough money to cover his, I did the same. I glanced over at Lucy. She gave me an inquisitive look as if to ask how things were going. I smiled weakly and gave her a little nod to let her know that I was okay. Side by side, Pablo and I sipped our beers in silence. The local news ended and some national news program came on. The screen alternated between various images of the war in the Middle East. There were tanks rolling across the desert and a marketplace where bodies were strewn around a charred sedan. A woman cried into a camera and then the picture went to a group of government officials giving an update from a clean blue room.

"I'm gonna go," I said.

"You said you were gonna go, like, ten minutes ago," he said.

I didn't know what to say. I just stood up and walked away. I was almost to the door when I turned and went back over to him.

"You're a coward," I said. "Remember that."

"Oh, and you're so honest about what you are," he said.

"At least I'm honest with myself," I said. "Which is more than you can say."

He gave me a look like he was about to say something else, but I walked away before he could.

Lucy ran out after me.

"Screw him," she said as she held me at the end of the alley. "You're too good for him."

We stopped by a liquor store and tried to buy a bottle of whiskey with our fake IDs, but got turned down. We bought some root beer instead and drove to the Lot, the empty parking lot of an abandoned hardware superstore on the edge of town. It was a popular nighttime hangout for Cedarville's more nocturnal crowd. Homeless people, restless thugs, and trailer park drunks all stumbled through the paved expanse at some point in the evening. Meanwhile my suburban peers marinated in the safety of their darkened cars, the orange glow of their lighters like signs of life viewed from across the galaxy. We were all watching each other in the dark, feeling one another's energy and canceling each other out with our own brands of lostness. Pablo and I had gone there to mess around a few times before, but I'd always been terrified, afraid we'd inadvertently stepped into an urban legend where I'd get home and find a hook hanging from my car door.

Lucy put on some French hip-hop and shook her shoulders back and forth along to the music. "French hip-hop makes everything better. I mean, how can you be sad or angry when some French dude with a Casio is rapping about loving your body down?"

"Pablo and I used to come here," I said. I was slouched in the seat, a stream of smoke from my cigarette snaking out my cracked window.

"It's hard to believe they haven't busted this place yet," Lucy said. "It seems like the perfect subject for a local new exposé. Maybe we should call the channel nine tip line. Do they pay for tips?"

"You're out of your mind."

"I'm just joking."

"I'm not in the mood for jokes."

"Oh, dude," she said. She took my hand. "I'm sorry. What can I do?"

"Nothing. That's just it. There's nothing anyone can do."

"Don't cry over him."

"I'm not crying."

"You look like you're going to."

"I don't understand him," I said. "Simple as that. I just don't understand."

A rush began in my torso and moved up into my head. She was right. I was going to start crying. I reached over and took her hand. She gave mine a good squeeze. I pinched the bridge of my nose as if that could stop it. She rubbed my knee and hushed me, told me it was going to be okay. I wiped my nose with the back of my hand.

"It's okay," she said. "Cry if you want. Let it all out."

Let it all out. If only I could. Letting it all out would involve me exploding like a firework, a beautiful riot of rainbow sparks bouncing around the car and lighting up the entire lot. Everyone would look over to see what was going on, and one by one they would understand everything I had inside me.

# Chapter 9

I woke up the next morning with a vague hangover and an aching sadness in my gut. In my first waking moments I couldn't place where it had all come from, but then the previous night came back in an avalanche of thought. I went into the bathroom and snagged an Advil and then went downstairs and ate yogurt, granola, and raspberries in my underwear at the kitchen table. My parents were nowhere to be found. Every now and then I glanced up at the television. News of Jenny Moore's disappearance had reached a national level. A tabloid journalist was interviewing a psychic in Portland who specialized in missing children. The newswoman asked her if there was any way, after such a long period of time, that Jenny Moore could possibly still be alive.

"It's possible," said the expert after a strange pause. She had an Eastern European accent and a short symmetrical haircut. "There aren't any rules for this sort of thing. When you cross certain borders, there is no telling what you may find. Anything is possible. Both the best and the worst thing about situations like these is that there is always room to be surprised."

The newscaster leaned forward in her chair. "Are you getting strong vibes one way or another about the fate of this young girl?"

She said, "I don't feel comfortable saying. Not here. Not on television. But I have been in touch with the police and the Moore family. And they are always in my prayers."

I didn't have to work that day. I put on my swimming trunks and went out to the pool. It was humid, at least ninety-eight degrees according to the heat index. A lawn mower buzzed from a few yards over and the scent of freshly mowed grass tickled the inside of my nostrils. I swam back and forth, forcing myself to stay under until my lungs felt like they might burst. After a while I got out and fell asleep on one of the chaise longues contemplating whether or not I could ever have the courage to drown myself, if maybe filling myself with water was the only way to fill the void.

I woke up sensing a presence. I assumed it was my mother coming to make me clean my room or ask me to change a lightbulb. But instead it was Fessica Montana standing just a few feet away. She looked guilty and lost, like she'd suddenly appeared in my backyard and didn't know how she got there. She was wearing khaki shorts, a frilly pink T-shirt that was a size too small, and a sequined yellow belt.

"The door was open," she said before I could say a thing.

"What are you doing here?"

"I thought I'd drop by. That's what friends do, right? They drop by." She looked over her shoulder at the water. "You have a pool."

There was something so pathetic about the way she said it. I felt embarrassed for her, but a part of me recognized her cluelessness. I thought back to riding in Alex's car, how every word that came out of my mouth sounded incredibly lame.

"Yeah," I said. I was already trying to figure out how to get rid of her. "We do. It's more of a hassle than anything, though. Leaves in the drain. Dead things. I need to take a shower, so you should probably—"

"What dead things?" she asked.

"Um, we've found a couple of mice. A bird once."

"Dead?" she asked.

"Yes. Dead."

"It just fell out of the sky?"

"I don't know," I said. "All I know is I had to get it out, and it was disgusting."

"Are there bird snipers in your neighborhood?"

"Bird snipers?"

"There are bird snipers in my uncle's neighborhood in Washington. They do it for fun. They hide in attics and shoot from the windows."

"Fessica," I said before she could say anything. "Why are you here? What do you want?"

"I wanted to see how things with Alex are going," she said.

"See if there's anything else I can do to help you. I still feel bad about what happened. I didn't mean to start any rumors."

"That's very nice," I said, "but you should probably go. My parents get weird if I have friends over."

I stood up and led her into the house, my hand on her arm.

"Friends over?" she asked. "So we're friends, right?"

"Sure. We're friends."

"I help you, you help me." I was pulling her through the kitchen. "We help each other out."

"Yeah," I said, not really getting what she was saying. "For sure."

"I mean, maybe someday we could sorta be more than friends, right? That's possible."

I stopped. "Fessica, come on. You can't be serious."

They were playing some home video of Jenny Moore on the refrigerator television. I went over and punched the mute button.

"Jeez," she said. "What was that about?"

"Fessica, I'm gay. We both know this."

Her eyes grew wide. It occurred to me that I'd never actually told her I was gay. In fact, Lucy was the only actual person I'd told. Her eagerness quickly gave way to a look of concern.

"But what about what happened in my bedroom?" she asked. "Did that mean nothing?"

"You attacked me," I said, gesturing at the ceiling like my dad when he was pissed. "You tried to stick your hand down my pants and I ran out of your house like I was on fire. What about that sounds like a romantic moment to you?"

She opened her mouth to let out a sound. But nothing came out. Her eyes got wet.

"Oh shit," I said. "Don't cry. Don't do that."

But it was too late. She let out a broken little cry. She limply held her arms out, ready to receive anything the world would offer her. I felt horrible and before I knew it, I was hugging her. My chin was on her shoulder, and I was staring at the television in the refrigerator, at a muted commercial for laundry detergent, and I prayed she wasn't getting the wrong idea. She started sobbing uncontrollably.

"Don't cry," I said. "Jesus, dude. Don't cry. I'm sorry. This isn't your fault."

"But I don't have anybody," she said between sobs. "I don't have *anybody*, Dade, and it makes me wish that I was dead. I wake up every day and I wish that I was dead. The only reason I don't kill myself is because the idea of it is so terrifying, and I'm scared I'll be so scared that then I'll screw it up and then people will have something else to make fun of me for."

"Jesus," I said. I pulled back and looked her in the eye. "Don't say that. That's horrible. You don't really think that, do you?"

"I do!" she screamed.

"Whoa, whoa, whoa," I said.

She pulled away. She wasn't crying anymore. She looked angry now.

"Maybe I'll do it now," she said. "Maybe I'll just go home and get it over with. No one will miss me. My parents won't. They have Jessica. What do they need me for?"

"Um, you're way cooler than your sister. Trust me on that."

She stared at my knees, her face locked into a hard grimace. I was hoping to maybe get a laugh out of her with that last line. No such luck. My annoyance with her gave way to a very real sympathy. My earlier thought of drowning myself in the pool was just a catnap away, and it was impossible to admit that it wasn't.

"You want to come upstairs?" I asked. "Hang out? It'll be fine. My parents won't care." She looked up at me and nodded solemnly, the faintest trace of a smile on her mouth. I grabbed two Cokes from the refrigerator and led her up to my bedroom. She followed behind, sniffling. She sat on my bed and sipped at her Coke while I went around picking up random articles of clothing off the floor and tossing them into my closet.

"What's this?" she asked.

I looked over and saw she was holding a soda can that Lucy had turned into a pipe a few nights beforehand.

"Gimme that," I said, going over and grabbing it from her.

"Sorry. It was just sitting there on your nightstand. What is it?"

"It's a pipe," I said.

"A pipe?" There was still the residue of sadness in her voice. Her throat sounded wet and clogged like a neglected storm drain.

"Yeah," I said. "You smoke pot out of it."

"Pot?" she asked. "I want to smoke pot."

I looked at her inquisitively. I really didn't think getting her stoned was going to accomplish anything, but there was something so pleading and expectant in her eyes that it was impossible for me to say no.

"Do you really want to?" I asked.

"Do you think it'll help? People seem to be really into it at school."

"I don't think it'll help, necessarily," I said. "But it'll distract you. And sometimes that's all you can ask for, right?"

"I guess," she said with a tinge of disappointment.

I put on a record by the Breathless Faggots and took the precaution of opening the windows, stuffing a couple of towels in the crack under my door, and lighting some incense. I still had most of the weed that I'd bought from Alex in my desk drawer. It was special to me. It was Alex Weed. Whenever Lucy and I would smoke it, she would say, "Mmmm. Tastes like sexy loser," and I would laugh. I placed a little bud on the constellation of pinpricks on the top of the can and turned around to offer it to Fessica. She was reading one of my notebooks that I'd left on my nightstand. I hurried over and grabbed it from her.

"Don't read that," I said.

She turned her eyes up toward me.

"Sorry," she said. "I didn't know you wrote."

"Well, I do."

"I didn't read anything in there. I promise. I just saw a few lines, that's all."

"Well, forget whatever you read," I said. "It's not finished."

"Can I read it when it's done?" she asked.

"Sure," I said. "When it's done I'll let you read it."

I handed her the makeshift pipe. She used the orange lighter on my nightstand and took a hit. She let out a massive, choking cough right into the can and blew the pot onto the carpet.

"Whoa," I said, stamping at the burning pieces with my bare feet. "Easy, partner."

The Breathless Faggots were singing that line about the times of our lives being outside of time. I kneeled down and picked up the pieces of Alex Weed off the carpet. They broke apart in my hand, black and spent. I held them in my fist and then went over to my trash can and brushed my hands together over it.

"I'm sorry," she said.

"It's fine," I said with a forced cheeriness that I hoped she mistook for the real thing. "Don't worry about it. You always cough your first time."

I repacked the bowl.

"Be careful," I said to her, handing her the pipe. "Don't inhale more than you can handle."

She handled the next hit much better. She kept watching me as she exhaled, as if trying to glean support from my presence. I gave her a thumbs-up as she sent a long plume of smoke across the room. She held the pipe out to me, but I shook my head. She set it on my nightstand and then leaned back and sprawled out across my bed.

"Your bed is so comfortable," she said.

"Thanks."

"I downloaded the Vas Deferens the other day. You like them, right?"

"Totally."

"You told me about them once, so I checked them out. I love them."

"Yeah, everyone loves the Vas Deferens."

"I like the song that was in that commercial. The one where he sings about the vast fields of ordinary."

She totally got the words wrong, but I didn't feel like correcting her. I just focused on doodling a big blue star on the back of an old notebook. She stared up at the Johnny Morgan shrine on my wall.

"You like Johnny Morgan a lot," she said.

"Totally."

"He's okay," she said blandly.

I stopped doodling and looked up at her. "I think he's really talented."

"Sorry," she said. She looked around my room. "So what kind of stuff do you write about?"

"Stuff."

"What kind of stuff?"

"Stuff about my life. People I like. And about how much I hate Cedarville."

"I hate it too," she said. "I can't wait until I graduate. I'm going somewhere far away. I'm going to start over. I'll be Francesca again."

I stopped doodling and looked up at her. She was still

looking around my room and taking everything in. I thought about telling her that I knew what she meant, that I also dreamt of starting over in a new place, but then I got worried that would give her the wrong idea, so I didn't say anything.

"Why did Pablo punch Bert McGraw that one day?" she asked. "What happened between you two?"

"Pablo and I don't talk anymore."

"Why not?"

"Because Pablo's a dick," I said.

"Did you and Pablo used to . . ." She trailed off. The way the sentence drifted out into silence somehow seemed like the most appropriate way to describe what Pablo and I used to do. In different circumstances, I would've laughed.

"We used to do a lot of stuff," I said. "But not anymore. Because Pablo's a dick."

"Is he gay like you?"

"I don't know. Well, no. Not like me. He is, but he isn't." I didn't know what I was trying to say. "I mean, he thinks he isn't. Or, I should say, he says he isn't."

"What about Alex?" she asked. "When are you seeing him again?"

"Who knows. I hung out with him once, but he hasn't called. I'll probably never hear from him." It wasn't until I said that last sentence that I began to realize that I really might never see him again. I wondered what this meant for the last few weeks. The thought that all this longing could be for nothing was too depressing to dwell on.

"Are your parents married?" she asked.

"They are," I said. The question sorta caught me off guard. "They shouldn't be, but they are. Are yours?"

"My dad left a couple of weeks ago," she said. "Just packed up his things and left. Jessica's been having a really tough time with it."

I tried to imagine Jessica feeling the same pain I'd felt when my father first told me about Vicki. I tried to imagine her sprawled on her bed, broken and helplessly staring off into space. The image came, but it didn't fit. It was hard to imagine Jessica feeling anything at all.

"I feel like I'm sad about so many things that I don't have room to be sad about this," she said. "Does that make sense?"

I nodded slowly. We stared at each other for a bit. Something passed between us, some sort of understanding.

"I don't think we need dads," I said. "My dad's a dick too. Dads are the appendix of humanity. They should just be taken out before they start causing problems."

"I love my dad. I miss him. I wish he'd come back."

I gave a little roll of my eyes and went back to doodling on my notebook.

"What was that for?" she asked.

"What was what for?"

"You rolled your eyes," she said. "Why?"

"I don't know," I said without looking up from my star. "I'm starting to think that getting attached to things is pointless.

That's how things get screwed up. People care too much about everything. Let it go. You'll be happier."

She was silent for about a minute.

"I should go," she said.

"Right now?"

"Yes," she said. "Right now. Is it dangerous for me to ride my bike stoned?"

"Are you stoned?" I asked. "Most people don't get stoned their first time."

"I can't tell," she said.

"Do you feel stoned?"

"I can't tell," she said again. "I need to go. I want to go home."

"My mom's out with a friend," I said. "I can take you and your bike home in her SUV."

"That might be a good idea."

∞

I backed my mother's SUV out of the garage and loaded Fessica's hot pink mountain bike into the back for her. We listened to the radio on the way there. Top 40 crap. She sat there with her arms crossed and her mouth fixed in a firm line. She was upset about something. It was coming off her in waves.

"Don't talk about my dad like that, Dade," she said when we finally pulled up to her house. "Don't tell me not to get attached to things. And don't tell me what I want. Ever. Not when it comes to my dad, not when it comes to me and who I am, not about anything else."

"What?" I asked.

"My dad is not an appendix. People aren't disposable. People's problems aren't disposable. You might think it's cool to say you don't care about anything, but you do. You care just as much as anyone else. Pretending you don't makes you just like Pablo and Judy and all those assholes. You're not lonelier than anyone else in the world."

She slammed the car door when she exited. I sat there, a bit stunned, a bit embarrassed. The honeyed glow of the sunset made even this ugly neighborhood look somewhat beautiful. She slapped her hand against the back of the car. She wanted her bike. I got out and opened the back for her. I started to unload her bike for her, but she shouldered me off to the side and did it herself. Jessica was on the porch painting her toenails. We made eye contact, and I didn't know what to do so I waved. She gave me the finger.

"Faggot," she said. She went back to painting her nails.

Fessica and I stood there in the street for a few moments. I wanted to say I was sorry, but I couldn't make myself do it. It felt weird having to be on the other side of an apology. I was so used to being the one who thought he was owed one. It was Fessica who spoke first.

"Faggot," she said. And then she turned and took her bike up toward her house.

# Chapter 10

Work the next day went by in a slow smear across my brain. It felt like I was stocking milk in the dairy for eight hours, but when I checked my watch, it had only been forty-five minutes. Thankfully, Pablo, Jessica, and Fessica weren't working that day. Part of me wished Fessica was there so I could apologize.

I hardly spoke to anyone all day and other than a few customers, no one spoke to me. I was left with my thoughts of everyone that had been playing a role in my summer so far—Alex, Lucy, Pablo, the Montana twins, Dingo. Even Vicki lurked on the edges of my mind, a smiling face in a photograph that stood for things too painful to think about. I ran through scenarios in which I impressed them all. I was a famous author being interviewed on a late-night talk show, and everyone was watching me from their homes. Lucy was pointing and saying, "That's my friend! That's my boy!" Pablo was scowling and jealous, but unable to switch the channel.

The imaginary host asked me what my book was about.

"It's about the summer after my senior year of high school. Everything in it is true. No names have been changed to protect the innocent, because everyone in it is guilty. Especially me."

∞

I was eating a piece of pizza in the break room when my phone vibrated in my pocket. I took it out and there was Alex's name on the screen. I felt a burst of pleasure in my chest.

"Hello?"

"Is Dade there?" There was noise in the background, like rushing traffic.

"This is Alex," I said. "Crap. I mean, this is Dade."

"Um . . . I'm Alex. You're Dade."

"Right," I said. Shut my eyes and sunk in my chair. I wanted to disappear. "You're Alex and I'm Dade. I think I got it."

Alex laughed. "Good. So now that we've got that straightened out, how are you, man? What have you been up to?"

"I'm good," I said. I tried to think what I'd been up to lately other than sitting around thinking of him. "Summer's good. How are you?"

"I'm good. I'm calling because Dingo's having a little get-together out at his place tonight. His band will be playing. There'll be, like, eighty kegs. You in?"

"I'm totally in," I said. I sat up straight. I was ready to go right then. "What time?"

"Come at ten?"

"Well, I'm at work now and don't get off until ten."

"No biggie," he said. "Come after. Things should really be hoppin' by the time you get there."

I thought of Lucy. "Can I bring someone?"

"Um, sure," he said a bit hesitantly.

"It's my friend Lucy," I said. "She's cool."

"Oh, word. Is that a lady friend? Someone you've got your eye on?"

It took me a moment to get the gist of what he meant, but when I finally did, I let out a laugh. "Oh, no, no. She's just a friend."

"Cool," he said.

He reminded me how to get to Dingo's place. I said good-bye and waited for him to do the same, but there was a click and he was gone. I immediately called Lucy.

"You have to go with me," I told her. "I can already feel myself turning into a mess. What do I say? How do I act? I can't do it on my own."

She let out a dramatic sigh. "I'd love to be your wingman, but Aunt Dana is a bit peeved about me being out so late so many nights in a row. She's forcing me to stay in for some quality time and watch the Grace Kelly DVD collection she ordered online. I told her that I loathe quality time, but that didn't make things any better."

For a moment I wondered how I would ever survive the evening alone, but then I realized I didn't have a choice. She wished me luck before we hung up.

"You're the best," she said. "Don't forget that."

∞

When I got to Dingo's there were about twenty other cars parked in the yard and along the dirt road that ran in front of the little house, and every light in the place was on. Music blasted from inside and diffused into the evening. I parked in the yard in a space between two cars, one of which was Alex's. The sight of it made my heart flutter.

There were a couple of guys around my age on the porch smoking a cigarette and passing a bottle of rum back and forth. They both had shaved heads. One of them kept running his hand over his head and laughing.

"Hey," I said. I noticed the caution in my voice and immediately hated it. "Is Alex here?"

"He's around here somewhere," said the other one. He looked me up and down with a coy smile. "Last time I saw him he was in the bathroom getting his head shaved."

I slipped between them and went into the house. There were about a dozen shirtless guys in the living room, all with shaved heads. The Jericho Bastards record was on, all razor-sharp guitars and nonsense lyrics. People were pumping their fists in the air and yelling along with the music. I kept stealing glances at the shirtless bodies around me. The tufts of hair under arms. Adam's apples and belly buttons. The vertebrae snaking up the center of muscular backs. It was then that I noticed my hard-on.

"Hey!" I saw Louis's head bobbing in the sea of bodies. He ducked under someone's arm and made his way over to me.

He had to yell over the music to be heard. "So glad you could make it, man. Alex said you'd be coming. There's tons of beer in the refrigerator. Band goes on in a couple of hours. Playing a ton of new songs. It's gonna be *sick*, man."

"I can't wait," I said. "Hey, do you know where I can find—"

He cut me off. "And remember how I thought Death Grip was a stupid band name?"

"Yeah."

"Well, dude, I totally got them to change it."

"To what?"

"We are now officially called Dingo and the Side Effects. Pretty cool, right? I'm Dizziness, Thomas is Vomiting, and if we get this dude that Dingo knows to play keyboards, he's going to be Diarrhea. Genius, right? *Super* edgy."

I told him it was and that I couldn't wait to hear the band and that I was going to find Alex. I made my way through the crowded living room to the bathroom.

It was an expectedly tiny room with an unflattering fluorescent light and bright white surfaces everywhere. Dingo was standing in the bathtub wearing nothing but a red Speedo. He had an unlit cigarette dangling from his mouth and his hip jutted out a bit in a pose that was decidedly effeminate. Thomas was sitting on the toilet, and Jay from Taco Taco was shaving his head for him. Everyone else's head was already shaved. The bathroom floor was covered with hair. Blond hair, black hair, brown hair, blue hair. There were even a few of Jay's dreadlocks in there. Alex was perched on the rim of the sink with his shirt off. The sight of him hairless caught me off guard, but after a moment I was swept back into how handsome he was, something that was unaffected by whether or not he had hair. He noticed me in the doorway and turned up one side of his mouth in a grin. His smile sparked something in his eyes that made me feel like I was the only person in the room, maybe the only one in the whole wide world.

"Dude," he said. He squeezed my shoulder and pulled me toward him. "Good to see you, man. Thanks for coming."

"Thanks for inviting me. Glad I could make it."

"Dade!" Dingo yelled, pointing at me. He was obviously on something. His eyes were narrow, almost closed, and his smile was flat and dumb. "I remembered your name!"

"Hey, Jay," Alex said, slapping me on the back. "It's our good friend Dade."

Jay gave me a nod and went back to focusing on the task at hand. Thomas seemed too nervous and uncomfortable to pay any attention to me. Jay ran the clippers along his head, sending tufts of red hair lightly to the floor.

"What are you guys doing?" I asked.

"We're having a party, man," Dingo said.

"You want to get your head shaved?" Jay asked, not taking his eyes off Thomas's head.

I had no desire to get my head shaved, but I was afraid of what Alex would think if I didn't do it. I thought of my parents. My mother would kill me.

"I'm not sure," I said. "I've never had a shaved head before."

"It's hot outside, man," Alex said. "You should do it. Dingo did it and then everyone started doing it."

"Yeah, I wish there was a bridge nearby so we could all jump off it," Thomas mumbled.

Dingo said, "Thomas is a big pussy. And there is a bridge nearby, buddy. I'll drive you there, Mr. Bad Attitude. You can go first, and then guess who will follow? No one."

Everybody started laughing except Thomas. He looked like he was going to cry. I felt bad for him, but I didn't know what to say. I looked over at Dingo. He seemed amused by how upset Thomas looked. I decided that Dingo was a dick.

"Yeah, you behind the wheel of a car," Jay said. "That'd be rich."

"I drive in a Speedo all the time!" Dingo yelled. "It's what I do! It's my thing!"

Everyone laughed again except Thomas. Jay finished shaving his head and gave him a good slap on the scalp.

"Don't you feel freer now, Tommy?" Dingo asked. "Don't you feel like all your problems have just melted away? Touch it. Rub your hand over your head. Do it. Give yourself some love."

Thomas unenthusiastically rubbed his hand over his head. Dingo brought one foot out of the tub and kicked around at the hair on the floor.

"Look at all our problems," he said. "All mixed up. Just one big mess on the floor. Start fresh. Start with nothing, man. Then work your way back. That's my motto." Dingo looked over at me. "Your turn, kid."

"And take off your shirt, boy," Jay said. "You look like a freak with it on."

Dingo was looking at me so intently, with such crazy eyes, that I didn't know what to say. At first I thought I would do it out of fear, but then I saw Alex's head and Jay's head and suddenly it didn't seem scary anymore. I wanted to do it, to jump off that cliff. In fact, I took off my shirt with such enthusiasm that everyone began to cheer. I took Thomas's place on the toilet. The music in the living room abruptly stopped and everyone out there groaned, but then the new Tomato Hoof record started and people started screaming along to the first verse. I made a mental note to download it the minute I got home.

After Jay was done, I got up and looked in the mirror. I looked like someone else. I remember thinking that the suburban boy with the mom-approved haircut was gone, although in retrospect it's clear that he'd been gone for quite some time. I felt like an active part of everything that was happening around me. I was suddenly part of their genus, and everything was beautifully and terrifyingly new.

"Let's get out of this cell," Alex said to me. "We'll catch up."

They were getting ready to spark up a joint. Jay asked us to stay and smoke some of it, but instead Alex and I went into the kitchen. A few guys were playing cards at the table. The counter was still covered with empty bottles, and a garbage bin in the corner was overflowing with trash. Alex grabbed four beers from the refrigerator. We went out back and sat on the steps. There was an intense light over the door that attracted all sorts of bugs. Out in the yard, a headless flamingo stood perfectly erect, its hollow plastic neck pointing straight up at the sky.

"How you been?" Alex asked.

"Good," I said. "Just working. Getting ready for school."

"College," he said.

"College," I repeated.

"Are you going to get one of those shirts that Belushi wore? The one that just says 'College' across the front?"

I laughed. "I highly doubt it."

"You should," he said. "That'd be funny."

All my nervousness had flown away. I found myself marinating in the now and enjoying the moment. Even Alex seemed different than he had the Taco Taco night, more relaxed and less surly. Maybe Dingo was right. Maybe all my problems had left with my hair. Maybe our hairlessness and shirtlessness were equalizers. We were aliens from the same planet.

"What are you going to study in school?" he asked.

"Probably English," I said. I kept staring at his mouth. It was impossible to look at it and not think about how amazing it would be to kiss him. "I want to be a writer."

"Really?" He was staring at me intently, his interest obviously piqued. "What kind of writer?"

"I write poetry. Some short story type things too. I'm still kinda . . . um . . . finding my voice, as they say."

"I've tried writing poetry before. It always turns out super terrible, so I just stick to reading it. I like a lot of the Latin

American stuff. This dude named Lorca is cool. Last summer I dated this guy who got me into poetry."

*Oh my fucking God! He* is *gay!*

It was suddenly impossible to swallow the beer in my mouth. My throat was spasming. I wanted to laugh both out of pure joy at this revelation and at how ridiculous I must have appeared.

"Are you okay, man?" Alex asked. He gave me a few concerned pats on the back. "You dying on me?"

I waved him away and forced myself to swallow the beer. It was painful, and after it was gone, there was a soreness in my throat like something was lodged there. I coughed a few times and took in some gulps of air.

"What was that all about?"

"I don't know." I coughed some more. "Wrong pipe."

"I hate that," he said.

"So do I," I said. I cleared my throat once more. "So, um, last summer. How was that?" I was completely shocked that we were having this conversation. It was so casual, just like the other night when the two guys at Cherry's started dancing together.

"It was good. I spent most of my time hanging out with David. That's the guy who got me into poetry and stuff. He was a good guy."

"How did you meet?

"On the Internet. He was older, in his thirties, but still really, really hot. And he was really, really smart. He was a high school English teacher. I was eighteen, freshly graduated, and he was smart and fatherly. Gave me great advice. But he was also fun.

And he looked like Keanu Reeves. But yeah, he got me into poetry. He saved me in a lot of ways."

"How's that?"

"I mean, I think everyone gets really close to that void, ya know? That loneliness that's so easy to fall into. It makes you do all sorts of stuff. It can turn you into someone who deep down inside, you don't want to be. He taught me that I was worth something, which I needed."

I wanted to tell him that I knew exactly what he was talking about, that I was in that void and he could save me. I wanted so badly to lean into him and let him put his mouth on mine, to press my chest against his. I wanted him to put distance between me and Pablo.

"Do you still talk to him?" I asked.

"Nah," Alex said. "He left Cedarville for some job in Florida. He was randomly in the state for some conference a few months back, and he sent an e-mail to an address that I never use anymore. I saw it a week after he left, when there was nothing I could do about it. I e-mailed him back and told him I was sorry. I explained that I'd missed the message, and that if he was ever in Iowa again that he should call me. He never replied. Maybe it's for the best. Things change."

He pulled out a cigarette and asked me if I wanted one. I said sure. He put both cigarettes between his lips, shielding the lighter's flame with his hand as he lit them. The glow lit up his perfectly stubbled face.

"You're gay, right?" he asked, handing me one of the cigarettes.

I smiled nervously. "Yeah. I am. Is it really that obvious?"

"Kinda," Alex said. He was suppressing a smile. "But who says that's bad? It's good. Plus, you're still guyish. You're not totally faggy."

"I don't like that word."

"Faggy?"

"Yeah. Faggy. Fag. Faggot."

"Sorry," he said. "I use it with these guys all the time. I usually just assume that people are okay with it. I forget sometimes."

"Don't change on account of me. Say whatever you want." I thought back to the night we met, when he told me I didn't have to say I agreed with him if I really didn't. I hoped this last comment didn't sound as spineless to his ears as it did to mine.

Alex laughed and shook his head. "You're a wild one, Dade. And by wild I mean not wild."

I nodded slowly, unsure what that meant.

"So Fessica seems to like you," he said in an obvious attempt to switch the subject.

"Why do you say that?"

"I stopped by Food World the other day and asked her where you were. She got that look in her eye when I mentioned your name."

He'd been looking for me? I forced myself to remain cool about this, to not pump my fist in the air. I wondered where I'd been. Probably swimming in my pool or driving around town or sprawled out on my bed and thinking about him. There was something beautiful about the idea of us reaching invisibly across town for each other.

"Yeah, I think she has a little crush on me," I said. "She came over to my house the other day unannounced. I was kind of a jerk to her. I feel bad."

"She's a sweet girl. Beyond awkward, but sweet. At least she's not her sister. Jesus Christ, that girl's a mess."

"How did you meet her?"

"I sell to her and her friends. I know her and the McGraw brothers and some kid they call the Sexican who's dating one of Jessica's friends."

"Pablo?" I asked.

"Yeah. That's him."

The thought of Pablo and Alex being in the same room together made my stomach twist.

"What a douche, that kid." He finished off his beer and opened another with the opener on his keychain. "Always telling me my bags are light. Don't tell me my bags are light, man. I'm the fairest dealer in this town."

He stood up. Something had changed in him. I could see it in his face. He looked blank and entranced, not there anymore. I was beginning to get the sense that his mind was like a jukebox and his emotions were plastic sleeves that displayed states of being instead of albums. I could almost hear the plastic slapping sound as his emotional catalog browsed itself, found nothing, and began to backtrack. He walked into the center of the yard and stared up at the sky. There in the moonlight he looked like something beamed down to earth from another galaxy, all lean muscle and wondering eyes with a shaved head that seemed to suggest he'd just been born a few moments ago.

"I wanted to be an astronaut when I was little," he said. "Can you imagine that? Me up in space? I bet being up there's a lot like being dead and alive at the same time. You are really and truly not in this world anymore. The only other time you can say that is when you're dead, and you can't even say it then because . . . well, because you're dead."

He glanced over his shoulder and let out a laugh. I suddenly felt so sad for him. I wasn't sure about his past, who he was, but right there is when I first sensed the sadness of Alex Kincaid. I felt the vacuum in him. It was the same as the one in me. It wanted, but it didn't know what it wanted, so it pulled at everything.

"I wanted to be an FBI agent," I said. "But I think that's just because I was really into this TV show about FBI agents when I was little."

"If you want to be a FBI agent you have to have never done any drugs, like, ever. They give you lie detector tests."

"I think there's like a ten-year gap or something."

"But still. I have a feeling the first ten years of my life are the only ten consecutive years of my life where I didn't do drugs."

"When did you first smoke pot?" I asked.

"Eleven." He wandered the yard, kicked at an old softball that was hiding in the grass. "It was with my dad. My mom found out and was all furious, but two months later all four of us were lumbering around the house stoned out of our minds."

"Four of you?"

"I have an older sister. She's in Europe. Has been for a while."

"What does she do there?"

"She ran away to get away from my parents. My dad's in jail now and my mom moved to Texas with some piece of shit trucker named Buck who was one of the reasons my dad got put in the clink in the first place. One of the worst people I've ever met. I've always wanted to get out of Cedarville, but I wasn't about to go with that guy. No fucking way. So I stayed behind. I live with my grandma now. It's just me and her and her cat Snowy. One big happy family."

He laughed nervously. I guessed he'd had to explain this situation before, and somewhere along the way he'd gotten into the habit of punctuating the whole story with a laugh to make things easier for everyone involved.

He asked if I wanted to go for a drive and I said yes. The idea of being alone in a car with him again sounded heavenly. We walked around the side of the house to his car. I felt the pricks of stray hairs all over my arms, neck, and back. They could've belonged to any of us. I ran my hand over my shaved head. I swore I could feel my hair growing back already.

We drove aimlessly across the darkened countryside. The engine rumbled and knocked under the hood, but Alex didn't seem to worry, so neither did I. We talked about bands we liked, television shows we hated. He told me about his grandmother and her church where people ran to the front of the congregation in mid-hymn and twitched with the spirit. He said that it never ceased to terrify him, that he didn't understand why anyone would want to voluntarily lose themselves in something when it seemed like life was all about trying to find yourself. I told him a little about my parents, about how lost they still were and how it sometimes felt like they'd given up trying to get unlost. I sarcastically said that maybe going to church would do them some good. Alex laughed and said that was doubtful.

"Wanna park somewhere?" he asked. "Get on the roof and watch the stars?"

I told him I'd like that. He pulled over at a random spot on the road.

"Let me grab my cigarettes and we'll go up," he said.

He flicked on the dome light and started looking for something in his glove compartment. I couldn't stop staring at his chest, at his nipples and the patch of hair that ran down to his belly button. He was rounded shoulders and muscled arms. He was perfect. I must have been staring too hard, because suddenly he stopped going through the glove compartment and just stared back at me. It was as if he'd just pulled the emergency brake on everything. The music moved, but everything else stood still. I turned away and looked out at the night, darker than ever thanks to the light in the car. He put his hand on my knee.

"Dade, it's okay."

I didn't reply. I was so thirsty and in shock about *his hand on my knee* that I almost opened up the door and ran into the night.

"It's okay," he said again. I looked over at him. "I get it."

He shut the dome light off. He leaned forward and kissed me. It caught me off guard, but my mouth reacted before my mind. I kissed him back. The underside of his upper lip was warm and soft. I pulled back and we stared at each other for a few seconds. Then it was me who bridged the distance, and we were kissing again, slow and deliberate like ice melting on a countertop.

# Chapter 11

The next day was one of those unbearably humid days where stepping outside was like stepping into an armpit. Mom and Dad were gone for the day, so Lucy came over and we made margaritas with twice as much tequila as was called for and hung out by the pool in our bathing suits. I told her about my night with Alex, about kissing him, about the way he'd played with my fingers during the last half of Dingo's set. She didn't make me stop talking about him. She let me go on and on. I told her that it all felt as if it were happening to someone else, like my memories of the previous night were someone else's memories that had been cruelly dumped into my head to show me everything that was missing in my life.

I told her I was scared I'd mess it up and that all of this would disappear as fast as it appeared. I talked about my shaved head and about his eyes on my face right before he leaned in to kiss me for the second time. I told her about the Tomato Hoof record I'd downloaded and listened to three times that morning and how every song on there reminded me of him so much that my stomach would cramp during certain melody lines and guitar parts, especially during the last thirty seconds of "Gravity Is Serious," where the lead singer keeps repeating: *I don't wanna be a part of the stratosphere / I don't wanna make policeman sounds.*

"I want to meet him," she said. "I want to meet this guy."

"We're hanging out tomorrow night, just him and me, but you'll meet him soon. I want you to tell me what you think."

"It's so hot." She spoke slowly, as if the temperature were affecting her speech. "I fucking love it."

"Summer's good, but I think I'm more of an autumn guy."

"Aw. How sensitive of you."

After Lucy left, I wandered the house in a daze. My brain was fuzzy from the tequila and the heat. The cool air of the house sharpened the sensation of the sunburn on my back and made it feel like my shoulder blades were giving off sparks. I had the Tomato Hoof record on at full volume. The walls bled guitars and drums, words and melodies. The songs were everywhere.

I was sitting in the kitchen wearing my bathing suit and a black hooded sweatshirt when my mother came home. I was watching some dating show on MTV and eating unwashed strawberries straight from the container. She walked in through the garage door and screamed.

I dropped the strawberry I was holding and looked over my shoulder at her. "What's the matter?"

Her mouth hung open and her eyes were wide and bugging out of her head. She looked somewhere between totally shocked and possessed.

"What do you mean what's the matter?" she asked. "What the hell happened to your hair?"

"Oh yeah. I forgot."

"What do you mean you forgot?" she asked. "You look like a serial killer. How could you forget?"

"What do you mean I look like a serial killer?"

"You look like a serial killer," she said again.

"So does that mean the entire Cedarville boys' swim team looks like serial killers?"

"Did you join the swim team?"

"No, but you know, this is what they do. They shave their heads."

She squinted at me like I was insane. "Then what are you talking about? What's gotten into you? Where's my son?"

"I wanted a change," I said. I got up and put the strawberries back in the refrigerator. "Can't things change? Do they have to stay the same all the time?"

I started upstairs and she followed.

"No. They don't. But when changes are made in my household, I would like to be made aware of them."

"Well, you're aware," I said.

I went up to my room and shut the door behind me, but she came in after me not two beats later. I pretended to occupy myself with the little things that littered my desk. Papers, pencils, a plastic toy robot I purchased from one of the little machines at Food World.

"Where were you last night?" she asked. "I heard you get home at five in the morning. That is unacceptable. *Unacceptable*. And this. Your hair. Did this happen last night? What were you doing last night that got you to do this? Was it that Lucy girl?"

"Lucy's my friend, Mom."

"Well, she's ruining your life. And friends don't ruin each other's lives."

"What are you talking about? How is shaving my head ruining my life?"

"If Lucy jumped off a bridge, would you?"

"I guess that depends on what was at the bottom."

"Har, har, Dade. Hardy frickin' har. You know, I smell the pot. Every now and then was fine. I could deal with that. But your room smells like a drug den."

"You're exaggerating."

"Give it to me," she said, holding out her hand. "Give me the marijuana. Now."

"It's gone," I lied. "I smoked it all."

"I don't believe you."

"Well, believe me. It's gone."

"What about the pipe or the joint or the bong or whatever it is you smoke it out of?"

"I don't have a bong, Mom. And besides, I'll be gone in two months and then I can do whatever the hell I want. I'll buy a hundred bongs if I want, and there's nothing that you or Dad will be able to say or do."

She gave me that wilting look, the look of death that she could sometimes whip out of her back pocket. She left the bedroom without even bothering to slam the door shut for punctuation. A minute later I heard her scream. It was different from the one that she'd let out when she walked into the kitchen. This was one of frustration, an animal sound shooting through the halls and rooms of the house. Then I heard glass breaking. I sat on the edge of my bed and shut my eyes.

*Don't go down yet. Wait a few seconds.*

I found her leaning against the kitchen counter and vigorously massaging her eyes with the palms of her hand. She'd thrown the bottle of tequila that Lucy and I had nearly finished against the refrigerator. What was left of the liquor had run down the surface of the fridge and pooled on the floor with the broken glass.

"Mom?"

She looked up. Her eyes were red. I couldn't tell if it was from crying or the rubbing. She gave me a defeated little smile, one that reduced everything to a petty, insignificant level.

"I'm sorry," I said. "I didn't think it'd be a big deal."

She reached into the drawer for her Marlboro Lights and lighter. She didn't even bother opening the window. She just lit up.

"I was driving home and I kept thinking about when your father and I first got married and when we had you. The farmhouse. I don't know why I wanted to live in a farmhouse so badly, but I did. Remember the chickens?"

"I remember."

"You were really young then. And your father was teaching high school PE courses, and he hated it, but he would come home and play his guitar on the porch and I'd be in the kitchen screwing up dinner. And you'd be there, all happy because you were a happy kid. And nothing made you happier than sitting there while your father played the guitar. Your father and I were young and in love and poor. We didn't have anything. We used to say that all the time, that we didn't have anything. Just you. And now look at us. I was thinking about that when I was in line at the grocery store the other day. I kept wondering what changed."

I didn't know what to say, so I didn't say anything. I pulled out an unused pair of yellow rubber gloves and a plastic Food World bag from under the sink. I put on the gloves and carefully picked up each shard of glass and placed them in the plastic bag. My mom presided silently over everything from the side. I used paper towels to wipe the tequila off the floor and the refrigerator, the fancy quadruple-ply kind that sucked up lots of moisture, and I thought of how this would make one screwed-up paper towel commercial. I took the bag out to the curb and threw it in one of our big rubber garbage cans. I tossed the gloves in as an afterthought. It felt like using them again would be bad luck.

When I went back inside, my mother was gone. Her unfinished cigarette was crushed out in one of the dirty bowls in the sink. The odor of the tequila, the cigarette, and the dirty dishes conspired to make the room smell like Cherry's. From above my head came the sound of my mother shuffling down the second-floor hallway. She moved with slow, sliding steps, the kind I made when I was an overtired four-year-old being dragged back to bed for the fifth time by my father. On the refrigerator television there were models strutting down a runway, flashes all around them as they walked with dramatic assurance. They had peacock feathers in their hair and wore neon makeup in tribal smudges across their eyes and mouths. Their faces gave away nothing. They knew exactly where they were going.

∞

Alex arrived at eight thirty the next night, half an hour after he said he was going to be there. I spent the extra time waiting on the couch, staring at the same patch of neighborhood through the picture window and just waiting for his car to roll into the picture.

"Who are you waiting for?" my mother asked. She'd been gardening and popping pills all day. They were lime green ones, ones I hadn't seen before. They must have been something new, something stronger and speedier.

"I'm going out with my friend Alex."

She stood silent in the living room for a few moments, eyeing me. Her mind was probably making connections between recent events and this name she'd never heard before.

"A new friend?"

"Yeah," I said.

"Does he shave his head too? Is that why you shaved yours?"

It was the first time she'd mentioned it all day. I didn't answer. I just kept staring, waiting.

"So you're taking his car? Not yours?"

"That's correct."

"Is he a good driver?" she asked.

"Very," I lied.

"Well, I think one of the many lessons I've learned over the last few weeks is that you're beyond coming home at a decent hour, so at least keep me updated. Send me a text message that says you're not dead or something. That'll make me feel better."

Alex's Citation pulled up just then and I hurried out the front door without saying anything. His windows were rolled down and he was blaring some wild speed metal. He waved at me when he saw me coming and I waved back.

"Get me the hell out of here," I said when I climbed into the car.

My mother was watching on the porch with her arms crossed. She was squinting intently toward the car like she was trying to see if she recognized my new friend from a wanted poster.

"Is that your mom?" he asked. He waved at her. She didn't wave back. Instead she just jutted out her chin and stared harder.

"Dude, c'mon. Let's go."

It was the time of the day where the sun was giving off its last brightness, one that seemed greater than anything all day. The rays came from low on the horizon, blinding us in some stretches and burning behind us on others. He was driving over the speed limit as usual. I was turned toward him in my seat, in love with the way the wind felt on my shaved head and the song on the radio, all buzz saw guitars and a guy growling in German.

"Where are we going?" I asked.

"I don't know," he said. He was sprawled out low in his seat, super relaxed and probably high. "Where do you want to go?"

"I don't care," I said.

"Somewhere new?"

"I've been everywhere. Take me somewhere I've never been."

"Oh, so he's been everywhere," Alex said to himself. He shot me a charming grin. For a moment I thought I might be too sullen to let it affect me, but before I knew it my scowl had melted away and I was smiling like a fool. He rubbed his hand over my shaved head. We drove out of the city in the opposite direction of Dingo's place. Before long, the sun had been reduced to a little glow far off to the west and Alex had to turn his lights on. We'd stayed quiet for most of the drive, and it took me some time to realize that's what I needed. I was glad he was able to recognize that, and impressed that he knew before I did.

"Bad mom business?" he finally asked.

"Sort of. It's always bad nowadays."

"That sucks. But I hear ya. I have those days. Or had them. Before my mom left."

"It's not exactly the same. I mean, I guess it is. But it's not. My mom's sick."

I'd never said it before, but suddenly it almost felt like I'd solved something. I'd put a word to it. She was *sick*. But the moment I'd picked that answer, a hundred questions grew in its place.

"We're all sick," Alex said. "I was thinking that the other night at Dingo's place when everyone was there going crazy and shaving their heads. I mean, I remember in high school seeing people who seemed like they had it all together. People like Jessica Montana or Judy Lockhart. Everyone thinks girls like them have a perfect life and that they fall asleep every night without any thoughts or fears or whatever. But it's not true. Everyone's got that thing in them that keeps them awake."

I sat there for a while thinking about what he'd said. I thought of how many nights I'd stayed up late wondering what the world had in store for me, if I'd ever find someone that I could fall in love with. I wondered if all gay boys had nights like these, if there was a time when even someone like Alex stared up at his ceiling and wondered the same thing.

"So where are you taking me?" I finally asked.

"Someplace you've never been." He looked at me and smiled. "Since you seem to think you've been everywhere. But don't worry. You'll be gone soon enough. Me, on the other hand. I don't know when I'm going to get out of here."

"What's keeping you around?"

"I tell myself it's my grandmother, but I know that's just an excuse."

"So what's the real reason?" I asked.

He tilted his head, pursed his lower lip, and made a little face. "I'm not exactly sure."

"You could make it somewhere else," I said. "It can't be that hard to leave. People do it all the time. Your sister did it. Plus, you seem like one of those people who could do anything if you put your mind to it."

"Yeah. I guess you're right." He smiled a little. "Sometimes I fantasize about New York. Chicago even. The idea of New York terrifies me, but I feel like maybe that means I should try it out. Go to where the fear is, right? Learn something new."

He drove me out past the towns that scattered the country-side beyond the Cedarville city limits, towns that consisted of little more than a post office, a gas station, and a bar. They all seemed abandoned, like the people living there had picked up and left. We were a mile outside the toy-like town of Whitfield (pop. 509) when Alex turned off the highway and onto a tiny road of packed gravel and weeds. In the headlights of the car I saw a rusted fence and beyond that were headstones. He'd taken me to a small rural graveyard.

"Are we supposed to be out here?"

"Probably not."

He navigated the road toward the back of the cemetery, where a fence divided it from a sprawling soybean crop, and shut off the car. There was just the buggy soundtrack of the countryside split with the distant rush of a semi on some unseen highway. Every sound he made—clearing his throat, removing the keys from the ignition, opening the glove compartment for a fresh pack of cigarettes—seemed huge. We got out of the car.

"Check out the stars," he said. They were abundant and bright.

"I forget how many there are sometimes," I said.

"Yeah. They're something. That's one of the reasons I come out here. It's like being at Dingo's house except the vibe out here is a little less intense, if you can imagine that." He was walking in front of me, determined on leading the way toward something.

I leaned in and checked the dates on some of the gravestones. They went so far back. 1932. 1920. 1899. I became humbly aware of my position in the void of time.

"Here it is," he said.

He was standing by a cross-shaped headstone. He leaned in and flicked his lighter to illuminate the date.

"John Arthur Ellis," he said. "Born 1880, died 1923. It's my grandmother's father, my great-grandfather."

He let the lighter go out and stood back up. He took a deep breath and slowly let it out. Something about it felt like he was reminding himself that he was alive. Without thinking, I did the same. He looked over at me and smiled.

"I come out here sometimes and talk to him," he said. "I obviously never met him, but my grandmother always tells me that I remind her of him. He was an inventor. He was always dreaming things up and trying to get rich off them."

"Did any of them work?" I asked.

"Nah. Supposedly he was a bit of a laughingstock around the town. But that never stopped him. He was looking for a way out. My grandmother told me he wanted to get rich and move to California. Live by the ocean. He died poor. Poor but happy. With my parents gone, sometimes I forget that I came from anywhere. That's why I come out here. To remind myself."

I was touched that he'd brought me here. I didn't know what to say. Up until then there was a part of me that wondered if maybe there was nothing more to him than an aura of danger and a disposable charm that he used to keep himself from getting into too much trouble. I was beginning to realize that like everyone else, he was searching for something, and like everyone else, he had no idea where he could find it.

"Thanks for bringing me here," I said. "It really means a lot to me."

"Does it?" he asked. He seemed genuinely surprised by this. "I'm glad. I wasn't sure if you'd get it. I thought maybe you'd think it was creepy."

"No," I said quickly. "Not at all. I like that there's these different parts to you."

"Good," he said, smiling. "It's hard to show people everything, you know? You never know what they'll do with it once they have it."

We sat on an old stump in the center of the graveyard, just big enough for two people. I wondered if he'd ever been out there with some other guy he liked. I thought about him out there with someone else, someone cooler and better looking who always said the right thing.

"They found that girl's shoe on a bike trail," he said. "I saw it on the news."

"Jenny Moore's?"

"Yeah. Her."

"Just one shoe?"

"Apparently. Bad sign. I feel like two shoes would've been okay, but just one seems bad."

"It's weird to think that she's out there."

"People've been saying they've seen her," said Alex. "I was at some party a few nights ago and this girl was going on and on about how she saw a girl that looked just like the girl in the yellow flyers sitting in the balcony of the Riviera."

The Riviera was an old movie theater downtown that played classic movies and art films. I had no idea how it did business, since its only patrons seemed to be the bespectacled members of the Cedarville High Cinema Club. Every year or so they threatened to turn it into a porno theater in an effort to make some money, but people would protest and money would appear and the matter would be put off for another year. I thought back to what Fessica had said about hearing someone say they'd seen Jenny on the golf course.

"Maybe it was a ghost," Alex said. "But I don't believe in ghosts, so screw that. This chick's also been known to eat a magic mushroom omelet before school, so who knows what kind of wavelength she was surfing at the time."

"I see those flyers all over town," I said. "Everything's haunted."

"I was always scared that I was going to be kidnapped when I was a kid. My sister was a hypochondriac, always thought she had bone cancer or a brain tumor. My big fear was kidnappers. I'd lie in my bed staring at the window and thinking that a man was going to crawl in and get me."

The scenario he'd just described flashed in my mind and I shivered. "I had that too. A little bit. Like, I got separated from my mom at the grocery store once and I was sure that I was never going to see her again. I don't know what I thought would happen. I remember crying, though, and everyone stopping to look at me. Everyone asking where my mother was."

"Had she left without you?"

"No. She was like one aisle over or something. But still."

"It's so weird to be young," Alex said. "I realize that now. I look back on when I was like eight or nine, and my brain worked differently. It was like I was hallucinating. The way my mind worked had so little to do with reality that it was sort of frightening. It's amazing I survived."

We paused to look away from each other and take in our surroundings. Any fear I'd had upon entering the cemetery had disappeared. I felt strangely at peace. I wondered if it was connected to Alex's great-grandfather, if maybe his kind spirit wandered the graveyard and kept everything in check.

"I've never met anyone like you before," I said.

He laughed. "Is that a good thing? Wait. Don't answer that."

"No. It's good. It's really good."

He put his hand under my shirt and rubbed my lower back. My skin tingled where his fingers were. I fell into him. I rubbed my face into the nape of his neck and moved my lips against his skin. It wasn't so much kissing as it was mumbling into his body. He took my face in his hands and really kissed me. The feeling of his mouth was so familiar and amazing that I wondered if every kiss in my life would lead back to him, to his cigarette and laundry detergent smell, to the stubble on his face. There was so much meaning in his hands, in the way they cupped my cheeks and kept me still.

We had sex that night in the grass. He kissed my ears and ran his hand over the stubble on my head. I kept waiting for the moment where he turned on me, the moment where he pulled a Pablo and everything was eclipsed by some dark malignant mass, but that moment never came.

Afterward we lay there side by side in just our T-shirts. Up in the sky the flashing red dot of a helicopter moved amongst the stars. The blades of grass scratched the back of my legs and bugs bounced off my naked thighs, but I didn't care. We'd been quiet for a long time when I said, "I'm scared that when you get to know me, you won't like what you see."

"Where did that come from?

"You know Pablo Soto?"

"The Sexican?" he asked.

"Yeah." I sighed. I could feel the entire story of Pablo gathering inside my throat and making it hard to speak. I decided to take it one word at a time. "We used to have a . . . thing. It was never all that great. And then things got worse."

"I'm sorry," he said. "What happened?"

"He's just a jerk," I said. "That's really the only way to describe it."

"Well, you don't have to sleep with him to figure that one out," Alex said with a sarcastic laugh.

"I guess you're right."

"But we all go blind," Alex said. "And scared. Everyone gets scared."

"Are you scared?" I asked.

"Right now?"

"Yeah."

"I don't know," he said. "Maybe."

"What are you scared of?"

He thought for a moment and then said, "I'm scared that I'll keep on not letting myself feel anything and I'll turn into my dad. Or Dingo. Or so many other people I know. I don't want my heart to become a dead nerve, you know? But at the same time, you've gotta numb that stuff sometimes, man. Sometimes not caring is the only way out."

I remembered what Fessica had said the other day about not letting myself become one of those people who stopped caring in order to protect themselves. I thought of my mother and her pills, my father and his distance.

"I think my parents are going to get a divorce the minute I leave for college," I said.

"Well, that's not always a bad thing."

"I know. It's probably for the best. But right now things suck. My father is having an affair and my mom just sits around painting and popping pills and pretending nothing's wrong, and then she freaks out from pretending nothing's wrong and takes more pills to pretend that nothing's wrong. It's a mess. I'm going to leave for school and my entire life is going to explode behind me. It's going to be like one of those scenes in an action movie where Johnny Morgan is walking toward the camera and a car blows up behind him."

Alex laughed. "I know exactly what you mean. Luckily you're walking away from it, though. At least you're not the dude stuck in the car who gets blown to bits."

He leaned over and kissed me. I got hard almost immediately, but he didn't. At first I was worried that I wasn't doing something right, and then a few seconds passed and I realized he simply wanted to kiss me. It was the first time someone had given me everything I wanted and asked for so little in return.

∞

There was no life as we drove through town. Everything was dark except for a twenty-four-hour convenience store, and in the blur of passing I tried to spot even one person behind its glass walls, but there was no one, not even at the counter.

I made him turn his stereo off when we pulled into our subdivision. He parked in front of my house and shut off his lights.

"Your neighborhood has such a weird glow," he said. "The

streetlights seem different than normal streetlights. Like space-ship lights."

"They import special lightbulbs from somewhere, France or something. The Neighborhood Standards Committee thought the old bulbs were sending out gamma rays that were damaging the lawns in the night."

"Uh, okay."

"I know, right? There was a petition and a protest and every-thing. It was insane."

He let out a snorting laugh and shook his head. He looked out at the neighborhood, at its perfect surfaces. The blades of grass, the clean black road, the sloping rooftops. Everything was something you could slide down.

"Up the street they have what they call a model home," I said. "It's a house that they show people who are thinking about buying here. For a little while they were having open houses every weekend, and they liked to have someone from the neighborhood there to talk about how wonderful the houses are. My mom had to do it a few times. They have like a cardboard television instead of a real one. And a cardboard family scattered around the house. The cutout of the dad is in the den. The one of the mom is in the kitchen. There's a little girl in one of the bedrooms."

"And the son?" he asked. "Is he in the basement listening to death metal and dying his clothes black?"

We both burst out laughing. He took my hand. Our laughter died off and we sat there for a little bit staring out the windshield at the neighborhood, both in some sort of trance.

"I should go," I said eventually. "But thanks for taking me out. I had a fun time."

"Fun date?" he asked. "Not too morbid for you?"

"Not at all. It was great." I thought for a moment. "I don't think I've ever been on an official date before. This was a good one."

"Your first date ever?" he said.

"Unless you count the time in third grade when I asked Gina Larsen to eat lunch with me on the jungle gym."

"How'd that go?"

"Terrible. She was the most stuck-up nine-year-old on the face of the earth and I was . . . a homo."

He laughed and moved in to kiss me again. We kissed for a long time. I didn't want to stop. I wanted to stay like that forever, to live in his car with him, kissing and touching while the real world trudged on outside the windows.

"I should go," I said when I finally pulled away.

"You're right," he said quietly, slowly settling into his seat. "Go on. Go inside. Sweet dreams."

I could feel him watching me as I crossed the lawn. He didn't pull away until I'd opened the front door and was stepping into my house. I was standing in front of the refrigerator trying to find something to eat when my phone vibrated. It was Pablo calling. I ignored it.

I poured myself a glass of lemonade and leaned against the counter, waiting to see if he'd leave a voice mail. But he didn't. Instead he sent a text.

## What r u trying 2 prove by not answering?

I shut my phone and put it back in my pocket. There was no room in that night for Pablo and his bullshit. I pulled a bottle of vodka from the cupboard and took it out to the pool with my lemonade. A cool breeze swept through the yard. All around, the leaves of trees rustled in the wind. I looked up at the moon, the only witness to the entire night. I longed to be back in the cemetery with Alex, lying in the grass and staring up at the sky. I wondered where he was right then, if he was home yet or if maybe he was driving around town on that disappointing nocturnal search for somewhere else to go that nearly every Cedarville teenager embarked on at some point.

Pablo texted again.

## I know you're awake, douche

It was immediately followed by another one.

## Judy says hi/die

I tossed my phone a few feet away, not caring if it broke against the concrete surface surrounding the pool. I chugged the rest of my drink and filled my glass a third of the way with vodka. I downed this in three big gulps and filled a quarter of the glass up again. I lay back and stared up at the sky and tried to make peace with the burning sensation that the vodka had left in my throat. I didn't know whether to be sad about Pablo texting me or happy about the night I'd had with Alex. I drank the rest of the vodka in the glass. I thought of science class and the way deadly storms were born when cold and hot air combined and how that same principle was behind the range of emotions I was feeling. I forced out a laugh just to see how it felt, and it came out forced and false and a little bit frightening. It didn't sound like me at all.

A few feet away my phone vibrated again. I didn't get up to check it.

∞

An especially forceful gust of wind woke me up. It was still nighttime. I didn't remember falling asleep. I didn't know how long I'd been out or what time it was. I tried to stand up, but when I did I grew so light-headed that I fell back onto the chair. I realized I was drunk. I remembered drinking the vodka and drinking it fast, and I wondered if maybe I'd had more than I realized. I clumsily reached for the bottle beside the chair. There was less than half left. I tried to remember how full it had been when I took it out of the cupboard.

It was then that I noticed a flash of movement in the corner of our yard, some little person scurrying away from the pool and toward the bushes.

*Is that a kid?* I thought.

It was. She was wearing a pink shirt and denim shorts. She looked over her shoulder at me as she got on her hands and knees and crawled into the bushes. For a split second I saw her face in the moonlight, young and scared and chillingly familiar.

It was Jenny Moore.

And she was gone.

I jumped up to go after her, but the light-headedness came back and I realized that my leg had fallen asleep, turned into a pillar of pinpricks and dead muscles. I stumbled over to the spot where she'd vanished. I kneeled down and tried to peer into the bushes, but it was too dense and dark to see anything.

"Jenny?" I said.

The word came out a garbled mess. My stomach made a noise that seemed distantly related to the sound her name had made, and before I knew it I was vomiting into the mulch.

"Don't be scared," I said, wiping my mouth. "I'm not gonna hurt you. I wanna help you. I wanna help them find you."

I collapsed onto the lawn. The sharp branches of the bush scraped my head. There was a loud chirping noise, and one of the last things I thought before passing out was that it wasn't coming from a cricket. It was coming from her. She was curled into a ball, farther back in the bushes where I couldn't see. She was making the noise in her throat and glowing from the inside.

# Chapter 12

It was my father who found me. He was kicking my leg. Hard.

"Dade Patrick Hamilton, get your ass up."

I could smell liquor and vomit and soil and spices from my mother's herb garden. I lifted my head and put a hand to my cheek. A thick stickiness mixed with pieces of mulch.

"That's right," my father said. "Wake up, kid. You and I are gonna have a long talk."

I slid backward out of the narrow space under the bushes where I'd passed out. The sun was so fucking bright. It seemed to be as much to blame for my pounding headache as the previous night's booze. The blades of grass were cool and sharp on my feet. My shoes were gone. When had that happened?

"Jesus Christ," my father said when I stood. "Look at you."

"Yeah," I mumbled. "Look at me."

"Who told you that you could shave your head?"

"Well, I would've asked you, but you haven't been home. You've been out. And about. Out and about, as they say." I was swaying back and forth a bit and my words felt misshapen. I think I was technically still drunk. He gave me a firm palm to the shoulder, a weird sort of frat boy shove.

"Get your ass upstairs, young man, and clean yourself up. Then I want you downstairs in the kitchen, and your mother and I are going to have a very long, very severe talk with you." He went back inside and left me there in the yard, basically lo-botomized and in a heavy amount of physical pain. My head. My fucking head.

I showered and went down to the kitchen. My mother and father were at the table, each with cups of coffee, which some-how made the whole thing seem like an intervention.

"Food World called," my mother said. "You were supposed to be there this morning at eight?"

"Oh. Shit. Yeah."

"I told them you were sick." She leaned closer to me.

"What the hell has been going on?" my father blurted. "I leave the house for a few days and suddenly my kid is acting like he needs to go into AA."

"I've been under a lot of stress."

"What kind of stress?" he cried. "How can you be under any stress? What in the hell do you have to be unhappy about? I'll tell you what *I* have to be unhappy about—"

"Tell me what you have to be unhappy about, Dad."

"I'm unhappy about the fact that you're obviously making terrible life decisions, that you're obviously drinking too much, that you're probably using drugs—"

"I know he's using drugs, Ned. His room smells like a rap video."

"What does that even mean?" I asked.

"It means that there are going to be some big changes around here," my father said. "And I don't care if you're only going to be here for another month. I have no qualms about making this month the worst of your entire life."

"Obviously, Dad. We all know you have no problems making anyone miserable."

"Dade, don't talk to your father like that."

"Why not?"

"Because. It's disrespectful."

"Who cares. You have to earn respect. Isn't that what you always say, Dad?"

My father's jaw dropped and the look in his eyes suggested that his anger level had reached new heights.

"What is that supposed to mean?" he finally said.

My mother said, "Ned, I don't think—"

"No. I want to hear what this little smart-ass has to say."

"You've sucked all summer, Dad," I said. "Admit it. You've started seeing this woman, and you're expecting Mom and me to just be okay with it, and it's not fair. I don't know how you've convinced yourself that you can just be gone all the time with *Vicki* and think that everything will just go on like normal. I'm not the fuckup, Dad. You are. *I'm* fine."

"Dade," my mother said. "*Fine* is not the word I would use to describe you, considering the state you were in forty minutes ago. Do you know how scared I was when I looked outside and saw you lying on the ground? I thought you'd been killed or attacked by something."

"This isn't about me passing out in the bushes."

My father said, "Well, what is it about then?"

"It's about a lot of things. It's about your and mom's problems and how they're affecting me and how you don't realize that. Or you don't care. One or the other."

"Dade, the issues with me and your father are between him and me. They have nothing to do with you."

"They have everything to do with me!" I said loudly. "I can't believe we're spending my final days in this household like this. Mom, I know you're miserable. And Dad, I don't know about you. I have no idea what's going on your head."

There was a pause in the conversation. My mother gazed at the hydrangeas in the middle of the table, her lips slightly parted as if at any moment she was going to start telling the flowers what they were, explaining their function on the planet. My father stared out at the backyard, his body jiggling slightly from the way he was bouncing his leg under the table. It was a nervous habit of his, something that always made him look like a kid. It coupled well with his momentary speechlessness.

Then I said it.

"Mom and Dad, I'm gay."

My mother sat up a little bit straighter. Her lips were moving, but she couldn't find the words. My dad shook his head and looked at his lap. Of all the moments, this is the one where our house chose to be silent. No air conditioner kicking on. No ice tumbling in the freezer. No barking dog or Jehovah's Witness ringing the bell. No telephone call or Food World commercial with its annoying jingle. Nobody said anything for a long time and then I said, "Tell me it's okay. Tell me that it doesn't matter."

My dad kept bouncing his leg and shaking his head to himself.

"Tell me it's okay. That's been my biggest fear. That it won't be okay. I need to know that it'll be okay."

My mom said to no one in particular, "I don't know."

"I knew," my dad said. "I always knew. I hoped I was wrong, but apparently I wasn't. I knew."

"Tell me it's okay," I pleaded.

"It's okay," said my mother. She was trying to smile, trying to act like this wasn't what it was. "It's fine. I just wasn't expecting it, that's all. Do you have a special friend?"

"We talked about it, Peggy. Many times. Don't act like this is a surprise."

"A special friend?" I said. "Like a disabled kid I play baseball with?"

"Watch your tone with your mother, young man."

"Talking about it is one thing," she said, getting teary eyed. God, it sucks seeing your mom cry. It's gotta be one of the worst things in the world.

I said, "Don't be sad, Mom."

She got up and stood beside me and held me against her

chest. A whimper escaped her mouth. I wondered how present she was in the moment, if the significance of the moment had been blurred by any number of pills that she'd taken that morning. Or maybe she was far from the moment but could see it and feel how far away she was from it and that's why she was crying. Or maybe she really cared.

"Peggy, let him go."

"I love you, Dade," she said softly. She was speaking into the top of my head. Her hair fell around me, touched my ears and the tip of my nose.

"Peggy, let him go."

"Mom . . ."

I noticed my father had stopped bouncing his leg, and somehow the energy of the room had shifted. He wasn't looking at either of us. He was just staring out at the yard. He was done with this conversation. But my mother and I stayed like that for a bit longer. It felt good to touch my mother, to be touched by her. It woke up something inside me that was linked to before I was born. It was like my body could remember being inside her and kept reminding itself that it didn't have to be afraid.

∞

After I saw Jenny, it was hard to think about anything else. I kept thinking I saw her everywhere. She was every little kid at Food World. Every late-night noise belonged to her. She was coming up the stairs, walking down the hall to hover at my bedroom door. I was tempted to blame it on the alcohol, but it was all too real.

*You saw her,* I kept telling myself. *That was her.*

I dreamt about her, but even in my dreams she didn't want to be found. I'd be following her down some street that was my street but not my street, and I'd ask her where she was, what it all meant. But she kept her back to me and just moved forward. I could never catch up. It was useless to try. That Tuesday after I first saw her, I made Lucy go with me to the Riviera, the old theater on the south side of town where Alex had said someone had seen her. She hadn't appeared again by my pool, and the Riviera seemed as good a place as any to find her.

We sat in the back row of the balcony. It was an older theater, gorgeous and grand, and from where we sat it seemed like we were floating above everything. When we walked in, the film had already started. It was some weird black-and-white French film with people sitting in a room and flinging nonsense dialogue back and forth. There were individuals scattered amongst seats down below, all slouched low and clearing their throats during the movie's quieter moments. A few of them were even smoking, the clouds from their cigarettes climbing and twisting in the light from the projector. One of the girls in the film was a gorgeous black girl with heavy eye shadow.

"Why the sudden interest in foreign cinema?" Lucy said quietly as she opened the bag of gummy bears she'd bought at the front counter.

"Just because." I kept looking around the balcony. There was a college-aged couple a few rows behind us making out, but that was it. It was a Tuesday afternoon and the theater was fairly empty. There was no ghostly girl anywhere.

"How are the 'rents?" Lucy asked.

"Good," I said. "It felt good to finally tell them. My dad already suspected I was gay. Which is fine. It's true, so who cares. It feels weird to have it out there, though. Like, where do we go from here? In some ways it's like they have to get to know me all over again."

"Well, congrats on coming out," she said. "That's a big deal."

"Thanks," I said. "No one's said anything about it since. I love the whole *if we don't talk about it, it'll go away* way of thinking."

"Parents. Can't live with 'em, wouldn't exist without them."

I nodded slowly and said, "Lucy, I need to tell you something."

"Sounds serious."

"It is."

"Serious it away, Mr. Serious."

"You know Jenny Moore, right?"

"Yeah," she said. "The missing girl."

I paused. "I saw her."

"What?" she asked.

"I saw her. In my backyard."

"Were you on something?"

"No," I said. "Well, I drank too much after my date with Alex, but this was so real. Lucy, I saw her."

She let out a sigh. "Dade, I hate to say it, but you sound crazy."

"Lucy, you have to believe me."

She stared straight ahead into the flickering glow of the giant screen. Her mouth moved slowly as she chewed on her candy. Someone who didn't know her as well might have thought she wasn't paying attention, but I knew she was actually thinking.

She turned to me. "Dade, either you're the most fucked-up guy on the face of the earth or the most special. I think that more and more every day."

"Um, thanks, I think."

"You're very welcome."

"You believe me, though, right?" I asked. I needed her to believe me. For some reason I thought that if she believed me, then I was sane, but if she didn't, then I was crazy. It was all on her.

"I don't know," she finally said. "If you need me to, I will. I trust you. But this is a stretch. You gotta realize that, right?"

I sighed and fell back into my seat. I hadn't realized that I'd been pitched toward her, practically falling at her feet.

"People have seen her here," I said. "That's why I wanted to come."

"But what does that mean?" she asked. "Why would she choose you? Why would she choose anyone? Does this mean she's dead? I don't get it."

On the screen a man stood up from his chair and lunged toward the black girl. She backed away dramatically. At first it looked like she was going to start crying, but then she let out a laugh.

I said, "I've asked myself that a hundred times since it happened. I have no idea. It scares me to think about it, though. To be associated with her."

"Do you think she's trying to tell you something?"

The thought brought a bowling ball feeling of sick to my stomach. It was completely possible that she was trying to tell me something, and it was hard to imagine that it could be anything good. I wondered about all the other people who'd claimed to have seen her. Had they really? And if so, did she talk to them?

"I can't talk about this," I said. "Forget I said anything."

"Dade—"

"No. Seriously, Lucy. It's not you. You've done nothing wrong. You're a good friend." I covered my eyes. "You listened. That's all I asked for, but now we gotta switch the subject. In fact, can we go?"

"Yeah, sweetie," she said, standing. "Let's go."

The walls of the theater hall were covered with red velvet wallpaper and the floor was worn black linoleum. I felt dizzy as we took the grand staircase to the foyer. I couldn't feel my legs, and I didn't want to look down for fear that I'd see they weren't there. So instead I looked up at the chandeliers. They were huge and ornate. They looked like sculptures of sea urchins made of crystal and light.

When we were outside, I looked around at the parking lot, at the sky. I took in the dirt and shit smell of the Midwest air, the stuff coming in from the patches of farmland just a couple of miles up the road. I wanted to see her right then. I wanted Jenny Moore to appear to me at that moment, to tell me what it all meant.

There was nothing to do, so we drove around town. There wasn't much talking, just singing over the wind as it came through the windows. I let Lucy drive. It felt strange to be slouched in my own passenger seat, like I was witnessing a scene of my life from someone else's perspective, watching someone else navigate without a destination in mind.

"Let's go to Taco Taco," I suddenly said. "If he's there, you can meet him."

"I get to meet him?" she said. "I finally get to meet the famous Alex Kincaid?"

"Yes. You get to meet him."

"Hurrah!"

"But you have to be cool. We have to be really, really cool."

"Are you saying I'm not? Dade, I am the coolest person you have ever met in your entire life. Do I need to show you my music collection again? Do I need to take you to a better, gayer gay bar? Fuck this Alex kid. I'm so cooler than he is."

"You're not. Trust me. And there's nothing wrong with that. Few people are as cool as Alex Kincaid."

"Well, if I weren't a lesbian, his name alone would turn me on. But that's not enough."

"I know, right?" I said. "He totally lives up to the hotness of his name."

"You're in love."

"What?"

"You're trying to play it cool. And you're doing a good job of it, actually, which makes me proud. It means you're making progress. But I can feel it coming off you. You love him."

"It's not love," I said. "I don't believe you can fall in love so fast. I think you have to build it."

"Wow, how mature," Lucy said. "Dade Hamilton's growing up."

We rolled into the parking lot of Taco Taco. The strip mall lights had malfunctioned and were flickering wildly, making the whole parking lot look like an empty dance floor. Lucy parked near the door. Alex was behind the counter and Jay was out in the dining area. There was no one else around, and they were tossing a foam football back and forth.

"Is that him?" she asked.

"Yeah. Behind the counter."

"He's cute. Total sexy loser."

"Don't say he's a loser. He's not a loser. He's a good guy."

"You know what I mean," she said.

"I do. But still."

"Sensitive."

"What now?" I asked.

"What do you mean what now?"

"Should I go in?"

"Um, yeah. We should both go in."

The door gave a little buzz when we walked in. It was barely audible over the heavy metal they were blaring over the speakers. For a second they didn't acknowledge our presence. Alex finished throwing a pass toward Jay, then he looked over and noticed us and his face lit up with this magical smile, and for a moment I thought that maybe Lucy was right. As strange as it sounded, maybe I really did love this boy.

"Well, well, well," he said over the music. "Look who it is."

"Hey, it's Dave!" Jay called out.

I could tell he knew better, so I didn't bother correcting him. Both of them were grinning stupidly with bloodshot eyes. Lucy yelled, "You guys look like you've been smoking pot all night."

Alex reached under the counter and turned the music down a bit. "You guys want a burrito or something?"

"A Deus ex Mexicana?" Jay said.

"I'm okay," I said. "I think. I may change my mind."

"Who's the chick?" Jay said.

"I'm not a chick. I'm a lady."

"Well, then. Who's the lady?"

"This is my friend Lucy," I said.

"Nice to meet you, Lucy," Alex said. He was sitting on the counter, gently kicking his legs back and forth. He looked so cute in his baggy cargo pants and the ancient-looking yellow T-shirt that he was wearing wrong side out. "Dade told me that you're a cool cat and I trust his opinion. Do you want a quesadilla? A chimichanga?"

"She should have a Deus ex Mexicana," Jay said, pointing at

Lucy. "I've never seen a girl eat one before. It would be interesting to see."

"What in the hell is a Deus ex Mexicana?" Lucy asked.

"Something you don't want," I said.

"I'd take a taco," she said. "Two tacos."

"Two tacos for the lady," Jay said. "I'm on it."

He jogged to the counter and swung his legs over in one smooth motion.

"So what brings you here?" Alex asked.

"We were just driving around, doing nothing," I said. "Thought we'd stop by."

"Glad you did." He was looking at me with this mischievous grin. It was a look that seemed to serve no other purpose than making me insanely horny. And it was working.

"So, Alex," Lucy said. "Dade's told me so much about you."

"He's mentioned you too. Good that we're finally meeting."

"He really likes you."

"Lucy," I said in a warning tone.

Alex laughed. "I like him too."

"Good," she said. "Because if you break his heart, I'll cut your Taco Tacos off."

"Sounds painful," Alex said. "But I catch your drift. I don't think you have anything to worry about. And in turn, I don't either."

The sly grin never left his face. "What are you two doing tonight?" he asked. "Wanna start trouble?"

"What kind of trouble?" Lucy asked. "Sounds like it could be fun."

"Bert McGraw is having a party at his parents' house," Alex said. "After Jay and I close up, we're going to stop by. I need to make an appearance. Should be huge. Ten kegs. Kids from every high school in eastern Iowa. Or at least all the stupid ones."

Jay came out of the kitchen with a bag of tacos. He handed them to Lucy. "The SUV crowd. The cool kids. The rich kids. The preps."

"Shell necklaces and too much cologne," Alex said.

"Guys with too much gel in their hair," I added.

"It's always too much gel," Alex said. "Even a single drop of gel is too much."

Lucy jumped in. "Even the mere thought of gel is too much."

Jay smiled at her. "There you go. Lady Lucy's getting the hang of it."

"You know, I'd really rather not see Bert McGraw," I said. "The last time I saw him he called me a faggot in front of the entire Cedarville High lunchroom."

"Screw that guy," Jay said. "If he does or says anything to you, come find me."

"No, find me," Alex said. He curled his arm in front of himself and flexed his bicep. "I've got bigger muscles."

"I'll be fine," I laughed.

"Totally," Lucy said. "And actually, if he does say anything, come find me. I'm stronger than both of these fools combined."

# Chapter 13

It was almost midnight by the time I turned my BMW onto Bert McGraw's street. Alex was in the front seat with me. Lucy and Jay were in back. Bert lived on Cedar Glen Way, a street that ran through a subdivision called Cedar Glen Terrace. It was known around town that if you lived in Cedar Glen Terrace, you were hot shit. The houses were huge, set back far from the street with sprawling lawns that their owners probably referred to as *grounds*. A few had circular driveways in front and one even had its row hedges trimmed to look like a line of horses bucked back on their hind legs. It made me think of Fessica and all the horses in her bedroom. I made a mental note to find her in the next few days and apologize. We parked at the end of the row of cars that lined the streets. The red pickup truck in front of us had a Cedarville Warriors decal on its rear windshield, a big blue *W* outlined in red.

"School pride confuses me," Jay said.

"Let's go in, get our business done, and leave," Alex said.

"Sounds good to me," Jay said.

Bert's massive house was all noisy and lit up, a box of music and light and crowd noise. A hundred pointless conversations blending into one. There was something almost apocalyptic about the way kids were coming toward the house from both ends of the street like blank-minded zombies slouching toward the scent of beer. Of course Bert McGraw was such a douche cougar that he had his younger brother Chip working the door. Chip was basically a younger version of Bert, a short bulldog-looking dude with psychotic eyes. We huddled in with the other people waiting to get in the door.

"This party is so gonna get busted," Jay said.

"You okay?" Alex asked.

"I'm fine," I said.

"You look green."

"Really?"

Alex laughed. "A little. You can wait in the car, you know. I don't think you have to, but—"

"Dade'll be fine," Lucy said. "You'll be fine, right, Dade?"

Somehow hearing her saying this swept away the small amount of nervousness I felt. I *would* be fine. No one was going to say or do anything. I was here with friends. If anything came up, they'd be there to help.

"She's right," I said. "I'm fine."

It was our turn at the door. Two of Chip's friends were standing in front of it with their arms crossed, two chubby fifteen-year-olds trying to act like they were tougher than they really were.

Chip stood off to the side, a clipboard and cell phone in his hand. A metal baseball bat rested at his feet.

"I don't know you guys," he said flatly. "Not familiar. Explain?"

"I know your brother," Alex said. "We're old friends. Is he around?"

"I need a name," Chip said. "No one gets anything without a name."

"Jesus Christ," Lucy said.

"I'm Alex Kincaid. But you can call me Jesus Christ."

Jay put his hand to his mouth, but not before letting out a little laugh. Chip gave us a hateful glare and made a call on his phone. After a brief conversation he hung up.

"So do we get the bat?" Alex asked.

"No," Chip said. His friends were still leaning against the door and staring at us. "Bert says you get in. But any excuse to use the bat, I will."

"What the heck, man?" Lucy said. "What did we do to you?"

"Well, I don't like dirtballs," Chip said. And then he looked directly at me. "And I especially don't like faggots."

I looked over at Alex. I thought back to the cafeteria, when I'd looked over at Pablo after Bert had called me out during lunch. The same silence that had blanketed me then now blanketed me and my three friends. Chip went on staring at me angrily while his fat friends snickered to themselves. I waited for Alex to make the next move.

"Come on," Alex finally said. His voice was quiet, serious. "Let's go inside."

His friends parted. Jay led the way through the front door with Lucy and me close behind. I could feel Alex close behind me and then I couldn't, and I looked back and saw him talking calmly to Chip McGraw, just a few inches from his face. Chip was staring back at him coolly, his anger slowly turning into something else, something more dangerous. The corners of his mouth were slightly perked in a small, menacing smile.

"What did you say to him?" I asked once Alex had caught up with us in the foyer.

"Nothing. Let's make our rounds and get out of here."

The main hall was crammed with people standing around, their voices mixing with the hip-hop that was playing all through the house. The floor bounced under my feet with each thump of the bass. A curved staircase led up to the second floor, where a line of girls stretched along the railing, their fingers loosely holding plastic cups over the crowd of people below them as they took note of the comings and goings. About half of them whispered and looked down at us, specifically at Alex. He looked up at them and gave a little wave. Three of them broke from the line and hurried down the stairs.

"Gotta do some business," Alex said, patting me on the shoulder. "You three mingle or something. Worst-case scenario we'll meet up back here in half an hour. Text me if there's trouble. Stick together."

Alex broke away and met the girls at the bottom of the stairs. They all had wads of cash in their hands. I thought about how so many of his relationships seemed based on drugs. I wondered if we'd ever create a bond that would be stronger than that, a bond that would set us apart from that world.

"Let's find booze," Lucy said. "Otherwise this is going to be unbearable."

"I hear that," Jay said.

The three of us made our way through the crowded house and into the backyard. The McGraws' pool was bigger than ours, and yes, it made me just a little bit jealous. People were splashing each other and wrestling over inflatable rafts and beach balls. Others were lying on the chaise longues, smoking cigarettes and pot, pointing at the antics going on in the water. There were clusters of kids everywhere engaged in loud conversations, girls screaming yes and no and laughing and guys high-fiving and roughhousing. There was a table off to the side covered with bottles of booze and mixers, red plastic cups and bowls of sliced lemons and limes, and standing right beside it were Judy and Jessica. We all noticed each other at the same time.

"Those girls with the hooker makeup don't look happy to see us," said Jay.

"Me," I said. "They're not happy to see me."

"I could take them," Lucy said.

We went over to the table and made ourselves drinks without saying anything. I focused on mixing the perfect vodka and cranberry. I could feel them off to my left, staring.

"Hey," Judy said. "Hey you. In the green shirt."

I looked over at them, trying to give off the impression of someone who didn't care.

"Nice haircut, blowjob," Judy said.

"Nice tits, slutbag," Lucy shot back.

"Who in the hell are you?" Jessica said.

"We're with Alex Kincaid," Jay said. "So leave us alone. We'll be gone as soon as he's done."

"Alex is here?" Jessica asked. She turned to Judy. "Do we want anything?"

"Since when did you guys start hanging out with Alex Kincaid?" Judy asked us.

"We're his friends," Jay said.

Judy rolled her eyes.

"Whatever," she said. She looked directly at me. "Hey, blowjob. If I see you even *looking* at my boyfriend, I'll fucking eviscerate your spleen."

"Why don't you tell *him* to stay away from *me*," I said.

"Like that would ever happen," Jessica said, cocking a nostril in disgust.

"Watch your mouth," Judy said, stepping toward me.

"Okay," Jay said. "Time to move to a different area of the party."

We retreated to a less populated area of the yard.

"Those girls are super pleasant," Jay said.

"Ignore them," I said. "I think Judy's just pissed because somewhere she knows that her boyfriend is still after me."

"Scandalabra," Jay said.

"This party is like a mixer of suck," Lucy said. "It's like the place you'd go to meet people you'd never want to meet."

We stayed quiet for a bit, just watched everything happening around us. Jay whipped out his new cell phone, some skinny silver thing he'd ordered from Japan that played MP3s and took crystal-clear video. He showed Lucy how it worked. I just stood back and watched it all. From the outskirts of the party the whole thing looked sorta beautiful. Everyone was so happy. Even Jessica and Judy had stopped sneering and were now pouring tequila shots with Travis Peabody and the hotness that was Darnell Jackson. Their mouths all hung open in laughter. Someone shot a bottle rocket out one of the windows toward the top of the house, and everyone started whooping and yelling. Two more came out in quick succession, almost like echoes. Twin whistles sailing over our heads and popping out over the neighbor's yard.

Jay looked up. "I've said it once and I'll say it again. This party is so gonna get busted."

"I sorta want to get in the pool," Lucy said. "Is that terrible?"

"I'd get in the pool," Jay said. "Dade, would you get in the pool?"

"I'm not getting in the pool."

"Jay, Dade *has* a pool. He's over pools."

"I'm not over pools," I said. "I'm just not taking my shirt off in front of any of these people."

"I'll get in the pool with you," said Jay.

"Did I say I was getting in the pool?"

"I feel like that's where you were going with it," Jay said.

Lucy stared at the people splashing around in the water. She bit her lip and shouted, "Screw it! Who cares?"

Jay let out a loud yell and pulled his shirt over his head. He'd barely passed it over to me before he was kicking off his shoes and dropping his pants. His hot pink briefs seemed electric against the dark brown of his skin. People were looking over at us. Lucy took off her shirt to reveal a leopard-patterned bra. And then her pants. She was wearing lacy turquoise panties, somehow weirdly unexpected. They ran and jumped into the pool. The rest of their clothes lay on the ground in two strangely controlled piles, as if their owners had simply evaporated. The two of them came up from underwater, laughing at the spontaneity of it all. I smiled too. *It's the summer*, I thought. They waved and I waved back.

I retreated farther toward the back of the yard. There was a private little area there, a stone bench hidden behind two large Japanese lilacs. I ducked into the hiding spot and took a seat there with my drink and Jay's blue T-shirt. The area was no larger than fifteen feet in diameter, with branches dangling just over my head and the sweet smell of lilac wrapping my head in an invisible cocoon. The noise and lights of the party went on beyond the branches and the leaves like some other world, one that wasn't as meaningful as my new small one. I was still holding Jay's blue T-shirt. I rubbed it between my fingers. It was the kind of T-shirt that made you jealous, it was that perfectly worn in. Without thinking, I brought it to my face and sniffed it. It smelled like fancy cologne and boy. I wondered where Alex was. I imagined him talking to some girl, charming her with his grin and listening to her talk about something pointless like her job at the mall or her new haircut before they made their transaction. Or maybe he was in a tiny room somewhere with Bert and some of the other guys playing straight and sharing a joint. Everywhere my mind put him made him feel far away and not mine.

"Hey. I thought that was you."

I looked up. Pablo was standing in the small entrance to the space. He was buttoning the last button of his fly, probably after pissing somewhere in the dark recesses of the yard. Typical Pablo. His body was loose, lacking his usual rigidity. He was probably drunk or high or both.

"Hi," I said in the least friendly tone I could muster.

"I didn't expect to see you here."

He came forward and sat beside me on the little stone bench. It was a lover's bench, designed to inspire closeness. It was made for two people, but was actually only big enough for one and a half. My right arm pressed against his left, his familiar mass of muscle, skin, and bones pulsing next to me. I hated the way I could feel myself yearning for him whenever he came around. I wondered how long I'd have to wait until there was no trace of him in my heart or mind anymore.

"Isn't this breaking the rules?" I asked. "Aren't you afraid Judy is going to see us?"

"I'm just saying hello. Isn't saying hello allowed?"

"You made up the rules," I said. "You tell me."

"Well, I say it's allowed." He was smiling, trying to be charming. It had been so long since he smiled at me like that.

Compared to Alex's winning grin, it was nothing. At least there was real affection and a genuine desire for connection behind Alex's grin. Pablo's was just a mask to throw me off.

"I've missed you this summer," he said. "I've really, really missed you."

"Good," I said. "I hope you have."

"Why you gotta be so mean?" he said.

"Why should I be nice to you after you were such a dick to me at Cherry's?" I said.

"Oh, come on," he said as if he'd completely forgotten about us running into each other there. "I was caught off guard. I was nervous."

"I thought you said you couldn't be like that," I said. "I thought you were dedicated to Judy and a normal life and that whole idea."

"I was," he said. "I am. I just went there to make sure."

"And are you?"

He waited a few seconds before speaking. "I don't know."

"Well, I met someone else," I said. "So whatever you decide in the future, keep me out of it."

He shot me a look of disbelief. I would've said he looked hurt, but I wasn't sure that Pablo Soto could ever really feel pain or rejection.

"Fine," he finally said. "Be that way. See if I care."

"I'm sure you won't," I said. "You never do. It's impossible for people like you. I'm finally over you. I've finally met someone who wants to be with me and doesn't make me feel ashamed of who I am. I'm not sure even the best version of you could offer me that."

I didn't realize how fast my heart was beating until I was finished speaking. I finally felt bigger than our situation, bigger than his confusion. He stared at me in shock. It was clear he hadn't expected there'd be someone else. We sat there in our little pocket of silence like some fucked-up version of *Romeo and Juliet*.

*What if he moves in and kisses me?* I thought. *Would I want that?*

But he didn't move in and kiss me. Instead he just stood and ducked out of the little space and walked slowly back to the party. I opened my mouth to call out for him, but I couldn't do that and still feel good about myself. I decided to let him wander off on his own, to let him be sad. Of course, this was all assuming that his sadness was real, which was a question that perhaps even he would have trouble answering. I wondered where he would go now, whether or not he would tell anyone we'd spoken. I hoped that someone had noticed us together and that somehow it would get back to Judy.

After a while I stood up and went back out into the yard. Lucy came jogging up to me, her clothes in her hands.

"Hey, kid," she said. "What's up?"

"Just watching," I said. "Where's Jay?"

"He met some girl. Can you believe it? They're in the pool splashing each other like dorks."

I searched for Jay among the people in pool. There he was,

flirting it up with Decora Whitman. He had his arms around her waist and was pulling her backward through the water.

"She's not bad," I said. "A little dim, but we all are. I approve."

Lucy rubbed her hand over my head.

"How's it going? Is something wrong?"

"No," I said. "I'm fine."

"You seem spaced out."

"I'm fine," I said.

"Are you sure?"

"I just ran into Pablo." I sighed. "But it's fine."

"You did?" she said. "Where is he? Was it okay?"

"It was fine," I said. "He's gone now. He said he missed me."

"What did you say?" Lucy asked.

"I told him that it was too late for that."

"Nice," she said. "Screw him. But next time someone like that tells you they're sorry you should say, '*Sorry* is the exact word I would use to describe you.' My mom said that to my dad once. It was amazing. I use it all the time now."

I burst out laughing. God, I loved her.

"Yeah, fuck him." The moment I said it, I realized I didn't totally mean it. Yes, fuck Pablo Soto for putting me through hell, but God help him for being so confused, for not knowing what he wanted.

"Let me put my clothes on and then let's go inside," said Lucy. "Rumor has it that there's pizza in the kitchen, and I have major munchies."

We left Jay in the pool with Decora, waving as we passed.

He gave us a little nod, never breaking from the deep conversation it looked like they were having. There were only a few other people in the kitchen. There were three untouched pizzas on the kitchen table, their boxes open like oysters showing off their pearls.

"It's like a desert mirage," said Lucy. "But it's not a mirage. It's real and it's my life."

She grabbed a slice of pepperoni and green pepper and shoved about half of it into her mouth. A glob of sauce hit the floor with a splat.

"Text Alex," Lucy said with a full mouth. "See where he's at."

I got out my phone and sent the message.

"So how are things with him?" Lucy asked. "With Alex. Are you feeling good? Feeling okay?"

"Yeah. I hope he gets done doing his thing, though. I want to kick it with him. We're still in that phase where we're getting to know each other. I feel like we need to do more of that."

"He's cute."

"Very," I said.

"Cuter than Pablo."

"Obviously," I agreed.

"Not that that matters . . . but it does."

My phone vibrated in my pocket. I took it out and flipped it open. It was a text from Alex. "He's outside, apparently."

"Let's go find him," said Lucy.

We went back outside, and within a few moments I spotted him. He was at the far end of the porch, looking out over the backyard with Darnell Jackson. They were drinking beer from plastic cups. Darnell pointed at something in the distance and they both started laughing. I wondered how long they'd been out there, why he hadn't called. Had he been purposefully avoiding me? A feeling of jealousy welled up in me like a toxic stomach-ache.

"Who's that hot boy that he's with?" Lucy asked

"Darnell Jackson," I said. "The patron saint of hot black guys."

"He's hot."

"Thanks for pointing that out."

"Well, you agreed."

"You're supposed to say he's not. To make me feel better."

"Dade, for better or worse, I'll never lie to you," Lucy said. "And don't be so insecure. Alex likes you."

It was stupid for me to feel jealous. Darnell was anything but gay. He'd been dating Matrisha Barnes since freshman year and was actually a decent guy. He'd once called Jessica a stupid-ass trick during study hall, which earned him some big points in my book, but still, even the thought of Alex being mildly interested in anyone else, even on the level of superficial attraction, was torture.

*Calm down, Dade,* I thought to myself. *He's just talking to someone. Get a grip.*

He turned around and noticed Lucy and me. He smiled brightly, and eagerly waved over. All that freaking out for nothing.

"Darnell, this is my good friend Dade and his friend Lucy," Alex said.

"I went to school with you," I said, extending my hand.

"Totally," Darnell said. "I remember Dave."

"Dade," Lucy said.

I turned to Alex. "So, how are things?"

"Great," he said. "Business is good. I'm done. We can leave whenever."

Darnell excused himself and drifted off into the backyard.

"Jay's in the pool with a girl," Lucy said.

"I noticed," Alex said. "Good for him. He's a good guy."

"Yeah, I like him," Lucy said. "Is it freakish that I'm having an okay time?"

"Not at all," Alex said. "It's a party. You're supposed to have fun."

"Well, now that I have your permission," Lucy said, "I'm getting back in the pool where the girls in bikinis are."

"You're supposed to wait twenty minutes after eating before you go swimming," I said.

She laughed and gave me the finger as she bounded off the porch.

"How are you?" Alex asked.

"Fine."

"Just fine?" he said. "Not great?"

"I ran into Pablo."

"Was it okay?"

"It was fine," I said.

"Are you sure?"

"I'm sure."

"When you say that things are fine so much, it sounds like a lie," Alex said.

"Well, I'm not lying," I said. I gave him a serious look, hoping this would end the conversation. "Things are fine."

That last time it felt like a lie. The truth was that my encounter with Pablo had unnerved me. I found myself wondering if I'd been too mean to him. I thought about going off and finding him, seeing if he wanted to talk. Not about us or our situation, but just about life in general. The end of the summer was growing closer every day and pretty soon he'd be gone.

Alex and I watched the party from the porch. Lucy stripped down to her underwear again and jumped into the pool. A big group of people were dancing in a corner of the yard. The thought occurred to me that so much of life is reenactment, people doing things that they saw other people do in the hopes that it could somehow make them rich or happy or popular. I wondered if people would be happier if they just were who they really were, if they didn't try and find themselves in other people. I could feel Alex watching me out of the corner of his eye. He slipped his arm around my waist and pulled me toward him.

"Sorry. I just really wanted to do that. Is that okay?"

His mouth was right against my ear. Somewhere in my mind I could actually see his breath winding around my outer ear, then disappearing into the canal like water down a drain. A hard shiver went down my spine. I felt plugged in.

"I guess," I said. "What if someone says something?"

"No one will," he assured me. He took my hand. "And if they do, I'll kick their ass."

He leaned in and kissed my neck, causing my body to suddenly relax. I hadn't realized until then how rigid I was. Whatever song was playing ended, and "Some Boys Keep Their Heads Down All the Time" by the Diligent Frenchmen came on, and I had one of those moments where life suddenly feels perfect and meaningful, one of those moments that's so pure and focused that you sorta start to freak out because it can't last forever.

People walked by as they went in and out of the house. Some of them glanced over at the two boys holding hands on the porch, some of them didn't. The few that did looked more confused than anything, as if they were wondering how in God's name we hadn't gotten our asses kicked yet. A tipsy, bookish-looking girl wearing glasses and a Tomato Hoof T-shirt did a double take and stopped to say, "I just want you two to know that you are the cutest couple ever, and I really support all of what's happening here." She stumbled drunkenly into the house without another word. We laughed.

"Oh shit," I said, extracting my hand from Alex's. "Look who it is."

Bert McGraw was standing by the pool with a couple of other guys from the football team. All three of them were giving us a death glare.

"We should probably go," I said.

Alex laughed and took my hand again. "No. No way. Screw

them. Plus, I just sold him a fat sack. Kicking my ass would be such bad manners."

After a couple of moments Alex told me to come with him. He pulled me into the house, through the crowded kitchen and the dining room, where a whole other spread of alcohol covered the dining room table. A red wine spill on the floor. A piece of lime stuck to the wall. I couldn't stop laughing. He took me to the second floor and led me down the hall to an overwhelmingly green guest bedroom. He pulled me into the closet and shut the door behind us. He clicked on the overhead light. Nothing in there but us, a vacuum cleaner, and the ugliest fur coat I'd ever seen. I was still laughing, and now he was too.

"What are we doing?" I asked.

"I scoped this spot before I came downstairs," he said. "I knew we'd need one eventually." He started kissing me. All I could do was kiss him back. He slipped his hands under my shirt and felt around my chest. He bit my lower lip just a little. Just the tiniest bit.

"Alex."

His name just fell out of my mouth. Like so many of the things I said.

"What?" He started kissing my neck.

"I don't know. I just felt like saying your name."

He laughed and kissed me again.

"Is that weird?" I asked.

"Not at all."

He moved back in and kissed me again. Slower this time.

So slow, it wasn't so much a kiss. It was more like he was trying to tell me something, something that couldn't be put into words. He touched my face with both hands, made a little noise in his throat, a whimpering gasp that drove me wild. I fell into him, begging him with my body to make that noise again.

∞

Jay lost his amazing blue T-shirt that night. He ended up giving it to Decora Whitman. He told her it was a token of his love, a symbol of the hope that they would someday be together forever, deeply in love until the very end. She laughed and rolled her eyes, and Lucy, Alex, and I all laughed and applauded when she put it on over her bikini and walked away. Jay shook his fists at the sky. Out front, Lucy jumped on Jay's back and he took off down the street toward the car, zigzagging back and forth as he ran. Lucy let out one of those insanely loud girl-squeals that echoed throughout the neighborhood.

"Don't drop her," I called.

My phone vibrated. I took it out and flipped it open. It was a text message from Pablo.

## I see you leaving with him

I slowed my step and looked back at the McGraw residence. There were a few people talking on the street, a few people in the yard. No one I recognized as him. Alex noticed and slowed down too.

"Did you forget something?"

"No. I just thought I heard someone call my name."

He laughed. "They were probably saying *Dave*."

"Yeah. Probably."

Alex took off screaming down the street, arms outstretched like an airplane. He went straight for Lucy and Jay like he was going to knock them down. They both screamed, and at the last minute he veered toward my car. Lucy hopped down and collapsed into a pile of laughter. My phone vibrated again.

### I can see you

# Chapter 14

I spent the next day locked in my room writing poetry about Alex. It was a sunny day, humid and in the high eighties, but I didn't care. I was determined to stay indoors, wear all black, and write poetry about the boy I was obsessed with. I imagined Lucy watching all this from the foot of my bed and saying, "Do it, Dade! Young gay love! Surrender to the cliché!"

I wrote nine poems about him, the shortest being four lines ("Sprawled out on the front lawn / Looking up at an ordinary sky / It could fall on me and somehow be / The day I didn't die") and the longest coming in at just over seven pages. Late in the afternoon I decided it was all shit. I took everything I'd written and burned it in my bathroom sink. I sprawled out on my bed and sent Alex a text message saying hello. Just that. Hello. I'd just pushed send when there was a knock at my door.

"Come in," I said, sitting up.

It was my dad. He was still in his work clothes. Fancy pants, a short-sleeved shirt, and the yellow Brooks Brothers tie my mother had bought him the previous Christmas. He sat on the edge of my bed and gave me a weak smile.

"Hi," he said.

"Hey."

"It smells like smoke," he said.

"Well, I haven't been smoking."

"No," he said. "Like paper burning."

"Oh," I said. "I burned some poetry in my bathroom sink earlier."

He gave a muted sigh and turned his eyes to the floor as if he'd been brutally reminded that he'd never understand me.

"Dinner tonight at the country club?" he asked. "We haven't been for a while."

"Um . . . sure."

"Great."

He seemed relaxed, like he was trying to be kind. Was he coming to bury the hatchet? Was there a hatchet to even be buried? For some reason I started thinking of how weird it was that I would always be his son and he would always my father, that there was nothing that could ever change that. I didn't know whether this permanence was comforting or terrifying.

"I want to talk to you," he said.

"Great."

"Nothing bad. Just talk to you." He considered his words before going on. "Dade, I want us to be friends."

"Okay. Whatever."

"No, scratch that. Not friends." He thought for a moment. "I want to know what you're going through. I want to understand this. As your father, I want to be there for you and your . . ." He gestured loosely with one hand until he found the word. "Gayness."

"My gayness?"

"Your homosexuality. I guess that's a better term."

"Well, you didn't seem too keen on understanding it the other day."

"I was more angry about the fact that I found you half naked in the yard. The two got confused. You know, I love you too. Your mother's not the only one."

Love. People threw that word around like crazy. I thought about the poems I'd turned into ash. We sat there in silence for a few minutes. My dad looked around my room. At my posters, my books. Scattered clothes and the pile of crap my mother had bought me the other day. He let his gaze linger on the Johnny Morgan shrine on my wall.

"Is he your type?" he asked.

"Dad . . ."

"I want to know." He pointed at a shirtless picture of Johnny. He was smiling cheesily into the camera. "Is he your dream guy? I mean, I'm assuming that's why you put it up."

"Dad, seriously. This is super awkward."

"I just wanna know."

Through the wall I heard the opening strains of "Never Forget." My mother in her meditation room. Fleetwood Mac. She was probably drinking.

"I'm gonna take a shower," I said, getting up. "And then we can go to dinner."

I went into my bathroom and shut the door, leaving him there on the edge of my bed. I thought I heard him say my name. I imagined him on my bed, lost among my things. My discarded clothing and my Johnny Morgan shrine. Dog-eared books by the Beats, by tragic female poets of the early twentieth century. My Andy Warhol calendar and the piles of *GQ*s that I'd stolen from him over the years. All those little parts of my life that made up who I was. I looked in the mirror and stared at my reflection, until I was in the head-clearing trance that comes when you stare at something for a long time, and then I turned on the shower and told myself that he hadn't just said my name in the next room, that I'd imagined it.

∞

All through dinner with my father I kept staring out at the golf course and thinking of the previous evening. I wondered where Alex was, why he hadn't texted me back. My father and I hardly spoke through dinner, so in that respect everything was back to normal. The only way this night out differed from the other was that my father wasn't allowing me to drink. I was stuck with soda.

"So your mother and I are going on a trip," he said after Cindy had brought our key lime pie.

"When?"

"Next week."

"That's soon. What for?"

"To work things out. We have a lot to talk about, Dade." He

leaned forward, made a steeple with his fingertips that signified some sort of serious plan was being put in motion. Such a Ned Hamilton move. "Your mother and I do. We have some decisions to make."

"Well," I said, "I guess it's good that you're finally going to actually make the decisions."

"Yes. Making decisions is a decisive step in the right direction."

The type of phrase he would probably have on his tombstone.

"What about that woman?"

"Vicki?" he asked.

"Yes. Vicki."

He cleared his throat. "Vicki and I are no longer seeing each other."

"That's good to hear."

"It was the right thing to do."

"I agree."

We were quiet for a moment.

"So where are you going?" I asked. "Is this trip happening for sure?"

"For sure. We're going around Europe for a couple of weeks. We've wanted it and now's the time to have it. Now's as good a time as any. We'll be back a week before you head off to Michigan, so don't worry about that."

"Don't worry," I said with an obviously forced smile. "I wasn't."

"Dade, your mother and I need to know that you're going to be okay here on your own."

"I'll be fine," I said.

"Mrs. Savage is going to be checking in on you while we're gone, but she won't be babysitting you. Because you're not a baby. Obviously. But she'll be checking in."

"Obviously."

"No drinking, Dade," he said. "No lawn shenanigans. There's a part of me that's apprehensive about leaving you here."

"I'll be fine."

"If you honestly want your mother and me to try our best to work these things out, then we need to be able to trust you."

I didn't really see what one thing had to do with the other.

"Fine," I said. "I'll be fine."

"And I want you to know that your mother and I are fine with your homosexuality. We are. Really."

I nodded. For some reason I didn't believe it. I don't know why. Maybe it was because my father was the kind of person who told himself things over and over until he believed them, who could justify almost anything. What I wanted was for it to *really* be okay. I wanted him to really not care, to maybe even be happy about it. Instead he was acting like I was making a bad career choice, like I was passing up an English degree at Fairmont in favor of a bartending certificate at the local community college.

"Did you really always know?" I asked.

"I had my suspicions."

I took a bite of pie. My father looked out over the golf course as he always did. The sun was just beginning its descent. His sun, his sky.

"Beautiful evening," he said.

"So it's okay?" I said.

He looked back at me. "Yes. It's fine."

I nodded slowly and went on eating.

"Do you have a boyfriend?" he asked.

"Um . . ."

"You don't have to tell me if you don't want to," he said. "I just figured—"

"No," I said. "Actually, there is someone. It's just that it's hard to describe exactly what he is."

"Oh. Okay. I get what you mean. What's his name?"

"Alex."

"Alex," he repeated. "You know, I always thought that maybe you and Pablo were . . ."

"Pablo and I were just friends, Dad. Nothing else. And we're not even that anymore. All that is through."

"You know, I never liked him."

"That means a lot to me, Dad. It really does."

"He was a scowler. He was always scowling."

I thought back to the previous night, of Pablo somewhere off in the shadows watching as I left with Alex.

"Yeah," I said. "And he still is."

∞

When we got home we found my mother in the living room reading some book called *Finding Your Awareness*. My father sat down beside her and put his arm around her, then leaned in and kissed her on the cheek. She gave him a sideways glance and strained smile. I fought the urge to retreat to my room and instead took a seat on the sofa across from them.

"How was dinner?" my mother asked.

"Dinner was great," my dad said. "It's always good to spend time with Dade."

I looked off into the dining room, the kitchen. There were no other lights on on the first floor. I hated when the house was lit like this, when the idea of even going into the kitchen carried some weird abstract terror. I thought of walking upstairs, seeing Jenny on the first-floor landing, and literally dying of shock.

"Did you have the sea bass?" my mother asked.

"I had steak. Dade had scallops."

"You love scallops," she said.

What to say to that? "Um, yeah. Totally."

"Did your father tell you about our trip?" she asked.

"He did. I told him I was jealous."

"Rome, Paris, Florence."

"It'll be great," my father said. "New beginnings."

"New beginnings."

Weren't kids supposed to hold out hope for their parents, to believe until the bitter end that they weren't going to get a divorce? That's what the after-school specials always said. But right then, all I wanted was for it to be over. What I wouldn't have given for one of them to go upstairs, pack their things, and walk out the door toward a happier existence. I didn't care which one. Somebody just needed to do it, for all of our sakes.

"Can Alex come over for dinner sometime before you go?" I asked.

"Who's Alex?" my mother asked.

My father said, "Alex is Dade's friend."

"My special friend," I added. Both my parents shot me a watch-your-tone look.

"Boyfriend?" my mother asked.

Who knew? He hadn't answered my text from earlier. I thought of him out with some other guy, driving around in his car with him, making out at stoplights. No, he wasn't like that. I pushed the thought away.

"It's sorta indefinable right now, but I guess he's on the boyfriend track. Maybe."

My mother looked over at my father. He was looking at me and grinning broadly. It was hard to believe he was actually there in the moment. His smile seemed forced, like it was hiding something.

"I'd like you to meet him," I said. "He's become sort of a big part of my life."

"How long have you known this boy?" my mom asked.

"A few weeks."

"How did he become such a big part of your life in such a short amount of time?"

"I don't know," I said. "It just happened. You know?"

My mother looked over at my dad.

"Young love, Peggy. You remember when you and I first met, don't you?"

"Is he the one that convinced you to shave your head?" she asked.

"That's a complicated question."

"What do you mean?"

"Leave him alone, Peggy."

My mom shot my dad a look and then looked at her lap, at the book butterflied between her thighs. She'd been outvoted. She said, "Well, if he's such a big part of your life, I guess we should meet him."

My father played absently with a piece of my mother's hair. She went back to reading, ignoring us both. How long would he do that? How long would she let him? My phone rang in my pocket. It was Alex. I got up without saying anything. I hurried upstairs, answering when I got to the top.

"Hey," I said.

"Hey."

"What are you doing?"

"I'm at home," he said. He let out a sigh. "Just doing nothing. I was just thinking about you, thought I'd call. I got your text earlier, but there was a massive guacamole spill in the kitchen at work, so I was cleaning that up forever. What are you doing?"

I smiled. So he thought about me. I wanted to know more. What did he think about me? Did he think about us making out? Or us just sitting and talking? Or did he turn me over in his mind and wonder when he'd know things like where the scar on my right shin came from or what my favorite ice cream flavor was?

I stretched out on my bed and smiled up at the ceiling fan.

"Do you ever just lie on your bed and think?" I said.

"I did a lot of that this morning. My grandmother calls it being antisocial."

"My mother calls it meditating. My mom used to be really into meditation, but now I think she just uses her meditation room as a place to hide and sling back the booze."

"A hiding spot?"

"Somewhere to go where my father and I won't come looking for her."

"Wow. A meditation room? Really? Next thing you'll say is that you have a bowling alley in your basement."

"No bowling alley. But who knows. One of them could suggest an addition." I paused, took a deep breath. "Hey, my parents are leaving town. Having an emergency marriage-rebuilding vacation."

"Sounds urgent."

"Sirens everywhere," I said.

"Where are they going?"

"Europe."

"Urgent *and* fancy."

"No kidding. Family vacations with us usually involve going to some crappy colonial place where they show you how to make your own jelly. Now they're going to Europe without me. Figures."

"Ultrawack. So when do they leave?"

"Next week." I said. And then I let out what I'd been thinking about since my father mentioned they were going on the trip. "You should sleep over." I winced at the phrase *sleep over*. What was I, twelve?

He laughed. "Yeah. I'd love to sleep over."

Somehow the words seemed less juvenile coming out of his mouth, more romantic.

"So I have another question," I said.

"And what is that?"

"Do you want to come over for dinner tomorrow night?"

"Dinner?"

"Yeah," I said. "With my parents. They kinda want to meet you."

"Oh."

An awkward pause. I winced again.

"Yeah," I said. "I hope you don't think that's weird. It's not like I think we're going to get married or something." I instantly regretted mentioning the word *married*. "Sorry. I didn't mean any of that. Or I did, but just not the stupid parts."

"No. I get you."

"It's just that I want you to, like, know me."

"No. I know what you mean. I do." He paused before going on. "Sometimes I think about you and I think about this town and I want to run away with you. Get you out of here."

This is what those pop songs were about. All those bad clichés. This is why people spoke in low voices when they talked about the serious parts of falling in love. I imagined climbing down the side of my house, climbing down a trellis we didn't have, and running to his car as he revved the engine in defiance of everything we were about to leave behind.

"No. I know what you mean. Is it bad that there's part of me that's jealous of that girl that disappeared? Jenny Moore? I feel like she's okay. I know that sounds weird. I was really scared for her for a long time, and now I feel like she's just in a better place."

"You mean, like she's dead?"

"No. Not dead. That's not what I meant." I rubbed my eyes. "I guess I don't know what I mean."

He laughed. "Are you drunk?"

"No," I said. "I meant that she's just like somewhere else, you know? Not dead. Just not here."

He laughed again. "Dude, I'm trying to follow you. Honestly, I am."

I sighed. "I want to tell you something. But you can't get freaked out."

"Okay. I'll try."

I waited a few seconds and then I said, "I saw her. I didn't want to tell you this before because I didn't want you to think I was crazy, but I saw her. Jenny Moore. I saw her in my backyard the night we were in the graveyard, after you dropped me off at home."

"I don't know, man," he said with a nervous laugh. "You've gotta realize how that sounds, right?"

"I told Lucy," I said. I don't know why, but it felt like him knowing this would help. "She believes me."

"What did you see?"

"She ran across my backyard and disappeared in the bushes. It was just a flash, but it was there. I'm sure."

"Wow. That's some heavy shit. I—I'm not sure what to say."

"I shouldn't've said anything."

"No. I'm just . . . you know. It's a lot to ask someone to believe."

"I can't doubt myself on this one. It happened. All those other people saw her. Why can't I?"

"You sound convinced," he said.

"I am."

"Well, in that case, then I guess I am too."

"Really?" I asked, a bit shocked.

"The world is a weird place," he said. "Who am I to say I know everything that's going on in it? I don't. I know I don't."

"I feel the exact same way."

There was a fat silence, one that seemed almost reverent of all the things in the world that couldn't be understood.

"So dinner," he said. "I work tomorrow night, so I can't. But the next night I'm free."

I smiled. I'd forgotten this whole conversation had started because I asked him to dinner.

"Great," I said. "I'll call you or text you with the details. Exact time and all that. Is there anything you don't eat?"

"So polite of you to ask, but no, there's nothing I don't eat. I'm a growing boy. Some would say I'm a food vacuum."

I laughed. "Well, cool. Sounds like a plan. I should really go now."

"You should."

"I should."

"You know what's funny?" he said. "If we did get married, your name would be Dade Kincaid. How funny is that?"

"Well, if you took my last name you'd be Alexander Hamilton. Are you saying that's not equally funny?"

"Um . . . is it bad that I don't know who that is?"

I laughed. "Are you serious?"

"I know he's a history guy, but that's it."

"He's on the ten-dollar bill. He was the first secretary of treasury."

"Not fair. You're fresh out of high school. And you didn't get your education from Cedarville South."

"Fair enough. I should go."

"I should too. I promised my grandmother I'd do the dishes."

"Okay. Well, I'll get in touch with you about dinner."

"Looking forward to it," he said.

I hung up the phone and he was gone. Like he'd just been in the room a moment ago and had disappeared. I stretched out on my bed again. I stared up at the whirling blades of the ceiling fan. I thought of all the times I'd told it I was gay. That night I told it I was falling in love.

∞

I had to work the next day. As always, I took the entrance around the back of the store. The purple-haired woman from the bakery was there, blowing the smoke from her Capri toward the metal bread racks waiting to be retrieved by the bread deliveryman and scratching the inside of her wrist with a construction orange fingernail. I'd never noticed her name tag before. It said Orla. Beside her name was a yellow chick sticker, probably from last Easter.

It was around noon when I was stocking the milk and heard someone enter the dairy cooler through the blue swinging door. I looked up, expecting to see my supervisor. Instead it was Pablo. I froze, unable to do anything or even move. He didn't appear angry. In fact, he seemed eerily calm.

"Yo," I finally mumbled.

He just kept on staring at me.

"I got your text the other night. Sorry I didn't write back."

Nothing.

"Fine," I said. "Don't answer me."

He walked slowly over to me, stood just a few inches away. How could someone's face register almost nothing? I couldn't tell if he was going to hit me or start crying or ask me to borrow a dollar.

"What are you doing here?" I said. "I thought you were working up front today."

"So was that your new whatever?" he said.

"That's none of your business."

He spit in my face. It caught me off guard. My jaw dropped as a new kind of shock radiated through my body, especially in my chest. The pang of heartbreak mixed with anger and humiliation. I wiped the spit from under my left eye.

"Why are you doing this?" I whispered. "If you don't like me like that, then why are you doing this?"

The question seemed to be too much for him. I could read the frustration in his eyes, the inability to really explain what was going on.

"So you have nothing to say?" I asked. My lower lip was quivering. I wanted to cry, but not because I was sad. I wanted to cry because I was so angry. "You just spit in my face and that's all that you got?"

Nothing.

"Sad," I said. "Beyond sad. Tragic."

I turned around and went back to stocking the milk, shoving it toward the front of the cooler to be taken moments later by customers. The endless refilling. I thought back to English class, to the tale of Sisyphus.

I heard the rattle of his belt coming undone followed by the sound of his zipper. I turned around. His pants were partially down his thighs and his dick was hanging out.

"Dude." His voice came out quiet and mangled, like an injured animal flopping painfully out of its hiding spot, and the massiveness of how sad it is to want someone suddenly fell on my head like an anvil in some comically violent cartoon.

"Oh my God." I turned and hurried out of the dairy cooler. The back area of Food World was a maze of pallets stacked with products. Ketchup, paper towels, grape soda, macaroni and cheese. All on cardboard flats and wrapped in plastic. Their noisily bright colors flashed by in the corner of my eyes as I hurried toward the back door. Twice I checked over my shoulder to see if Pablo was following me, but he wasn't. Of course Orla was still sitting on an overturned milk crate at the back door and smoking.

"See you later, Dade," she said in a wobbly voice as I hurried by.

As if we'd spoken a hundred times before. As if all of this was normal. And then I thought, *How did she know my name?*

The Cedarville Warriors cheerleading squad was hosting its annual car wash on the far edge of the parking lot. All the girls were in tiny shorts and bikini tops. Someone's car stereo was playing some terrible Top 40 bubblegum crap. The girls were using the hose on each other, almost completely ignoring the gold Suburban they were supposed to be washing.

I got in my car and put the key in the ignition. I was technically supposed to be at work until three, and it was just a few minutes before noon. I sat there, ready to turn the key or pull it out. I wasn't sure which I should do. Out the front windshield was a little grassy hill that led up to a small road, one that allowed easy access from the Food World parking lot to the mini mall across the way. Chain restaurants, a cell phone retailer, a women's clothing store called Dress Explosion.

I suddenly felt the need to not be in the car. The interior was hot and stuffy. I grabbed some cigarettes from my glove compartment and stepped out of the car. Outside was hot too. I was already sweating. When had this started? My back was soaked with perspiration. I longed for the cold of the milk cooler. Did I want a cigarette? I'd thought that I did, but at that moment it sounded gross to me. I threw the pack on the ground. There were still at least ten cigarettes left, but that didn't stop me from stomping on the pack over and over again.

I put my hands in my pocket and leaned against the trunk of my car and stared out across the parking lot. Cars and cars as far as I could see. I thought of the homeless guy I spotted at the car dealership lot when I was driving to Cherry's with Lucy, of the way he gazed out in awe at all the cars.

*You don't want to be part of our world.* I was sending the voice in my head to wherever he was. *You think you want it, but you don't. It all comes at a cost.*

The cheerleaders squealed. One of them was hosing down her friend. Two suburban dad types were standing on the outskirts of it all, chuckling and nudging each other. I wanted to levitate away from it all. I wanted people to look up and see it happening. I wanted people to point up at me and say *That boy is floating away.* And then I wanted Pablo to come outside and wonder why everyone was looking up. I wanted him to follow everyone's gaze and see me, the last thing he expected.

# Chapter 15

At seven thirty the next night I was waiting on the couch for Alex to arrive. There was the subtlest suggestion of evening, just a little shift in the angle of the sun that meant it would be setting in the next hour or so. I was wearing my favorite pair of jeans and a polo that my mother had purchased for me during our shopping spree a few weeks back. At the time I'd hated it, but that night it felt right. Pink with a fat lavender strip across the torso. I felt my mother hovering in the space where the living room met the dining room.

"Yes?" I asked.

"Your father wants to know if he should start heating the coals."

"He'll be here soon. It's just now seven thirty."

"Are you nervous?" she asked.

"A little."

"Well, I am too, if that makes you feel any better."

She'd already had three glasses of white zinfandel. And that was just what I'd noticed. How many pills had she taken that day? What parts of her were my mother and what parts of her were Peggy Hamilton, static-headed suburban housewife, a walking cocktail? Despite all this, I couldn't be all that hard on her. I did drugs and drank for reasons that were more similar to hers than I wanted to admit. I thought back to one of my first nights out with Alex, the night when I thought I saw Jenny out by the pool.

"Can I have a beer?" I asked.

"Are you going to pass out in the yard?" she asked.

"It depends on how the evening goes," I said.

"On second thought, why don't you have an Arnold Palmer," she said. "I've got a pitcher of iced tea in the fridge."

It was just then that Alex rolled up to the house. My mother saw my expression change and looked over her shoulder out the giant picture window that looked out on the neighborhood. His crappy Citation looked so out of place against the backdrop of perfect houses. He stepped out of the car wearing baggy black pants, a short-sleeved dress shirt, and a blue and yellow striped tie. He was carrying something.

"Are those flowers?" my mother asked.

I smiled. They were.

He ambled slowly across the lawn toward the house, his eyes on the ground. Was his mouth moving? It was. He was talking to himself. Probably giving himself a pep talk. I broke into a wide grin and went for the door. I opened it before he could even ring the bell. He'd shaved. He didn't look like the guy from *Lube Jobs 4* anymore. He looked like my boyfriend.

"Hey," I said.

"Hey," he said. He handed me the flowers. "These are for you."

It was a bouquet of carnations, the kind we sold in the floral department at Food World. I knew how much a bouquet of carnations cost, and in fact, I'd once overheard Judy and Jessica talking about how if a guy ever gave them carnations they'd never speak to him again. But for some reason the memory of that just made me like him even more. He'd gone out on a limb for me, stopped at some grocery store on a whim with the idea that he was going to make this night as special for me as he could. He was going to prove himself to me in front of my parents. It felt wonderful.

"No one's ever brought me flowers before," I said.

"Really? Pablo never brought you flowers?" I laughed and shushed him.

"Come on in," I said.

I remembered my mother. She'd melted away for a moment. She was still standing by the couch. Her smile was a bit forced, but it was hard for me to get upset about it. This was all new. And at least she was smiling. She came over and put out her hand.

"Hi, I'm Peggy Hamilton. Dade's mom."

"Hi, Mrs. Hamilton," Alex said, shaking her hand.

"Call me Peg. Actually, no. Call me Peggy."

"Okay. Peggy."

My mom laughed nervously. Then I started laughing nervously and Alex did the same, and all I could think about was moving away from the door, going farther into the house, and making the evening as comfortable as possible.

"Let's go out back," I said, leading him into the kitchen. "I think my dad is playing Grill Master. Should be fun to watch. You thirsty?"

"Yeah," he said. He mouthed "Beer?" I shook my head.

"You want an Arnold Palmer?" I asked.

"What's an Arnold Palmer?"

"Half lemonade, half iced tea," I said.

"Um, sure," he said. "Sounds great."

"I'll make them and bring them out," my mother said, coming into the kitchen behind us. "Go on outside. Alex, you can meet Dade's dad."

Alex and I went out back. My father was staring at the smoking grill with a weird sort of grimace on his face like he didn't know what was going on but was prepared to at least attempt to disprove anyone who suggested such a thing. He looked up when he heard the sliding door.

"I accidentally bought the crappy coals and not the good ones." He looked Alex up and down. "You must be Alex."

They both put out their hands and shook.

"I am," he said. "And you're Dade's dad."

"Call me Ned."

"Okay." Alex shoved his hands into his pockets and rocked back on his heels. I remembered the first night we'd met, how he'd done the exact same thing on the sidewalk that ran in front of the Montanas' place. "Nice pool."

"Alex brought me flowers," I said. The moment I said it, I wished I hadn't.

My father waited a moment and said, "Well, that was nice of you. Nobody ever brought me flowers. Dade's mother brought home this wonderful fern when we first got married, but I think it was more for both of us. Not for me specifically."

"I have some more in the car if you want them," Alex said, pointing his thumb over his shoulder in the direction of his car.

"Oh. Um, no. I'm all right."

"Dad, that was a joke."

My father looked at me and then let out a laugh so loud that I gave a little start. Alex gave me a look of wild amusement.

"Of course," my father said. "Of course." He turned back to the grill and poked around at the coals. An awkward silence fell over the three of us, like he'd suddenly forgotten we were there.

"So what's for dinner?" Alex said, circling the grill and putting himself in my dad's line of vision. There was nothing on there, just a heap of coals that were barely burning. They both looked at it like that evening's meal would magically appear there at any second.

"Kabobs," my dad said. "Lots and lots of kabobs."

"Nice," Alex said.

"Should we sit?" I asked.

The dining area in the corner of the yard was already prepared. The lime green plates were out, the ones my mother only used when we were eating outside. She had put out silverware, cloth napkins, salt and pepper shakers.

"So," my father said after we sat down. "Alex." His name hung there in the air for a few seconds. Alex nodded at my father. He wore a good-natured smile, a less charged version of the smirk he offered those he was trying to in some way seduce. "How old are you?"

"I'll be twenty-one in November," he said.

"So you're twenty."

"Yes. Twenty."

"Dade's eighteen."

"Yes. I am aware of that."

Just then my mother came out with drinks. She placed an Arnold Palmer in front of each of us, smiling brightly as she did so. There was something weirdly ceremonial about it, as if she was glad for the chance to play perfect homemaker in front of someone new.

"No further schooling for you, son?" my dad asked while she did this. "Dade said you weren't enrolled at any of the local colleges."

"Not right now," he said. "Maybe someday. I'm just working. Saving money."

"Saving money is good," my mother said, taking a seat.

"Where do you work?" my father asked.

"I work at Taco Taco. It's over on Edgewood and—"

"I know where Taco Taco is," my father said.

"We have two locations," Alex explained.

"Is that so?"

"Yup yup."

"Your mother got sick on Taco Taco many years ago," my dad said in a slightly accusatory tone.

"Mine?" Alex asked. I couldn't tell if he was joking or if he actually thought my father was referring to him. My dad shot him a weird look.

"No," he said. "Dade's mother."

"Me," my mother said, raising her hand demurely.

"I don't remember that," I said.

"You may not have been born," she said.

We all reached for our beverages and went through the awkwardness of drinking them together. It was an accidental camaraderie followed by a long silence.

∞

Dinner was kabobs, salad, corn on the cob, and some mushroom rice medley thing that my mother always served when we had people over for dinner. She asked Alex about his family and work, and he gave her sterilized answers, things to appease her inquires but nothing to alarm her. I kept stealing glances over at my father. He appeared to be pouting about something. I wondered if all this was his worst nightmare, if he was sitting there thinking about how he'd always wanted a jock who'd bring the head cheerleader home for dinner. Instead he got some lazy, skinny, thrift-store-loving kid who brought home some dude that worked at a taco joint.

"Ned, did you hear that?" my mother said.

Both my father and I looked over at her. I'd also missed whatever had just been said.

"No," my dad said. "What?"

"Alex's sister is in Europe," she said. "That's where we're going. Isn't that something?" She looked at Alex. "Dade's father and I are going to Europe next week. I can't wait."

"Ah, yes," my dad said. "It'll be great."

His words came out empty and emotionless, and he went back to his food without saying anything else. The silence that followed was unbearable. Alex gave me a look that seemed to ask what was going on. I gave a subtle shake of my head to indicate he should ignore it. My mother needlessly cleared her throat and reached for her wineglass.

"It's hard to believe Dade will be leaving for school in less than a month," she said. "You know, Fairmont is the same school—"

My dad suddenly shot up, pushing the chair back noisily as he went. He grabbed his plate and headed for the house.

"—where Dade's father went," my mother went on, her eyes following my father. She took another gulp of her wine. "I remember going to visit Ned—"

"What's his problem?" I asked after he'd slid the glass door shut behind him.

My mom shrugged, shook her head, and waved her hand all at the same time. "I don't know. You know how he is."

"This is embarrassing," I said. "What the fuck?"

"Don't say *fuck*, Dade," my mother warned.

"Should I go?" Alex asked. He was already halfway out of

his seat, his thumb once again pointing over his shoulder in the direction of his car and the nonexistent flowers he'd brought for my father. "I don't want to intrude."

"No," I said. "Stay."

"Stay," my mother said. "There's still dessert."

"Unless you'd rather go," I said. "I understand if you want to."

"I want to stay," Alex said. "If that's cool."

"It's cool," I said. I stood up and grabbed our plates. "We'll go up to my room and finish." My father's plate was in the kitchen sink, but he was nowhere to be found. Alex and I took two spoons and an entire container of strawberry ice cream up to my room. We were at my bedroom door when I realized that I was about to escort him into a realm where everything was mine, covered with the fingerprints of my existence, and unable to be explained away or blamed on someone else. I thought of my Johnny Morgan shrine. It suddenly seemed childish and obsessive. I gave a long, hard blink, and silently wished that we'd walk in and find it had magically disappeared.

"Nice digs," he said as we walked in. Despite my wish, dozens of Johnnys grinned and posed on the far wall. "Love the high ceilings. Makes my room at my grandma's look like a jail cell."

I laughed lamely, unsure how to respond. I perched on the edge of my bed with the ice cream and spoons as he walked the perimeter of my room. He closely examined the postcards I'd taped to the wall, images by Lichtenstein, Warhol, and Cindy

Sherman. He briefly perused my bookshelf, hums of interest coming from his throat as he scanned the titles.

"What's all this?" he asked when he came to the pile of stuff my mother had bought me for college.

"Stuff for my dorm," I said.

"Ah," he said. "Your dorm. I keep forgetting."

"Keep forgetting what?"

He went over to my desk and flipped open my laptop. "Can we put some music on?"

"I'll get it," I said. I put on a collection of *Vasectomy* B-sides that I hadn't listened to in a while. The sad opening chords of "Lava Lamp" started and I returned to my bed.

Alex noticed the Johnny Morgan shrine and laughed. "Love it."

I felt my face get hot. I looked away. "I should take that down. It's lame."

"Whatever," he said. He came over and sat by me. "Johnny Morgan's a hot piece. I'd hit it."

He took the ice cream from me and opened it up. We sat there eating it and listening to the music and not saying anything.

"So what did you mean that you keep forgetting?" I finally said. "You keep forgetting that I'm going to school?"

"Yeah," he said. "Michigan's far."

"It's not that far," I said.

"Far enough."

I didn't like the way he said it, like he'd already decided something about what was going to happen to us after the summer ended. He was looking around my room, not completely invested in the conversation. It occurred to me that we'd been alone for over five minutes and we hadn't kissed yet. I put my hand on his knee. He gave me a smile, warm and maybe a little bit forced. It felt like a consolation prize. I moved my hand away.

"What's wrong?" I asked.

He furrowed his brow. "Wrong? Nothing's wrong. Am I acting like something's wrong?"

"Frankly, yeah. A little. Did dinner freak you out?"

"No. Not at all. The food was good."

"I'm sorry about my dad."

"Don't be. God only knows how my parents would've acted in the same situation. At least your dad had the courtesy to just get up and leave instead of causing a scene. Mine probably would've just gotten drunk and thrown something."

"We went out to dinner the other night, and he said he was going to try," I said. "He said he wanted to understand everything."

"Bummer."

He was holding the ice cream and looking distractedly around my room. I was convinced that he was plotting his escape. Why hadn't he kissed me yet?

His phone rang. He took it out of his pocket and checked the caller ID. He gave me a look that asked if he could take it, and I gave him an overly permissive nod. He stood up and moved slowly to the corner of my room and answered.

"Hey, Jarvis," he said. "How can I help you this lovely evening?"

Alex took the liberty of opening my window and lighting up a cigarette. He leaned far out as he blew the smoke into the night. It vaguely pissed me off, but I didn't know what to say. I lit some incense and went over to my closet. I took off my collared shirt and tossed it on the ground near my shoes. I was over that shirt, over this night in general. All I wanted was for Alex to leave so I could call Lucy and commiserate with her about how crappy the evening had been. I went through my clothes, noisily pushing the hangers down the rod as I went, until I finally settled on a tight green T-shirt that bore the logo of some heating and cooling business, one of my favorite thrift store purchases.

"Hey, man," I heard Alex say to the caller. "I should go. I'm at a friend's. But I'll be there in thirty. We can talk more later. . . . Okay, peace. . . . Right, I won't forget. . . . Okay. Bye."

"You gotta go," I said for him as he hung up.

"Yeah." He came over to me and kissed me on the forehead and rubbed my shoulders. There was something so condescending about it. I suddenly couldn't wait to get him out of the house. "I gotta go."

"Okay," I said. "Go."

The words came out a bit more defiantly than I wanted them to. He leaned back and gave me an inquisitive look. I looked everywhere but in his eyes. He put his hands on my shoulders and tried to steer me into looking at him, but I kept my focus on everything behind him. My bed, the Johnny Morgan shrine, the spoon on the nightstand resting in a puddle of melted strawberry ice cream.

"What's wrong?" he asked. "Did I do something?"

I finally let my gaze meet his. "It's just that nothing about tonight has gone the way I wanted it to. My dad was a jerk and now you're leaving. I guess I just had this idea of how things would be, which was a huge mistake, but one I make over and over again. You think I would've learned my lesson by now."

"Hold on," Alex said. "I had a great night."

"Well, you're being all distant," I said. "And a kiss on the forehead? What's up with that? And you're at your *friend's* house? Is that what I am? Who's Jarvis?"

"I'm sorry," he said. "I don't know Jarvis that well. He's only bought from me twice before, and he doesn't need to be all up in my business. He doesn't need to know whether or not you're my friend or boyfriend or whatever. And I'll admit, dinner freaked me out a little. I'm not good with parents as it is, and then to have things go down the way that they went down . . . well, I got a bit rattled. I'm sorry if I went into my shell. But what do you expect?"

What did I expect? We stood there in silence for a while, each with our arms crossed and our eyes wandering. I started tapping my foot.

"I'm sorry," I finally said. "I guess I wasn't being totally fair."

"Don't sweat it."

We felt each other out with our eyes and then moved in for a hug. He squeezed me tight and rolled me lightly back and forth in his arms. I liked that he was a little bigger than me, that he could put his arms around me and make me feel safe. He kissed the top of my shaved head.

"Your fuzz feels funny on my lips," he said, not moving his mouth.

"Your lips feel funny on my fuzz."

"Do they?"

"They do."

He blew out a puff of air that vibrated his lips against my scalp. I laughed at the sensation and the noise it made and pulled away from him.

"Go," I said. I moved back a bit, laughing as I went. "Go off and do your drug business."

"Oh, it's like that, is it?" He was smiling and grabbing out for me, but I kept slapping his hands away playfully. "Come back here. I want a kiss."

"Leave me alone. I'm still mad at you."

"Then why are you smiling?"

"I'm not," I said.

But I was. He rolled his sleeves up to his shoulders and got into a wrestler's crouch. He snarled at me, bared his fangs like a scrappy little dog, and then lurched forward and tackled me and brought me down onto the bed. We laughed for a second and then he moved in and we were kissing. He brought his hand up and touched my face and kissed me again. I decided right then that for the rest of my life I would tell people Alex Kincaid was the first boy I kissed. Those few that I'd stolen from Pablo wouldn't count.

# Chapter 16

Lucy and I met up later and went to our diner. I'd called her for an emergency meeting the moment Alex left. We sat in our usual booth and ordered a plate of cheese fries and a couple of Cokes. The counter was lined with truckers all looking up silently at images of the war on the mounted television. A big-haired waitress moved up and down the counter filling coffee cups and water glasses as she went. There was a Sting song coming from the speakers in the ceiling. Near the entrance a redhead in a very short orange dress was in the phone booth crying into the receiver.

"So my dad, like, disappeared after dinner," I said.

"Where'd he go?" She was pulling apart two clusters of French fries that were attached with a web of bright yellow cheese. "To that chick's house?"

"He said that things between him and Vicki were through," I said. "But really, who knows. It's just that we went out to dinner the other night and he acted like he was going to try to be there for me, but when it all came down to it, he just couldn't keep his word. Typical. And then Alex was being distant. And then there's my mom acting like a happy robot woman, which I guess isn't the worst thing in the world, but it just adds this air of stress to the whole situation."

"It's a big deal," said Lucy. "Meeting the parents and all that. I'm sure that's why Alex freaked out. This is new for your parents too."

"I guess," I mumbled. "I just want to skip it, you know? I want it not to matter. I've spent so much time worrying about being gay and telling people. I want to move beyond that. I want to worry about other stuff."

"Good luck with that," Lucy said. "It's always going to matter to someone. And didn't you say you and Alex were talking about Fairmont and stuff?"

"Yeah. A bit."

"Well, think about that," Lucy said as if it was the most obvious thing in the world. "If he likes you half as much as you like him, then I'm sure the idea of you taking off forever doesn't exactly put him in the best mood."

I stirred the ice in my Coke. "I never really thought of that."

"Way to overlook the obvious, kid." She smiled and leaned forward. "So tell me more about dinner. Tell me the good stuff. Is it love? Could you love this guy?"

"I don't know. I still feel like using that word might jinx it all. Like if I say it's love, he'll call and tell me he doesn't ever want to see me again."

NICK BURD

Lucy laughed. "That's not how the universe works, Captain Negative. Good things happen."

"This might sound crazy, but I can't wait to get out of here and go to college and be done with everything. I'll miss Alex a ton, and if there's a way to make this work, I'm willing to try. But it's time for me to get out of here. I feel done with it. The next month can't move fast enough."

"Yeah. Cedarville sucks." She looked around the diner for emphasis. The woman in the phone booth had shielded her eyes as if she was trying to hide from everyone in the restaurant. Three out of the six truckers at the counter were showing major ass crack. "I can't wait to go back to California. I mean, L.A. sucks, but at least it sucks in a much more sophisticated way than this place. This place is just . . . *ugh*. New York City is where it's at. I'm gonna apply for college out there."

"New York City doesn't even seem like a real place to me. Nothing outside of here does. It's all just a fuzzy dream."

"Isn't it?" she agreed. "This town wipes out the idea of anywhere else. It's sort of magical like that."

"Have you been to New York before?" I asked.

"Never."

"Me neither," I said.

We picked at the fries in silence. I used my straw to stir the melted ice and watered-down soda concoction that my drink had become. A few minutes later another Sting song came over the speakers and Lucy lip-synched along, squinting her eyes and tilting her head up to the ceiling for maximum adult-

256

contemporary emotional emphasis. She stopped after a bit and laughed and then went back to just sitting there, sometimes watching the cars out the window as they took the ramp up to the interstate.

"I like how I can just be quiet with you," I said. "When we're here. Or driving. It's always the same. I can just sit and be with you and not have to worry. I mean, don't get me wrong, I love talking to you. But there's this great comfort in being quiet."

"I know what you mean," she said.

"I'll miss you when you go back to California. You're my first real friend."

She smiled and reached across the table for my hand. She squeezed my fingers.

"You're the sweetest," she said. "You're a great, great guy, Dade. Alex is lucky. And I'm lucky. Anyone who knows you is lucky."

I was tearing up before I knew it.

"Oh no," she laughed. She was getting teary eyed too. "Don't cry. I'll cry if you cry, and I don't cry."

I laughed and wiped my eyes. "I can't tell if I'm crying because I'm happy or sad."

She got up and came to my side of the booth. She put her arm around me and pulled me close. I reached around her and hugged her back.

"The truckers are staring," I said after a few seconds.

It was true. They were. The whole row of them was doing a bad job of pretending not to look at us.

"We just got engaged," Lucy shouted over to them. "I just asked this man to be my wife."

The men at the counter traded confused looks. I burst out laughing.

"We're glad you and your ass cracks could share this moment with us," she went on. "Seriously. We really are. Those are some serious cracks and this is a serious moment."

∞

Three days later I was sitting on the couch in my swimming trunks and an old baby blue T-shirt as my parents buzzed around the house in preparation for the trip. Their suitcases were packed and waiting by the door. They would be leaving for the airport at any moment.

"Has anyone seen my pills?" my mother called from the kitchen.

"Which ones?" I called back.

"The blue ones."

"What are they called?"

"I can never remember the name. The new ones that start with a *P*."

"Prednisone?"

"Prednisone? That's a steroid. I don't take steroids. Where did you hear that word?"

"I take steroids now, Mom. I think I'm going to join the Fairmont football team. It'll be a good way to meet girls."

My mother came into the living room. "Tell me you're joking," she said demandingly. I gave her a pointed look. She started to go back into the kitchen, but she turned around after just a few steps.

"And meet girls?" she said. "I thought you were gay."

"I am gay, Mom. It was a joke. Ha-ha. Get it?"

She went back into the kitchen. There was the sound of drawers opening and closing. "I'm stressed out and trying to leave, Dade. And your father can't find his passport. Please don't play tricks on me when I'm like this. Not now."

"But you're always like this," I muttered to myself.

I just sat there staring out the picture window. Alex was due to arrive in thirty minutes. Hopefully my parents would be gone by then. I could hear my father's footsteps above me as he moved from room to room looking for his passport.

Mikey Sanchez from four doors down came racing down the street naked. Not ten seconds later his mother came running after him wearing an apron over a flower-pattern dress and one yellow rubber glove.

"Ah!" I heard my mother say. There was the unmistakable rattle of pills in a bottle and then a drawer sliding shut. "Found 'em."

Just then my father's voice came through the intercom.

"Peggy?"

"Yes?"

"Why was my passport in your sock drawer?"

"I hid it when I was angry with you."

"Well," my father said through the intercom, "I found it."

I glared at the luggage by the door.

When would they be gone?

It was August and the house was cool, but under the coolness was a persistent throb of heat, like there was a window open somewhere in the house that was preventing everything from dropping to serious frostbite levels. Or maybe it was just so hot outside that the summer was winning over everything. I wanted to open the door and feel the heat hit me like a blast of water, like something from a submarine movie where the tragic sailor opens the door and is met with a surge of ocean water. Let the summer run through everything, let it flood the house.

My mother came into the living room and sat by me on the sofa.

"Are you nervous about being by yourself? Remember that Mrs. Savage is there if you need her. Go have dinner at her house. Don't eat junk. Don't pass out in the yard."

"I'll be fine, Mom."

"You and Lucy can swim in the pool," she said.

I could tell there was something she wanted to say to me. There always was with her. I sorta understood that for the first time right then. What was the thing she was constantly not saying and what did it have to do with me? It wasn't that she loved me. She said that often enough. It was something else. Something that mattered more, if you can imagine that.

*Just say it*, I thought to myself, despite the fact I didn't know what it was. *Just come out and say it.*

She rubbed her palm over my head.

"Your hair's coming back fast," she said.

"I need to cut it again."

"But there's hardly anything there."

"I liked the way it felt when I first shaved it."

"Oh, grow it out," she said. "I like it longer."

"I kinda like it short. No?"

"Whatever you want, I suppose. But I like it long. It feels like it's you then."

"It's still me," I said.

"I suppose."

She took my hand in hers and put it in her lap. She let out a sigh and looked out the window. "Every time I'm about to get on an airplane, I start to think about everything. It's the world we live in now, I guess."

"Nothing'll happen. Cars are more dangerous than airplanes."

"I've never flown over the ocean before."

"I'm sure you're above the clouds," I said. "You probably can't see anything."

"It's still there, though."

Outside Mrs. Sanchez came walking back down the street, her naked son squirming in her arms.

"That child is going to grow up to be a nudist," my mother said.

"I think he already is one," I said.

My father came into the living room. He was wearing khaki shorts that stopped just above the knee and a navy blue polo tucked in at the waist. His sporty-shaped sunglasses hung around his neck on a bright yellow cord. Summertime leisure gear for dads. His face had that magic ease to it, the one he could put on at a moment's notice in an effort to make everything seem okay.

"We all set to go?" he said.

"I think so," my mom said. "I think we're off."

I stood and gave her a comically huge hug. Then I went over and gave my dad a sideways squeeze. He brought his hand up behind me and rubbed it on my head, letting out a little laugh as he did so.

"Emergency numbers are on the refrigerator," my mother said. "Dr. Kennedy's office, the fire department, poison control center, oral surgeon—"

"In case of any teeth-shatteringly good times."

"—the alarm company, the Savages'. I think that's it. And don't say *teeth-shattering*. It makes me nervous."

"911?" my dad asked.

"911 is on there," my mom said, totally missing the joke.

"Super," I said. "We're set."

"I can't think of anything else," my mother said.

She looked nervous. Pensive. It would've been terrible form for her to bust out a pill right then and there, but I'm sure she was itching to do just that. So I gave her another hug.

"I'll be fine, Mom," I said into the side of her head, into her hair. When did I get taller than her? I always thought that at times like this. "Have a good time. Don't worry about me."

"Dade'll be fine," my father said. "Man of the house." He

opened up the front door and a surge of warm air entered the house. I helped them take their luggage out to the driveway, where my father's Audi was parked. He'd gone out early that morning and had it washed, as if it were important that their trip to the airport be in a sparkling car. That was how my father's mind worked. The quest to make things perfect must be perfect in all respects.

My mother put her sunglasses on before getting in the car. She rolled down the window and mouthed good-bye as they were backing out.

"I love you, Dade," she added. "Very much."

My father lifted his hand from the steering wheel and waved at me like I was some kind motorist who'd just allowed him to merge into his lane. I waved back as they pulled into the street, straightened out, and drove away.

From my pocket came the sound of my new Vas Deferens ringtone. A text message from Alex.

### R they gone yet?

# Chapter 17

That week the house felt more like home than it ever had before. Having my parents and their problems out of the house made me realize how much space they took up.

I was making me and Alex breakfast at one p.m. in nothing but my bathing suit and I was suddenly overcome with the urge to stop everything and allow myself time to breathe and simply exist. I just stood there staring at the scrambled eggs. A million watts of sunlight were blasting through every window, and I could feel the blood moving through my body and sustaining my existence. Alex sauntered in from the backyard, the blue and yellow plaid bathing suit he borrowed from my father dripping water on the floor. He came up behind me and put his arms around my waist and kissed my bare shoulder.

"You're such a good housewife," he murmured into the back of my neck.

"Don't interrupt," I said, nudging him away. "Scrambled eggs are an art. I need focus."

He tugged at my bathing suit. "I wanna play."

"Stop," I said. "I need *focus*."

"That's not what you need. You need to play."

I tried elbowing him away several times, but he kept tugging at my suit. I finally thought *Screw the eggs* and moved the pan to an unlit burner.

We made frozen margaritas and took turns doing readings from my mother's self-help books while standing on top of the kitchen table. We read from *Finding Your Awareness*, *The Secrets of Intuition*, and *How Can I Love Me if I Don't Even Know Me?*

"'What one must realize,'" Alex read in a fake British accent, "'is that in the absence of hope, there lies hope itself. The vast expanse that many people mistake for a desert of utter hopelessness and despair is actually the rich field from which a bountiful crop of faith will eventually spring. And like any other crop, faith needs time to grow. And time, dear friend, is your friend too.'"

"I hate the way he refers to his readers as his friends." I was leaning back in my chair and stirring my margarita with a grape Popsicle. "It's so patronizing."

He held up the back cover of the book to show me the author photo. He was a mustached man with giant red-framed eyeglasses. "Dude, Dr. Harris B. Harris is your friend. He wants to help you. And me. He wants to help us."

∞

We kept getting calls on the landline from a blocked number. Sometimes there were as many as five or six a day. I'd answer and there'd be only a long silence as I asked who it was, what they wanted, and then finally a click as the caller hung up. The first few times I thought it was my parents trying unsuccessfully to reach me from somewhere abroad. But after a while I ditched that theory and assumed it was Pablo or Fessica or maybe even Vicki.

"Maybe it's Jenny Moore," Alex once said before making a ghostly moaning noise and waving his arms around. I told him it wasn't funny, but he just laughed and rolled his eyes and told me to lighten up.

Once we got one of these calls at five in the morning. Alex was passed out next to me in bed. I deliberated not answering, but with each one came the fresh hope that after the call I'd realize something that I hadn't before. Maybe something basic like the caller's identity. Maybe something deeper and more cosmic.

"Who is this?" I asked the silent void. "Seriously. You're not accomplishing anything by just calling and not saying anything. Tell me what you want."

No sound. Not even breathing. At least there would've been comfort in that. I would've known that it was an actual human being on the other end. But now every time we got a call, I thought of Alex's sarcastic suggestion that it was Jenny Moore. The idea of this sent a shiver down my spine.

"Jenny?" I said.

The person hung up immediately.

∞

Alex introduced me to *The Difference Between Wright and Wong*, a cop show from the early eighties that they showed at three thirty a.m. on channel 321.

"This is easily one of the most underrated shows in the history of television," he said. We were on the floor of the family room in a tangle of sheets, blankets, and pillows. I was struggling to keep my eyes open, but he was wide-awake. The opening sequence had just begun and already he was completely immersed. "I used to watch this show with my dad. He loved it. I met the actor who played Detective David Wright at the state fair when I was, like, seven. I bet I still have his autographed picture somewhere. God, what I would give to get this channel at my grandma's place."

The two detectives were speeding through Chinatown on a little black moped. Detective Wong was driving and Detective Wright was holding on to his waist and shooting at a black sedan that was chasing them. The horns in the chase music kept pulling me out of sleep.

"Which would you rather be?" Alex asked. "Wright or Wong?"

My eyes were barely open. "I don't know. I've only seen, like, two half episodes in my entire life."

"I think you'd be Wright. Wright is careful, levelheaded. He's the partner that talks to the chief when shit goes wrong, like when a stakeout ends with a giant explosion and a dead hooker. Only Wright can talk him down. And Wong knows the Chinese underworld really well, sorta like I know the Cedarville underworld. So I think it fits."

I thought about pointing out that Dingo and his gang of loser friends could hardly be referred to as the Cedarville underworld, but I fell asleep before I could.

∞

That night I dreamt it was me and him on that moped. We were flying through a bright neon Chinatown of my mind. There were puddles in the street and I was having trouble steering the bike. It leaned in ways that defied gravity. It was all I could do to hang on. Even in my dreams there was music: cheesy horns, intense percussion, and a bass guitar humping away at a single note. "You're such a good housewife," Alex whispered into my ear before going back to shooting at the invisible thing following us.

∞

Lucy and Jay came and went as they pleased. The house became our post-adolescent clubhouse. There were epic barbeques at dusk. There were marathon Ouija board sessions between the four of us in my mother's meditation room, where we tried to conjure the ghosts of dead rock stars and poets.

One night Alex and Jay stayed up late doing God knows what while Lucy and I slept upstairs. I woke the next morning to find a long crack in the sliding glass door. Alex and Jay were eating frosted cereal in the kitchen, bags under their bloodshot eyes.

"What happened?" I exclaimed. "My parents are gonna kill me!"

"He fell," Jay said.

"I fell," Alex repeated. "My head did that."

I didn't know if believed them or not, but I quickly found myself thinking that maybe I didn't want to know.

"This needs to be fixed," I said.

"I already called some glass place," Alex said. "They'll be here between two and four. I'll pay for it."

"Oh," I said. I hadn't expected this, but it was a pleasant surprise. It still wasn't enough to completely smother my irritation.

I leaned against the counter and rubbed my eyes. This was not the best way to wake up. They went on eating their cereal in silence. I found myself glaring at Jay more than Alex. I felt a bit jealous of Jay, jealous that the two of them had been up all night together wreaking havoc in the house. I looked over at the refrigerator and noticed it was covered with magnetic letters. Amongst the jumbled nonsense someone had spelled *Dade Kincaid is not afraid.*

"Where did those come from?" I asked. "Did you go out and *buy* refrigerator magnets last night?"

The two of them looked dumbly at the phrase spelled out on the fridge.

"I'm not sure," Alex said slowly. He paused for a moment. "I don't think so, although a chunk of last night is a bit fuzzy."

"To say the least," Jay said.

"But I'm thinking yes," Alex said. "We must have."

"At least you're thinking," Jay said. "That's more than I can say for myself."

∞

Lucy and I sat out by the pool and watched Jay and Alex rough-housing in the water. We talked about what would happen after I left for school and she went back to L.A.

"We'll still be friends," she told me. "Distance has nothing to do with friendship. Think about someone like Pablo who was right beside you for such a long time, but did you ever feel close to him? Distance is meaningless. No one's that far away unless they choose to be."

I watched Alex and Jay as they jumped on each other's backs and tried to hold each other's head underwater. I wondered how well I really knew him, how close we really were. Maybe my perspective was all messed up. Maybe we were really miles apart.

"Have you two talked?" Lucy asked. "You and Alex. About after the summer."

I shook my head. "I think about it sometimes and it makes me sad."

"Yeah," she said. "Well, what are your options?"

"I don't have any," I said.

"There are always options, Dade."

"Not going to college isn't an option," I said. "I'm not staying in Cedarville. And it's not like he could come to school with me and sleep in my dorm room closet or something."

"Try not to think about it," she said.

"This is helping," I said.

"What is?"

"My parents being gone. Having the house to ourselves."

I considered what I meant exactly before going on. "I feel like we're in a beautiful bubble."

"How long after they get back until you drive to Michigan?"

"Two weeks."

"Right around when I head back to L.A.," she said.

Alex and Jay had worn themselves out and were playing dead in the pool. Lucy let out a little laugh at the sight of it.

"That's the sad thing about bubbles," she said. "They burst."

∞

One night I dreamt that someone was in the house. I didn't know who it was or if it was even a person. In fact, I was pretty sure it wasn't a person, that it was some sort of force moving through the halls. In the dream I was in bed with Alex and I could feel the thing coming up the stairs. I was afraid to speak too loudly, so I kept whispering Alex's name in an attempt to wake him up. I nudged him and hissed his name, but he stayed fast asleep.

"It's coming up the stairs," I whispered to no one.

Then, in the dream, my phone rang. It was my mother. She asked if I was at home.

"I am," I said. "Are you coming up the stairs right now? Someone's on the stairs and I don't know who it is."

She said she wasn't in the house, that she was in Europe with my father and that she was calling to tell me to get out of the house as soon as possible. Her voice was calm when she said this, so calm that it seemed like it couldn't really be her calling.

"Why? What's going on? What is it? Do you know what it is? Is it what's been calling the house?"

She said it was and that I needed to climb out the window. I could feel it moving on the other side of the walls. The thing was at the top of the stairs now, almost to my door.

"What about Alex? I can't wake him up. I can't leave him here."

She told me to forget about Alex and to save myself.

"But we're the same person," I said. I wasn't just being dramatic. It was clear in the dream that he and I were in fact the same exact person.

My mother said that even though it felt that way that it wasn't true. She said I had to get out of the house.

"But I can't leave him." I was hysterically crying at this point.

Yes, you can, she said. In fact, you have to. You really don't have any choice.

It had its hand on the doorknob.

"But I can't. I can't do that."

Do it. You have to. Go.

# Chapter 18

It was a little after five in the morning. Outside my windows, the dawn was shifting the black of the night sky to a clean dark blue, Alex was sound asleep right next to me, his bare back just inches away. I reached out and put my finger to his left shoulder blade. Yes, he was real. Both him and his snoring were very real.

I got out of bed and wandered the house. The blue predawn glow coming through every window made the house feel ghostly and electric. It reminded me of the black-and-white horror movies, zombies lurching across the cornfield under some weird hybrid of day and night. The television in the refrigerator had been left on all night, muted and pouring its visuals to an inanimate audience of all the things that made up our kitchen. The cupboards, the granite countertop, the state-of-the-art faucet, the butcher's block, the kitchen table where I sat down with my parents and told them I was gay. How did these things exist when we weren't here? What did they do when everyone was fast asleep?

*They enter our dreams, that's what*, I thought to myself as I opened the fridge. How many times had I dreamt dreams that took place in this house? In this very kitchen even? Maybe that was these things' way of talking to me in my sleep. They were sending me benign reminders of their existence. I thought back to the dream I'd had the previous night, the one with my mother telling me to get out of the house.

I grabbed a carton of chocolate milk and drank it while leaning against the counter. The light in the house seemed to be changing a bit each second, getting brighter as the day was being born. I pushed a button on the fridge to unmute the television. The sound came on just in time for me to catch the final strains of the Cedarville Sports Club jingle (*"—ville Sports Cluuuuuuuuuub . . . It just fits!"*).

What came next seemed like the reason I couldn't sleep. The reason the television had been left on. For reasons that exist far outside our realm of consciousness, for invisible reasons.

A News Channel 4 special report came on, all dramatic music and flying logos in the intro. Then anchorwoman Billie Yellowfield appeared on the screen. She'd possessed the same blond perm for as long as I could remember. As always it was frizzy and out of control, giving the whole thing the appearance of being some lost transmission from the eighties. She wore a crisp white blouse with a large red bow tied at her throat.

"Good morning. I'm Billie Yellowfield, here to bring you this breaking News Channel Four special report. Police are reporting Jenny Moore, the nine-year-old Cedarville girl missing since

June third, has been found safe and sound in a local supermarket, of all places. Channel four reporter Kip Bradley is on location at the eastside Food World where the young girl was found. Kip, what can you tell us about this strange turn of events?"

The screen split, and there was Kip Bradley, by far the sexiest anchor on any of the Cedarville news stations. He always had this look of muted incredulousness on his face, like he couldn't believe he was on TV. His oil-black hair was styled in a hipster pompadour that suggested he spent his downtime in dive bars drinking cheap beer and monopolizing the jukebox with rockabilly tunes. Behind him was Food World, *my* Food World, its red neon sign bright and frantic. Behind him police officers were wandering back and forth. A lone potbellied civilian stood gawking at the camera a few yards back.

"Yes, Billie," Kip said. "This is an amazing end to a situation that many people feared would end in tragedy. Police say nine-year-old Jenny Moore was found in the cereal aisle of this east Cedarville Food World. Now, the young girl was rushed to North Cedarville Hospital, but early reports coming in from people who saw Jenny said that she appeared to be fine, laughing even, and didn't look like a girl who'd been missing for the better part of the summer."

And then Orla the purple-haired woman from the bakery was on the screen, a microphone bearing the channel 4 logo aimed at her orange lipsticked mouth.

"Well, I just came in at four to put the bread in the oven like I always do and I saw her just sorta wandering up and down the aisle. She was opening cereal boxes, looking for the little toys they give away, and I thought it was strange that a little girl would be at a grocery store all by herself at four in the morning. So I asked her where her mom was and she just sorta looked at me. She was giving me an odd little smile and wearing a decoder ring she'd found. She was more interested in that decoder ring than telling me where she lived or who might be looking for her. After a few seconds I realized who it was, and by golly, I just about had a heart attack."

From off-screen an unmicrophoned Kip asked, "A good heart attack or a bad one?"

Orla gave a restrained chuckle and said, "Oh, a good one."

The live Kip returned to the screen.

"Police are still investigating this strange development in the case. Authorities have said they'll be reviewing the store's surveillance tapes and looking for clues about the young girl's whereabouts. There are more questions than answers in the air this morning, but there's something else floating around as well: an air of hope. And, yes, people have been throwing around the word *miracle* like you wouldn't believe, and for once, they just might be right. Stay tuned to News Channel Four for what I'm sure will be numerous updates throughout the day. I'm Kip Bradley. Billie, back to—"

I shut it off. My body suddenly felt heavy. I dropped myself into a chair at the kitchen table and stared out at the backyard. It was getting brighter out by the minute. A few leaves dotted the surface of the pool. I thought back to the night where I thought

I'd seen her. Where had she gone? I wanted to be happy that they'd found her, and I was, but it was smeared with something else, fear of the unknown, the place she'd been all summer long.

I took off the gym shorts I'd worn to bed and walked out to the pool. I put a toe in. The water was warmer that I thought it'd be. I fell in sideways and made a huge splash. It echoed throughout the quiet suburban morning that blanketed our backyard and all the others around it. No other sound to decorate it but the rapid chirping of the morning birds.

I floated on my back. Up in the sky an airplane soared overhead. Who was up there? Where were they going? The fact that they'd found Jenny safe and sound was like trying to grasp the meaning of infinity. I wanted to know where she'd been, what had happened there, and then I wanted her to show me where that place was.

I got out and lay on one of the chaise longues. I shut my eyes but I couldn't sleep. I hovered in a space just a few levels below full consciousness for God knows how long. The sun rose fully and warmed my skin, and somewhere a lawn mower started up. Slowly I sunk into unconsciousness. I dreamt in words, in conversations that scrolled quickly across the backs of my eyelids, conversations whose content and meaning I could never fully grasp.

∞

When I finally woke the sun was so bright that I had to squint for a good twenty seconds and even then the world was hidden behind a hot white glow.

*I've gone blind.*

I found Alex sitting at the kitchen table. He was wearing my father's ratty blue bathrobe and sleepily shoving a spoonful of Fruity Sugar Crisps into his mouth. He was on the phone with someone.

"I'll ask him," he said into the mouthpiece. His mouth was filled with cereal. The words sounded mushy. "That's fine. . . . Well yeah. . . . I'm sure he'll be down. . . . Oh my God, you should see him right now. He just came in from skinny-dipping in his pool. . . . I'm aware of what time it is. . . . Hey, look at what *you're* doing at nine in the morning. . . . Exactly. . . . *Exactly.* . . . Hey Dade, Dingo says yo."

"Tell him I said yo back."

"Dade says yo back. And I say yo too. To both of you. . . . It's a yoversation. . . . Yeah, I have no idea either."

He went on talking. I made myself a bowl of cereal and a cup of coffee and sat across from him. I looked groggily out into the backyard. So bright, but I couldn't wake up. How in the heck was Alex so awake? He was laughing at something Dingo was saying. He called him a fucker. A black fuzz ran evenly over Alex's head. His hair was growing back.

"I should really jet, Ding," he said. "Dade just sat down. I'm gonna ask him about tomorrow night over a nice gay breakfast."

I laughed through my grogginess.

"So that was Dingo," Alex said after he hung up. "Apparently he's been up all night writing songs with the guys and snorting

God knows what. He wants to know if we wanna have a little last-minute shindig tomorrow night. He was thinking maybe the band could come play out by the pool. That'd be cool, right? Get a few kegs, invite a few people over."

"It could be. I just don't want the house to get wrecked to all hell. Especially after what happened to the door."

"It won't," Alex said. "I promise. We won't invite too many people and we'll try and keep everyone outside. But we'll have, like, Lucy and Jay and Dingo and those guys. Is there anyone else you can think of?"

I stirred my cereal. The whole idea had that dangerous ring to it, like when you hear someone suggest something your mother spent a good part of your childhood warning you against. In my mind I saw a demolished lawn, vomit on my parents' bed, and fist-sized holes in the walls.

"We really gotta be careful," I said. "You and Jay and Lucy is one thing, but Dingo and a whole mess of people is another."

Alex shot me a look. "You can invite your friends too," he went on. "It's not like this is just my thing or something. It's your house. Do whatever. Set whatever rules you want."

"Fessica," I said. "I should really invite Fessica."

"Montana? You're kidding, right?"

"It would make her millennium. And it may make up for some things."

Alex smiled and rubbed my head affectionately. "See, Dade, this is why I love you. You're such a sweet guy. So nice."

*This is why I love you.*

He went back to eating his cereal. Yesterday's paper lay in disarray in the middle of the table. He grabbed the sports section off the top and reread all the things he'd read yesterday.

"Why are all football players hot?" he asked. "Not American football. Euro dudes. Soccer. Why are all soccer players so hot?"

"Um, did you just say you loved me?"

He put down the paper and looked over at me. "Did I?"

"You did. You said that you loved me because I was a sweet guy."

Alex gave me the sideways grin. The charmer.

He pulled on my arm. "Get up. C'mere."

I stood up and let him pull me over to him and place me on his lap. He kissed my neck and let his hands traveled all over my body. My legs. My arms. The small of my back. He dotted my neck with little kisses. I could feel his boner through the terry-cloth robe, but I wasn't feeling the same way. I wasn't sure I was completely behind the party idea, and the news about Jenny Moore had infected the mood of the morning. It felt like I was on some precipice in a dream where at any moment it would reveal itself to be a beautiful vision or a horrible nightmare.

"They found Jenny Moore this morning," I said.

He stopped kissing my neck. "Oh no."

"No, not oh no. She's alive. She ran away or something. Apparently she's fine."

"See, this is why I don't get invested in anything," Alex said. "I bet she's not even real. I bet the news stations made her up to boost ratings."

I tried not to laugh. "You're insane."

"You have no idea what kind of world we're living in, Dade Kincaid." He smiled at my new name and then sang, *"Dade Kincaid is not afraid of the things of which the world is made."*

I slapped him playfully upside the head and slid off his lap. I carried our dishes over to the sink and rinsed them out. Outside, the automatic sprinklers came on. The water hissed rhythmically like the opening beat of some ultramodern pop song. When would the girl start singing the lyrics that didn't mean anything? When would the chorus come and sweep us away in an irresistible wave of saccharine melody and recycled metaphor?

Outside in the pool a yellow raft drifted calmly. Had we always had that raft? We must have.

"So where was she?" he asked. "They don't know?"

"Not yet," I said. "I'm sure they'll figure it out."

"Maybe," he said. "How weird, though. And she's not talking?"

"I don't know," I said. "I guess not."

"I feel like we're married," Alex said. "Don't you? Not all the time. Just at times like right now. Like we'll be together forever."

"Maybe that's because you keep tacking your last name onto my name."

"Dade Kincaid? You like it. Admit it."

"I never said I didn't. I'm just offering an explanation."

He leaned back in his chair and put his hands behind his

head and looked out at the backyard. "What am I going to do when you go to college? Do you think Fairmont will hire me as a janitor? Everybody needs a janitor. I could sneak into your room and give you blowjobs while your roommate takes a shower."

My pulse quickened. I shut my eyes and tried to put myself in the moment. I had to bury it all over again. Bury it under the smell of the fresh-cut grass, the hissing beat of the sprinklers, under the image of Alex in my father's robe, the smell of coffee in the air, the weird hollow feeling in my chest that was distantly related to the discovery the police had made that morning.

"I still can't believe they found her," I said.

"You're really fixated on this, aren't you?"

I shut off the sink and turned to look at him. "I just feel like it means something. Don't you? Like, when people see Jesus' face in a tortilla or something. You know what I mean?"

"I don't. But that's fine. I like that about you. How you don't make sense sometimes."

∞

Later on I sat by the pool and wrote while Alex floated along on the yellow raft. He asked where it came from. I told him that we'd had it for ages even though I wasn't sure that was true. I found a page in my journal that said *Things and people may just appear, but they appear for a reason.* There was nothing else on the page. I didn't remember writing it. The handwriting didn't look like mine. It was messier. I wondered if maybe my father had written it, if maybe Fessica or Alex had. Jenny could've. That seemed just as possible as anything else.

Alex was wearing cheap sunglasses with hot pink frames. His head was turned slightly to the left. I was pretty sure he was asleep. There was something godly about the way he drifted across the surface of the pool, like a rock star being passed over the heads of his adoring fans. I wanted to call out to him. I wanted to tell him I loved him.

"What are you looking at?"

It was like hearing a statue speak. Apparently he hadn't been asleep. I didn't say anything for a while. I looked down at my journal.

*Things and people may just appear, but they appear for a reason.*

"You," I said.

He smiled, but I couldn't see his eyes and that made it seem too cool, too far away to be real. I suddenly had the feeling he was laughing at me.

"What's so funny?" I said.

"You," he said, mimicking my voice.

He brought his sunglasses up to his forehead. There he was. He screwed up his face and stuck out his tongue. I suddenly had the sensation that I'd dreamt all this before. It was stronger than déjà vu. Or maybe this had all been done in some eighties movie I'd seen. That's what he was. He was The Guy from all those movies they played on cable late at night. The one everyone wants, the one I had.

# Chapter 19

Lucy came over the next night at around six. I was up in my room trying on every item of clothing I owned. I couldn't figure out what to wear. There was a new pressure to the evening, one that I hadn't experienced in a very long time. The last party I'd hosted was my thirteenth birthday party.

Lucy was wearing white patent-leather go-go boots and an insane prom dress she'd found at a thrift store downtown. It was lime green with purple sequined zebra stripes. In the meantime, I was in black jeans and nothing else. I think just about every T-shirt I owned littered the floor around me.

"Fashion emergency?" she asked.

"I seriously have nothing to wear. You look like you're going on a disco drag queen safari."

"Aw, thanks," she said. "I was going to wear my hot pink wig, but Aunt Dana freaked out when she saw me. She said she refused to even let me walk two doors down dressed that way."

"What a buzzkill," I said as I sifted through the shirts I'd already vetoed twice. "Seriously, Lucy, I have nothing to wear."

She flopped down on my bed with her feet up by my pillow and her head dangling off the foot of the bed. "Where's Alex?" she asked.

"He's on his way here with Dingo and his band. They're bringing kegs too."

"Wow. A real live keg party. How frat boy of you."

"I know," I said. I gave up going through my clothes and plopped down on the floor. "I can't believe I'm throwing a party at my parents' house while they're out of town. Who am I?"

"Not the Dade Hamilton I met three months ago," she said. "So who's all coming?"

"Me. You. Jay. A bunch of people I don't know. Maybe this girl Fessica."

"The one that tried to unzip your pants?" Lucy asked. "Sounds hot."

"No, not hot at all. But I hope she'll come. I sent her a text this morning and I haven't heard anything back."

"What about Pablo? Did you invite him?"

"You're joking right?"

Lucy sat up. "Did you tell Alex about the other day?"

"About Pablo whipping it out in the milk cooler? No way. Alex knows very little about Pablo and me, and I prefer to keep it that way."

"Do you think he'll show up?" she asked. "What if he does?

What if he does and there's a fight between him and Alex. That could be romantic, right?"

"Don't say that. There's not going to be any Pablo drama tonight." I picked up a red T-shirt off the floor, the same tattered one I wore to Cherry's that night with Lucy. "What about this? Is it too casual?"

"For a poolside rock show? Hell, no. What if someone calls the police?"

"I don't know. We'll deal with that when it happens. Isn't that what you do in situations like these? Did you tell Dana that I was having a party?"

"I described it as a gathering. One with a band."

"She's totally going to tell my parents," I said.

"Who cares?"

I considered this simple question for a moment and then said, "You're right. Who cares?"

I tossed the red shirt aside and put on a white button-up along with a hot pink tie. I looked in the mirror, tried to see myself as someone other than myself. Of course I hadn't invited Pablo, but for some reason I found myself wondering what he'd think of the outfit.

*He's not going to come, Dade. He hates you. He doesn't want you. And you don't want him. Remember that.*

∞

They came in packs, in congested blobs, fused groups that arrived simultaneously and spilled into each other. Human pools of knowing and acquaintance. Every time I opened the door, there they were. Most of them were friends with Alex, Dingo, or Jay. The rest were friends of friends, people whose exact coordinates on the social line would be revealed later on during drunken conversations by the pool and result in a light shock and disbelief at how we were all connected. Someone would say that the world was small, that everything happens for a reason, that everything that happens, *happens.*

I stood at the kitchen sink and shotgunned beers with Lucy and Dingo's bandmate Thomas. I was determined to drink away the burden of my anxiety, because I was sure that ridding myself of this was the key to fitting in with everyone else. The less I worried about everything, the freer I would be, and that's what this was about. Freedom. That night there was nothing wrong with the world. There was no Bert McGraw, no Pablo Soto, no Fairmont waiting to tear me apart from the first real boyfriend I'd ever had. There was nothing outside of the three months of summer. June, July, and August.

Lucy belched hugely and then slapped me on the back. A smaller one came up through my body, the little brother of whatever Lucy had just let out. Thomas let out a lost-boy howl and the insanity of the fact that my kitchen was crammed full of people I didn't know filled me with the rawest sort of happiness, the kind that comes to life in your chest and gives off sparks. I wondered if everyone felt like this all the time, if I was the last one to arrive at this ecstatic destination.

The kids swimming in my pool were wearing their tighty-whiteys or nothing at all. My Ultimate Vas Deferens Playlist was blaring from every speaker in the house with everything from *Introducing... the Vas Deferens!* to *Emotional Aviary Death Watch* heartily represented. Lucy and I were in my backyard watching two Asian girls have a break-dancing competition when one of the sophomores who worked at Food World came up to me and put his hand out for a high five.

"Great party, Hamilton," he said.

I put my hand out stupidly and let him slap it.

"Look at you," Lucy said after he walked away. "Mr. Popular."

It was then that I saw them. Jessica Montana and Judy Lockhart. They'd just stepped onto the back porch along with four of their friends. They were looking around, their faces registering a nervousness I'd never seen on them before.

"Is that that bitch from Bert's party?" Lucy asked. She raised her glass. "Hi, ladies!"

It took a moment for them to realize we were talking to them. Judy gave us a strained smile and wiggled her fingers in a pathetic and somewhat snotty hello. I waved back, surprised by the fact that I was sorta happy to see them there. As much as I wanted to pretend that there was nothing outside of this summer, there was, and whether or not I wanted to admit it, this was sort of my last bash. In some ways, it wouldn't have been complete without them.

"Who invited them?" Lucy asked.

"Not me," I said. "But it's cool. Whatevs."

"Are you okay? Feeling good about things?"

I nodded. At first it was more to convince myself that things were fine, but then I realized that things really were okay. I was happy, and the most beautiful part of it was that it didn't seem dependent on anyone. My happiness didn't feel tethered to Alex or Lucy or anybody else. It was mine, independent of everything else.

"Let's go inside and check on the band," I said.

∞

Dingo and Alex had turned my mother's meditation room into the band's green room. The speakers in this room were turned off, as were the lights. Everyone was sitting on my mother's Balance Pillows. A shirtless Dingo was strumming an acoustic guitar while Thomas and Louis watched. Thomas was running his fingers over a new tattoo that ran across his abdomen: the word *Iowa* in a florid cursive font. There were two dark-haired girls passing a cigarette back and forth and giggling from behind their curtains of hair. Someone had lit my mother's candles, and the walls were a production of overlapping silhouettes. Dingo was singing a song about killing his stuffed animals. I made a mental note to burn sage in this room before my mother came home.

"Alex told me he's writing a concept album about the toys of his youth," I whispered to Lucy.

"Sounds completely cutting edge," she said. "In a masturbatory man-child sort of way. How can you kill toys? Toys aren't alive."

"I think Dingo probably had a very different childhood than most people."

"Can you keep it down please?" one of the dark-haired girls said. She was trying to sound authoritative, but her friend burst out laughing and then she did too. "We're trying to listen to this *amazing* song."

"It's fine, ladies," Dingo said, still strumming. "This is Dade's pad. He can do what he wants. Plus, my music is meant to exist in the hallways of life, and in the hallways of life, there is always distraction."

"I like the way this room feels," one of the girls said. "I feel like there's a portal in here somewhere."

"I'm heading downstairs to check things out," I said to Lucy.

"I'll stay up here and hold down the crazy," she said.

I left them there and went downstairs. The house was full of people. It lacked the anarchic vibe of Jessica's party earlier in the summer. There were no freshmen dancing on top of the coffee table, no frat boys howling like banshees when a big-breasted girl walked by. There were people chilling out everywhere, nodding along to the music. Out by the pool a group of thirty people were watching Jay juggle some oranges that he'd found in the refrigerator. I stood watching from the back porch. I wondered where Alex was, where he'd disappeared to.

And then I saw him. He was standing in the back of the crowd with Fessica. He was taller than she was and he had to bend down a bit to talk to her. At one point he was smiling and pointing over everyone's heads at Jay and his act. Fessica was smiling too, clutching a bottle of beer and looking a little less tragic than usual. After an eternity of ponytails she'd finally let her hair down, and it made me think she was making steps away from the place she'd been for so long. Alex noticed me and excused himself. Fessica looked over and saw me and waved. I smiled and waved back. Alex sauntered up toward the porch. His swagger, his boyish gait. Another thing I adored about him.

"You don't look stressed," he said.

"I'm not. It's a miracle."

"I figured you'd be a mess," he said.

"I did too. And I'm not even stoned. Shocker."

"Total shocker," he said.

He moved in and kissed me. He did this thing where he softly bit my lower lip, and there was always a split second where I thought he wasn't going to let go, where I truly thought he was going to bite my lip off out of some primal desire to quite literally devour me. I put my hands on his chest and I swear to God I could feel things moving around inside him. I decided it was his affection for me, a shimmering blue circuit of light that made his entire body give off some invisible force that rendered me completely powerless, a light and force that also lived in me.

∞

Time got rubbery. One minute it was eleven o'clock, the next it was almost two in the morning. The Vas Deferens playlist ended and Lucy put on some German synth pop. Two spike-haired boys moved the kitchen table into the garage and began break-dancing in the space where it used to be, leaving black scuff marks on the linoleum. I was too drunk to care. I told myself that I'd make Jay and Alex help me scrub that up the next morning. A crowd of people gathered around the break-dancing boys. People were clapping their hands and cheering. The house was singing in German. Somewhere I heard glass break. Someone yelled, "Party foul!" and everyone laughed like they'd never heard anyone say that before.

"Party foul!" I yelled, eight seconds too late.

A girl to my left looked over at me and let out a laugh.

"You okay, man? Havin' a good time?"

I looked over at her, gave my sagging eyelids a minute to open. Was she the girl from Bert's party who'd told Alex and me that we were the cutest couple she'd ever seen?

"Sucks that Dingo and the band got too messed up to play," she said.

"Um, yeah," I said, not knowing exactly what she was talking about. Had there been some announcement I'd missed? "Do you like Johnny Morgan?"

"The actor?" she said.

"Yes. The actor. The very famous movie actor. I'm in love with him. I believe that someday I will marry him. I believe it enough to make it happen. It will happen."

The girl burst out laughing and threw her arm around my neck. "Dade, dude, you are *toasted*."

"How do you know my name?"

My words felt like heavy things that just kept falling out of my mouth.

"I'm Sandra. We met earlier. Remember? We talked about

the Vas Deferens show I saw in Colorado with my cousin Roxy, who knew the drummer because—"

I walked away as she spoke. Stumbled is more like it. I needed to leave, needed to lie down. Where was Alex? Jay? Lucy? I should stay awake. This was my house. I had to keep things in order. Why had I gotten so drunk to begin with? If my parents could see me from Europe, they would ground me for the rest of my life. On my way up to my room. I passed a guy with blue hair wearing a T-shirt with Jenny Moore's face on it. Across the image was the word *found* in big red letters.

∞

I went into my darkened room and fell face-first onto my bed. Purple Christmas lights blinked all around me. What was a purple Christmas for? Who has a purple Christmas? I told myself that I was just going to close my eyes for a minute. I was just going to take a little nap. I would stick my big toe into the pool of sleep and that would be enough. Then I'd get up and go downstairs and make coffee, wake the hell up, become a new man.

∞

I have a fuzzy memory of Lucy kneeling by my bed and asking if I was okay. I made a noise in my throat. She asked me if I was okay again. I think I said Alex's name. Actually, I think I said Alexander Hamilton.

∞

I woke up in my underwear with my sheets pulled over my head. From the other side came an icy light, the earliest moments of dawn. I felt like I'd woken up in the middle of an operation and was being forced to confront my useless, semi-repaired body. Alex was right there beside me, lying on his stomach in his neon green briefs. His mouth hung open in some sort of dreamy awe like on the other side of his eyelids he was watching a film that explained all the secrets of the universe.

"Are you awake?"

The voice came from the corner of my bedroom. Pablo was sitting on the box that contained my new dorm refrigerator. Scattered around him were the smaller things from that day. The alarm clock and the hair dryer. Packages of underwear and socks. He looked like he'd been drinking all night too, but not here. There were dark circles under Pablo's eyes and a cut on his lower lip.

"You haven't answered any of my text messages," he said.

I sat up slowly. The vile taste in my mouth seemed to correspond not only with the large amount of alcohol I'd consumed the previous evening, but also with Pablo's presence, with the fact that the light coming through the window was exactly how it was the other morning when I'd gone downstairs and saw that they'd found Jenny Moore. A hundred Johnny Morgans watched from the wall, cutouts from different magazines. Different haircuts, different expressions, different periods.

"How did you get in here?" I asked.

"There's a guy and a girl out by your pool. Everyone else is gone. The front door was open. Wide open."

"What time is it?"

"Five something. Real rager, Hamilton." He sniffed loudly,

kicked his toe at the carpet. "You're a real dick, you know that?"

"What?"

"The way you left me there in the milk cooler." He gave out an awkward laugh, curt and sorta terrifying. "We fuck around for how long and then you just leave me all balled out?"

"I'm sorry," I said tentatively.

"Yeah, I bet you are. I bet you're real sorry." He was bouncing his left leg rapidly, a terrible habit he shared with my father. He nodded at Alex. "Who's that dickhead? Is that him?"

"That's Alex."

"Yeah, I know Alex."

"Then why did you ask?" I said.

"I wanted to hear you say it," he said. He sat there searching for something else to say, but he just ended up repeating himself. "You're a real dick, you know that?"

"You told me you didn't want to ever see me again. You *spit* on me."

He scratched at the inside of his wrist, some halfhearted distraction from the matter at hand.

"That was different," he said. He furrowed his brow at something, maybe at his imaginary itch or maybe he'd realized that what he'd just said didn't make any sense at all. He let out a sad little half laugh. "But I'm here now. I'm right here."

"I need water," I said, slipping out of bed. "And Alex is asleep. Let's take this downstairs."

Walking and being upright shifted the ache in my head from the back to the front. Pablo followed me downstairs, several paces behind and moving as slowly as I. The house was a mess. There were plastic cups scattered about and dirty footprints on the ivory carpet in the living room. My mother's giant potted plant had been tipped over, and the surrealist print in the foyer now had a forty-degree tilt to it. The kitchen counter was covered with empty two-liters of soda and seltzer water and bottles of cranberry juice and orange juice that contained less than an inch of fluid. The kitchen table had returned but it was upside down with its legs in the air like a dead horse.

I got a glass of water and we went out back. The backyard was in a similar state of disarray. Cups, napkins, assorted scraps of garbage everywhere, on the lawn, polluting the pool. Whatever couple Pablo'd been talking about was gone, but there was an army green bra near the pool just lying there like some listless amphibian trying its damnedest to make it into the water and failing. We each took a seat on a chaise longue.

Pablo nodded slowly, acting like he understood me. We were both staring out at the yard, at the pool. That moment marked the first time our interaction wasn't overshadowed by some huge emotion. I wasn't scared of him or desperately infatuated or even angry. I felt a sort of empathy toward him, and with that empathy came a new willingness to let Pablo be whatever he happened to be.

"You seem different," he said.

"How?"

"More like the you I think you really are. Does that make sense?"

"I guess," I said, a bit flattered. "You're probably right."

"It's been weird not seeing you this summer." I could sense him feeling for the next phrase, trying to find a way to say it so it didn't sound like what it was. "I missed you. They found that girl, you know? At work. Of course you know. It's been everywhere. Just found her. She just reappeared. I thought of you when I saw that. I almost called you."

"I thought I saw her one night," I said. "Right over there. On the other side of the pool. I thought all those people that claimed they saw her around town were just making it up, but now I wonder. I wonder if maybe she didn't really come back, that maybe the Jenny Moore they found at Food World is, like, the product of some mass hallucination, like maybe we all can't deal with the fact that the real Jenny Moore is gone, so now we've gone and invented her. Or I guess reinvented her. Brought her back."

"Things come back if you want them to."

He lit a cigarette and fell back against the chaise longue, silent for a moment.

"Your mind is a mysterious thing, Dade Hamilton," Pablo said. "A very mysterious thing."

He had this look on his face like he was seeing right through me and the smile of someone who'd just glimpsed some fateful light.

"Thanks," I said. "I'm learning that."

"So I'm not going to Western Iowa," he said.

"What?" I asked, surprised. "Really? Why?"

"I'm just not going there."

"So where are you going?"

"Somewhere else," he said. "Not there, though."

"What about Judy? What does she think of this?"

"I haven't told her yet," he said. "But she'll figure it out."

And then I noticed he was crying. He was still wearing that glazed smile, but there were tears in his eyes. Pablo Soto, crying in my backyard amongst the debris of a party I'd had the night before, while my boyfriend slept upstairs. Miracles everywhere. He wiped at his eyes and tried to hold it back, but he couldn't. He sat up and buried his face in his hands and he wept. I thought of something my mother sometimes said. *I couldn't have been more surprised if you set me on fire.* And I was on fire. The summer was on fire, a giant surprise.

"Are you okay?" I asked.

He suddenly stood up and started for the patio door.

"Walk me out," he said.

He was wiping his eyes with one hand and blindly waving me inside with the other. I was caught off guard. I had no choice but to follow him inside and through the war zone of the house. I wish I could've smiled about it. There was a Dade somewhere who wanted to smile at the state of his parents' house, at the way the summer had changed. Or maybe that Dade had changed over the summer. But it can be hard to smile at endings. The end of the party. The end of the summer. The end of the Pablo I'd hated for so long. I followed this stranger through the kitchen and the living room, into the foyer and out the front door.

He'd made himself stop crying. We stood for a bit like the

awkward couple we always were. I was in my boxer shorts. He was looking at his shoes. The cool of the early-morning air was laced with subtle streaks of heat. Suddenly he grabbed my arms and pulled me toward him, and for a moment the familiar fear of Pablo Soto welled up inside me.

Instead he kissed me. His mouth tasted like beer and beef jerky and salted peanuts, all sorts of convenience store junk he'd probably picked up sometime during his night of driving around thinking about whatever, maybe thinking of this moment, imagining it happening and repeating to himself over and over again that he was gonna do it. He was gonna kiss Dade Hamilton, really for the first time.

He pushed me away frantically, keeping his hands on my shoulders. His tearstained face now registered more fear than sadness. He lumbered off the porch toward his little gray pickup truck, an object that appeared in some of the family photos his mother had around his house. In one of them Pablo's father and another man are leaning against the truck shirtless, both men holding a beer, Pablo in his father's arms, a little baby reaching for some eternally unknown thing just out of the frame of the photo.

He started his car and took off down the street, the mufflerless engine sending a beaded roar through the suburban morning. I stood there watching, feeling like I'd been dropped into another life. I watched him turn the corner, listened to the engine fade as he navigated his way through the maze of our subdivision. And when that was gone, so was he. No one ever saw Pablo Soto again.

∞

The ringing of my phone pulled me out of my second sleep, the one I'd fallen back into after Pablo sped off down my street. My head still hurt. The clock on the wall said 11:41 a.m. In those piled moments upon waking I recalled Pablo's earlier visit as if it were a dream, an unfocused film projected onto an overcast sky. I glanced over at the refrigerator he'd been sitting on as if I would find some trace of him there, as if the slow aimless spirals of the dust motes were somehow confirmation that yes, he was there but now he was gone. This is what he left in his wake. Aimless pieces of the things we begin and end as. Beside me was Alex, a sprawled mass of beautiful boy in the bed beside me.

I checked my caller ID. It was Fessica. I didn't say anything when I picked up.

"Dade?" She sounded frantic, like she was looking over her shoulder as she ran from something. "Dade, can you hear me? It's me. Are you there?"

"Yeah," I said. "What is it?"

"Pablo's dead. Can you hear me? Pablo's dead."

It was as if the floor had disappeared. I became wrapped with the sensation of plummeting, riding my bed like a broken magic carpet into oblivion. There was a single stinging point of pain in my chest and then it spidered out, filled my entire body with an acidic ache. A pain that makes you sink.

"He can't be. He was just here a minute ago."

"He's dead, Dade. Judy's freaking out. Everyone's freaking

out. He got in a car accident this morning. People are freaking out, Dade. People are *freaking out*."

I could make sense of it. I could prove Fessica wrong. She didn't know anything. She'd never known anything.

"Dade, are you there?"

My hand went to my mouth. I was watching this all from my seat on top of my dorm refrigerator, watching myself react like some character in a movie.

"That's not true," I said. "That's not true. They're lying to you. They're playing some stupid fucking trick. Tell your sister she's a lying piece—"

"Dade, listen to me."

"I can't listen to you," I said. The panic in my own voice scared me. "It's a lie."

"What's going on?" It was Alex. He'd woken up. His hand was on my back.

"Dade, talk to me," he said. "You're scaring me. What's wrong?"

"Dade, it's true."

I made a sound that wasn't words, a nothing sound that meant everything. She said my name again and through the nothing sound I said his name.

# After

That was it. That was the end of my summer. It was my last real summer in a lot of ways, just like my father said. I could never set foot into June, July, and August without thinking of those months before I left for college, the summer I floated away.

Fessica was right. Pablo Soto died at 9:49 a.m. at Cedarville Memorial Hospital after losing control of his truck on Maple Creek Road and driving headfirst into a tree. He wasn't wearing a seat belt, and his truck was from the days before airbags. The police said his vehicle reeked of booze and there were no skid marks. They figured he was a drunken teenager too out of his mind to even think about breaking.

When I look back on that morning I remember a strange nutty taste on my tongue and a cramp in my stomach and the exact temperature of the morning air on my skin as Pablo leaned in and kissed me on my porch. In retrospect, I think I knew as he sped down my street that he was going to kill himself. It was as if I'd experienced this all before, maybe in some other life that I was now reliving with the hopes that I could get it right this time. That would explain the overwhelming sense of failure that I carry with me when I think of all the other ways it could've ended.

Alex tried to comfort me after I got off the phone with Fessica, but I couldn't bear to be touched by him. Not because of anything he'd done, but because somewhere buried in his touch was the idea of Pablo, the idea that any boy I loved would eventually disappear. He went downstairs and woke Lucy, who was asleep on our sofa, and it was when I explained it all to her that it crystallized in my mind and became real. Lucy sent Alex home and told him she'd call him later with an update.

Mrs. Savage called my parents in Europe and explained what had happened. They booked flights to leave that night. I stayed in bed with Lucy until they got back. That day and a half passed like a runaway nightmare, one that kept lurching over the borders of sleep and into my waking moments. Dana Savage would pop in now and then. She'd stand there watching us grieve with the heavy solemnity of someone who'd been there before and was all too aware that the sadness had to run its course like a fever.

I kept having this terrible dream that seemed like the cousin of the dream I'd had where the thing was coming up to my room. In this new dream I was in a pitch-black room that may or may not have been my bedroom. I could sort of see someone shifting around in the darkness, someone I was pretty sure was Pablo. He was crying and asking for my help, but when I reached out, I couldn't find his hand, and suddenly his voice and cries would be farther away and I'd have to keep on looking for him.

I'd wake up and my heart would be racing. I could tell from the light outside that time had passed and for some reason I found this completely terrifying. Lucy would jerk awake and plant little kisses on my cheek and whisper that everything was going to be all right.

When my parents returned my mother held me as I cried hysterically into her chest. My father watched awkwardly from the doorway of my bedroom. Somehow it was enough to feel him there, hovering on the outskirts. In fact it was exactly what I needed. I was thankful that he understood that, that he was aware of the nature of our relationship.

I only saw Alex once more after that. We met for coffee at a diner and I told him that I loved him, but that I had to go to Fairmont and start over again.

"I get it," he said. He was looking out the giant windows at the traffic rolling up the ramp toward the interstate. "I know I'd leave if I could."

"You could," I said to him. "You could go anywhere you want. You're smart. You could make it."

He shook his head and laughed. "You make it sound so easy. Trust me, if I could run away I would. But sometimes I think about my mom and my dad and my sister and I think about how they all ran away and how it didn't do any of them any good. The scenery might change, but you're still the same person deep down inside. You carry that shit with you."

He looked at me like he wanted to make sure I understood this. I nodded in solemn agreement and looked down at my cup of coffee.

"And I think about my grandmother," he went on. "I couldn't

do that to her. It's not her fault that life is complicated and filled with tough decisions and painful good-byes. All she's ever done is try and protect me from that. I think some love you can stand to let go of because it's ultimately for the best, but other types you have to stick with until the day you die even when it's hard. You have to think about that before you run away from wherever you are. And then when you know, you either stay or you go and pray that you're making the right decision."

We spent the rest of the time in silence. The other patrons buzzed around us and one soft rock track faded into the next over the speakers. At one point he smiled at me sadly and I smiled back and then I looked out at the traffic. I was one of them on the on-ramp heading toward the interstate. I wasn't leaving. I was gone.

On my way out of town I had my mother stop at Cedarville High. I told her there was something I had to see. The football team had already started practicing for the fall, and the sight of them running around the field in their blue and red uniforms made me think of Pablo. I got in through the rear gymnasium door and went straight to the last stall of the first-floor boys' room where I'd drawn the giant heart on the night of our senior prom, the one with our initials in the middle, but when I got there all I found was a giant square of paint just a shade darker than the original orange. A janitor had painted over it.

My roommate at Fairmont ended up being a Jewish kid from Chicago named Howie. On our first day of living together I found out that he loved the Vas Deferens as much as I did, and that was the beginning of what would become a close friendship. He was an inch shorter than me, built like a wrestler, and had shaggy dark hair, sleepy eyes, and a deep voice. He was majoring in religion and philosophy and was a writer like me. He was working on a nonfiction book about anarchy called *Recipe for Rebellion*. I rarely saw him in anything other than tight jeans, a white T-shirt, and an old pair of black Converse high-tops that were held together with duct tape. He wore fancy glasses, always had a tequila and pineapple juice just within his reach, and he liked to tell stories about the all-boys high school he'd attended in Chicago. It was only when I was very drunk that I found him even remotely attractive, but otherwise he was just my nerdily handsome roommate who spent an hour each night on the top bunk talking to his girlfriend in Vermont, the conversation falling to a whisper as it wore on and dissolving into a million soft proclamations of his love for her.

I told Howie I was gay our fourth night in the room together. We'd just crashed a frat party on the hill and we were drunk and listening to music in the room.

"Both my brothers are gay," Howie said. "You'd be hard-pressed to find someone who gave less of a fuck than me."

Four weeks later he was eagerly trying to set me up with a guy in his bio class. By second semester we were like brothers.

Three weeks after I started school my mother called me to tell me that she and my father were getting a divorce. It was one of the most anticlimactic conversations I've ever had. If I felt anything, it was only a sense of relief that it was all over. I was vaguely worried about how they would cope with wandering the desert of adulthood without the other's hand to hold, but then I remembered that they never appeared to give each other that much comfort in the first place, or at least if they had, those days were buried so far in the past that it was hard to consider them a meaningful part of their life.

My mom stayed in the house in Cedarview Estates. Sometimes its largeness made her lonely, but I think she stayed there with the secret hope that someday she would use every inch of it again, that maybe she would have another husband, maybe even another kid or two, and the house would have a life again. There would be splashes in the pool, bikes lying on their sides in the yard, and rubber balls rolling down the gentle slope of the driveway. Every few months she sent me checks with subtle commands written in the memo line. *For Healthy Snacks* they sometimes read or *New Winter Coat Money.* Once it even said *To Take a Nice Boy Out to Dinner.* I called her after that one to tell her that I loved her.

My dad became the merry bachelor. He started dating, which filled me with sympathy for the single ladies of Cedarville. He bought a condo in a new development across town and furnished it with nothing but a treadmill, a king-size bed, and a giant flat-screen television. Sometimes I pictured him walking on the treadmill and talking on his headset to some legal secretary across town while he watched a basketball game on mute.

Every now and then he'd drive up to Fairmont for football games. We'd drink hot chocolate in the stands and I'd stand up and cheer whenever he did. One night after a game we got drunk at a pub on campus and afterward when we were walking through the snow he stopped and held me and told me he was sorry. I told him that it was okay, that I knew he always did the best that he could, and then we trudged on back toward his hotel with icy tears sticking to our cheeks.

∞

Lucy came to visit in the spring. I showed her the buildings where I had classes and the little nooks around campus where I would sit and write. I told her I was working on a book called *The Vast Fields of Ordinary*. She begged me to let her read the first chapter, but I told her it was better to wait until it was finished, until all the little pieces fit together to make a whole picture.

I took her to the Laguna Lounge on a Wednesday, which was Lesbian Night. We sat at the bar with fruity cocktails and talked about the previous summer while the DJ played a string of ridiculous Fleetwood Mac remixes that reminded me of my mother. We talked about Alex and what would happen to him. We talked about Jenny Moore and how her and her family moved from Cedarville to get away from all the attention they were getting after what happened. One rumor was that they were living in a cabin in Maine. Another had them living on a reservation in New Mexico, where Jenny was receiving mystical training from a shaman. A few people even said the whole family had disappeared just like Jenny had, that she'd taken them to the place she'd been because it was so much better than this world. We never said Pablo's name, never once talked about the "accident," but he was there as much as we were, a ghostly listener a couple of barstools down who finally understood all the things he couldn't when he was alive.

∞

I stopped wanting to float away from my life, because in the end my life was all I had. I'd walk the Fairmont campus and look up to the sky and I wouldn't see myself drifting off like some lost balloon. Instead I saw the size of the world and found comfort in its hugeness. I'd think back to the times when I felt like everything was closing in on me, those times when I thought I was stuck, and I realized that I was wrong. There is always hope. The world is vast and meant for wandering. There is always somewhere else to go.

# LESBIAN, GAY, BISEXUAL AND TRANSGENDER RESOURCES

## Some Facts about LGBT Youth

∞

- Nine out of ten LGBT students (86.2%) experienced harassment at school; three-fifths (60.8%) felt unsafe at school because of their sexual orientation; and about one-third (32.7%) skipped a day of school in the past month because of feeling unsafe.

- LGBT students are three times as likely as non-LGBT students to say that they do not feel safe at school (22% vs. 7%), and 90% of LGBT students (vs. 62% of non-LGBT teens) have been harassed or assaulted during the past year.

  (GLSEN From Teasing to Torment, 2006)

- Sexual-minority youth or teens that identify themselves as gay, lesbian, or bisexual are bullied two to three times more than heterosexuals.

  (Nationwide Children's Hospital, Columbus, OH, 2010)

- LGBT youth in rural communities and those with lower adult educational attainment face particularly hostile school climates. (JG, Greytak EA, Diaz EM—*Journal of Youth & Adolescence*, 2009)

- Lesbian, gay, and bisexual adolescents are 190 percent more likely to use drugs and alcohol than are heterosexual teens.

  (Marshal MP, Friedman MS, et al.—*Addiction*, 2008)

- Lesbian, gay, and bisexual youth are up to four times more likely to attempt suicide than their heterosexual peers.

  (Massachusetts Youth Risk Survey, 2007)

Statistics provided by
http://www.thetrevorproject.org/suicide-resources/suicidal-signs

**Need help? Know someone who does?**

∞

The Trevor Project http://www.thetrevorproject.org/

The Trevor Lifeline: 866-4-U-TREVOR

The National Suicide Prevention Lifeline: 1-800-273-TALK

PFLAG: Parents, Families, & Friends of Lesbians and Gays: http://www.pflag.org